P9-DXL-168

A DARK DESCENT

ALSO BY LISA FIEDLER

The Mouseheart Trilogy
Mouseheart
Hopper's Destiny
Return of the Forgotten

Ages of Oz
A Fiery Friendship

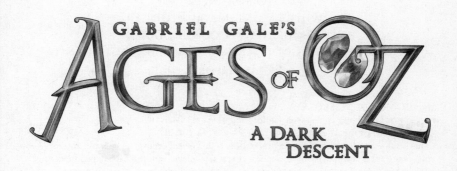

GABRIEL GALE'S

AGES OF OZ

A DARK
DESCENT

Written by LISA FIEDLER

Illustrated by SEBASTIAN GIACOBINO

MARGARET K. McELDERRY BOOKS
New York London Toronto Sydney New Delhi

To Rene,
A true sorceress and my most trusted comrade,
I have loved traveling this road with you.
And to Dean, for your clear thinking.
—Gabriel Gale

To Shannon,
where all my Magic begins.
And to our newest cousin, Taryn . . .
Marriage, like a good book, should be a page-turner!
—Lisa Fiedler

MARGARET K. McELDERRY BOOKS
An imprint of Simon & Schuster Children's Publishing Division
1230 Avenue of the Americas, New York, New York 10020

MARGARET K. McELDERRY BOOKS is a trademark of Simon & Schuster, Inc. For information about special discounts for bulk purchases, please contact Simon & Schuster Special Sales at 1-866-506-1949 or business@simonandschuster.com.
The Simon & Schuster Speakers Bureau can bring authors to your live event. For more information or to book an event, contact the Simon & Schuster Speakers Bureau at 1-866-248-3049 or visit our website at www.simonspeakers.com.
Book design by Debra Sfetsios-Conover and Irene Metaxatos
The text for this book was set in Sabon LT Std.
The illustrations for this book were rendered digitally.
Manufactured in the United States of America • 0418 FFG
First Edition
10 9 8 7 6 5 4 3 2 1
Library of Congress Cataloging-in-Publication Data
Names: Fiedler, Lisa, author. | Giacobino, Sebastian, illustrator.
Title: A dark descent / written by Lisa Fiedler ; illustrated by Sebastian Giacobino.
Description: First edition. | New York : Margaret K. McElderry Books, [2018] | Series: Ages of Oz ; 2 | Audience: Ages 12 and under only. | Summary: "After the defeat of one Wicked, the other Witches of Oz are ready for vengeance"—Provided by publisher.
Identifiers: LCCN 2017034400 (print) | LCCN 2017045895 (eBook)
ISBN 9781481469746 (hardcover) | ISBN 9781481469760 (eBook)
Subjects: | CYAC: Fantasy. | Witches—Fiction.
Classification: LCC PZ7.F457 (eBook) | LCC PZ7.F457 Dar 2018 (print) | DDC [Fic]—dc23 | LC record available at https://lccn.loc.gov/2017034400

1

WICKED LANDING

The tumult overhead was nothing short of Wicked.

Clatter and motion, fury and speed. Dark Magic seemed bent on tearing the sky to pieces in its desperate race to the south. Underfoot, the solidness of Oz felt close to crumbling.

The Witches are coming.

Miss Gage's warning rang in Glinda's ears, colliding with the sound of the enemy's approach: croaking and hissing from the West; a droning buzz from the East, and a deep lowing groan from the North.

Where moments ago the air had sparkled with the pure emerald light of King Oz's final thought, there was now a vicious melee of stingers and wings. The ground shuddered under a violent stampede of trampling hooves and swiftly slithering things. Billows of scarlet dust rolled forth as the menacing armies of the Witches advanced.

"*Why* are they coming?" Locasta asked, her violet eyes focused on the fracas above their heads, her fingers fidgeting nervously with the new gold bracelets on her wrists.

"To see for themselves that their rival in the South has been vanquished," said Miss Gage.

"Will they attempt to avenge her?" Ben rasped, his face pale.

Gage shook her head. "More likely they've come to celebrate her defeat."

As the commotion drew nearer, Clumsy Bear whimpered and covered his face with his paws. Glinda and the others watched as Ava Munch, the Royal Tyrant of the East, touched down. She was riding an insect of uncommon proportions—a weevil as large as a lion, with jagged legs and waving antennae. Swarming around Ava was a platoon of bulging-eyed creepy-crawlies: oversize wisp-wasps, mosquitoes and fruit flies, beetles and tumble-bumbles with iridescent wings. Out of the din they swooped, stirring up a small cyclone of dead leaves as they landed. Dressed in a sheath of blue satin, Ava hid her face behind her Silver Mask, as though she were ashamed to be seen in the hideous company of her own army.

Daspina the Wild Dancer of the West arrived next,

gracefully astride a spiny-tailed skink lizard. Flanking her was a legion of warty toads and scaly snakes, all of inordinate size. Draped in yellow scarves, the Wild Dancer shimmied in her saddle, her Silver Shoes catching the sunlight.

Finally, from the North roared Marada, the Wicked Warrior; her army was a careening herd of draft animals, each ridden by a Gillikin soldier armed to the hilt. The beasts—yakityaks, buffalopes, oxen, and bulls—came snorting and bellowing. The Witch used her Silver Gauntlets to yank back on the reins of her mount, and the gigantic yakityak skidded to a halt. Its pointy horns missed impaling Ava's weevil by less than an inch.

"Watch it!" Ava warned, removing her Silver Mask.

Marada growled and raised a gloved fist in a warning of her own.

Glinda spied a small, white-faced monkey scampering about. His presence among these creatures was inexplicable to her, and his wide eyes surveyed the scene, as if he, too, wondered what ugly twist of fate had brought him here. What Glinda found most stunning was that he had *wings*.

Sliding down from the skink, Daspina sashayed on dainty silver heels—first a few steps to her left, then a skip back to her right. "The Harvester is *quite* vanquished," she declared, as if there had been any doubt. "Gone to seed, one might say!" At this, she laughed and turned a pirouette.

"She was worthless," Marada spat. When she leaped

from her yak, the spurs of her heavy sandals left deep gashes in the dirt. "Ruling by delusion and trickery is not ruling. It is merely deceiving. She was as weak as the flowers she grew! I could have crushed her with one blow."

"And she was a terrible hostess," Daspina observed with distaste. "She never once threw a ball or cotillion, not even a pitiful little tea party."

"Still, her Magic was potent," Ava admitted in a grudging tone. "And there was an elegance about her. Handsome features. Good bones—"

"Good bones are the best kind to crush," Marada noted.

"—but she was more vain than she had any right to be."

At this, Marada whirled on Ava with raised brows. "*You* dare to call another vain?"

"*My* vanity is warranted," Ava insisted. "Aphidina was merely pretty. I stun."

"In more ways than one," Daspina conceded with a nervous giggle, eyeing Ava's mask.

Marada grunted; it might have been laughter. The sound made Glinda queasy.

Now the three Wickeds fell silent, looking out over the ravaged castle grounds, each with a glint of longing in her eyes. The monkey, who as far as Glinda could tell had no particular connection to any one of them, sped anxiously from steer to insect to amphibian, none of which paid him any mind.

"Surely I could collect immense amounts of taxes were

I to lease this land to the Quadling farmers." Ava's fingers twitched as if she could feel the gilt coins being pressed into her hands.

"And I could erect dance halls and bowling greens and gaming fields," Daspina twittered. "There would be garden parties and carnivals every day and every night if this were mine."

"The lists for training would go there," Marada planned aloud, pointing to where the Grande Allée of Symmetrees had stood just that morning, before Aphidina's defeat. "And there, rows of sturdy barracks for my soldiers."

"Don't you mean 'barns'?" scoffed Ava, gesturing to Marada's cattle grazing on what was left of the Haunting Harvester's grass.

"I would put my herd up against your pests in any battle!"

"Oh, would you?" Ava's eyes burned. "One well-placed sting on the rump would have your mount galloping back to Gillikin with his tail between his shaggy legs."

"*My* soldiers have fangs," Daspina boasted, her hips swaying with pride, "and venom."

For a moment, the three harridans stood motionless, hurling lethal glances at one another. Glinda shivered at the nearness of the Wickeds, thankful for the protection of the Road of Red Cobble beneath her feet; she was close enough to reach out and pull the mask from Ava's hand.

"This is a little too close for comfort," Locasta whispered. "I know they can't see or hear us, but I wish they'd just go back to where they came from."

"So do I," said Glinda, ducking back from the whipping hem of one of Daspina's scarves.

It was then that she felt the tickle—a soft, fuzzy graze against her trembling hand.

Startled, she looked down and saw that the monkey had crept to the edge of the Road of Red Cobble. The fluffy top of his head, swiveling from side to side as he took in the patch of road with great curiosity, was brushing against the tips of Glinda's fingers. Tilting his face upward, he met her green eyes with his enormous round ones. He blinked, as if trying to determine what her purpose was, there upon that patch of road.

Then he turned to Marada, and Glinda held her breath.

The monkey's wings fluttered slightly as he snapped his gaze to Ava, then Daspina. Glinda knew it would take no more than a single screech for him to alert this rancorous triad to her invisible presence, and she sensed he knew it too. But after a moment of eyeing the Witches, he seemed to decide against raising the alarm and returned his attention to the cobblestones.

Expelling her breath in a grateful sigh, Glinda watched the monkey tap his slender toes onto the red bricks, holding there a moment as if waiting to experience some sensation. But when nothing occurred, he simply shook his head in disappointment and trotted off. Glinda's eyebrows furrowed. The road had accepted him. But weren't these cobbles only welcoming—not to mention visible—to those who were worthy to travel them?

Her thoughts were interrupted by the words of the Royal Tyrant: "Perhaps I shall claim the South as my own so it will belong to me now and evermore."

"That simple, eh?" Marada let out an inelegant snort. "You think just because your lineage is noble you can claim lands at will?"

"You *are* quite the saucy former princess, aren't you?" Daspina snipped, gliding toward Ava. "Why should such a bountiful country as Quadling be *yours* for the taking?"

"Because," Ava drawled, returning the Silver Mask to her face, "*I* can do this!" A bolt of blue fury burned through the slit eyes of the mask, heading straight for the Witch of the West. But the Dancer was keen and graceful, and Glinda watched in horrified awe as Daspina quickly knocked her heels together. Three quick clicks of those Silver Shoes and she'd moved faster than sight or sound to the far side of the Tyrant.

"What was *that*?" Locasta asked.

"Those stolen shoes," Gage replied with a foreboding look. "It seems they allow the Dancer to skip from place to place without the bothersome inconvenience of utilizing the moments it would ordinarily take to do so."

"Well, they did belong to King Oz once," said Ben, who

was still holding Aphidina's Chainmail. "No wonder they carry such power."

"Power corrupted by the Witches," Shade added softly. "King Oz would never cheat time."

Glinda knew Shade was right; whatever Good Magic these pieces of silver contained before the Witches ripped them from the fallen king had been converted to Wicked long ago.

Now Ava turned the mask on Marada, but for all her immense bulk, the Wicked Warrior was agile; she dodged the blue bolt, then crouched low to hammer her heavy Silver Gauntlets against the ground. The terrain bucked up like an angry stallion, throwing both Ava and Daspina off their feet to land hard in the red Quadling soil—Ava sprawled on her back, and Daspina on her hands and knees. Fortunately, the red road beneath Glinda and the others remained steady. They all turned to Ben, clutching the chainmail.

"Careful with that," Locasta muttered wryly, and Ben slipped the silver mesh cautiously into his knapsack.

"Enough of this!" sang Daspina, executing another trio of heel clicks; this returned her instantaneously to the skink's side. "We were not sent here to battle among ourselves."

"More's the pity," Marada muttered, but she stood and swept the red soil from her gloves.

"Much as I hate to agree with the dancing fool," said

Ava, tucking the mask under her arm and frowning hatefully at the place where Aphidina's castle once stood, "she is indeed correct. We all know who will decide what is to become of Quadling. She ordered us here only to show us what Glinda Gavaria has done."

Hearing her name on the lips of the Wicked Witch of the East made the hair on the back of Glinda's neck prickle. But the true import of Ava's statement was not lost on Miss Gage. "*She* ordered them? Who's 'she'?"

The elusive and terrifying fifth Witch, thought Glinda, *that's who.*

Marada punched the knuckles of one gauntlet into the palm of the other. "Hah!" she barked. "I for one do not fear *children*. They are small and weak, scrawny and stupid. They cower and cry and have very little intelligence."

"This may be true of your little slavelings in Gillikin," Ava averred (and Glinda instinctively grabbed hold of Locasta to prevent her from bounding off the road to attack the Witch for her insult). "But children do grow up. They learn things. I realize that Glinda is presently no more than a pupa—"

Glinda's jaw dropped. "*What* did she just call me?"

"An insect," Ben clarified, "in its immature stage."

"—but once she is trained, she will surely be a force to be reckoned with." Stroking her weevil's glossy shell, Ava clung a little tighter to her Silver Mask and looked concerned.

"That is a most unsettling thought," Daspina remarked with a pout. "I believe I shall double the guards along my Winkie borders."

"I will do the same," said Ava. "It is in our best interests to keep the Sorceress larva out, for with the proper tutelage, there is no telling how powerful her Magic might become!"

Marada glowered and again surveyed the emptiness of the Harvester's grounds. "Perhaps we should teach this youngster-beast, this *Glinda*, a lesson ourselves. Let us not wait to hear the Krumbic one's plans for Quadling. Let's annihilate it!"

On the red road, the four friends, the bear, and the teacher froze. Even Feathertop, hovering over Ben's shoulder, stiffened in horror.

"Can they do that?" asked Ben. "I thought Ember would protect Quadling Country now that he's free."

"He can only protect the final thought and its power to birth Goodness," Miss Gage explained. "Quadling and those who dwell in it will never be completely invulnerable until Wickedness is abolished entirely."

"Great." Locasta rolled her eyes. "No pressure."

"Destruction is always an excellent idea, Marada," said Ava, returning the mask to her face. "Even if it was *yours*. I say we begin by torching the village."

Daspina twirled and clapped her hands. "Oh yes! A bonfire! How lovely. And how Wickedly injurious."

Marada clasped her big hands above her head in a gesture of certain victory. "And while the village burns, I shall capture as many Quadling prisoners as my soldiers can carry and bring them back to Gillikin as slaves."

Locasta went ashen. "We have to do something! The Quadling citizens will be caught totally unawares. They can't possibly defend themselves against three Witches."

"Neither can we," Glinda murmured, feeling helpless and afraid.

Until her eyes again fell on the little monkey, whose curious face was now turned skyward.

She followed his gaze, and her heart filled with hope.

Just overhead was a twinkle of green—a piece of King Oz's final thought, glowing emerald against the blue and red of the sky. Suddenly Glinda's whole mind echoed with the king's wise words: *That moment in which all is lost is the same moment in which begins the battle to regain it.*

And *that* moment, it seemed, was *this* moment!

Heart racing, Glinda reached into her sash and drew Illumina.

"What are you doing?" asked Ben.

"Beginning the battle," Glinda replied. "I think I can infuse the ground with Oz's last thought."

"Excellent plan," said Gage. "It won't keep them out of Quadling permanently, but with any luck, it might shock them enough to send them scurrying now."

"Hurry," Locasta advised. "They're preparing to ride."

Indeed, Daspina was prancing past in a flurry of yellow silk, the toes of her silver slippers a mere inch from the Road of Red Cobble. "I shall collect every crystal punch bowl and silver candlestick in the South," she announced, as she slipped into her saddle. "These will be the spoils that adorn the tables at my next banquet. And I shall kick the teeth out of the mouth of any Quadling who attempts to stop me."

Glinda aimed Illumina toward the bobbing green orb overhead.

"More to the left," Locasta coached.

"Now higher," said Ben.

"Gently," Shade advised in a hushed voice.

Glinda guided the tip of the sword toward the orb until the ball of light balanced upon it, quivering like a green flame on a candlewick.

"You got it!" Locasta cried as Glinda lowered Illumina cautiously out of the sky.

Just then Marada came marching past them with such gusto that the road shook; Glinda stumbled and nearly lost her grip on Illumina. Ben gasped; Shade ducked into the collar of her cape. But Glinda held fast and the orb remained perched on the point of the sword. Gage, Locasta, and even Clumsy Bear shared a sigh of relief.

"Are you sure this is going to work?" asked Locasta.

Glinda wasn't sure at all. But if all were to be lost, it would *not* be because she failed to take the chance.

Plunging the tip of Illumina into the dirt at the edge of the red cobblestones, she sank the green orb into the soil. Blazing streamers of green light erupted beneath the hooves and underbellies of the Wicked armies, and the surge of Goodness threw the Witches from their saddles. Daspina twirled in the air; Ava shrieked and Marada flailed. All three hit the ground with a sickening *thud*.

"Good Magic!" Ava howled, slapping at her satin sleeves as if they were engulfed in flame.

Lumbering back toward her yak and leaping into the saddle, Marada bellowed, "Retreat!"

"Retreat?" cried Daspina as she scrambled onto the skink, blowing on her singed fingertips. "So . . . no punch bowls, then?"

"Not unless you are willing to pay for them with your blistered skin!" Ava shot back, leaping onto her giant weevil. "Fly!"

"Slither!" Daspina commanded, snapping the lizard's reins.

Marada spurred her yak so violently that the animal grunted in pain. The rest of the draft beasts followed, thundering northward as Daspina sped west and Ava and her flying creatures veered east. With the monkey flapping frantically to keep up, the three armies formed a thrashing mass that briefly covered the setting sun.

From below, on the safety of the red road, Glinda, the Protector of Oz, watched their escape. She knew they could not feel her furious gaze upon them.

But they will, she vowed silently.

And soon.

When the Witches were out of sight, the Road of Red Cobble sank back beneath the grass. Glinda wasted no time; she spun on her heel and headed for town.

"Wait!" called Ben, galloping along beside her. "Where are we going?"

"To find Mythra."

"Mythra?" Locasta echoed. "But you already found her in the Reliquary."

"That was a *statue*," Glinda corrected, doubling her pace. "This time I need to find her for *real*. You heard what my mother said before she ran off on that yellow brick road. 'Find Mythra.' And that is exactly what I'm going to do!"

"Glinda," began Miss Gage, who, along with Clumsy Bear, struggled to keep up with Glinda's speed.

But Glinda had already climbed over a stone wall and leaped across a narrow creek, marching faster and more furiously as she went. Ben, Shade, and Locasta stayed close at her heels, while Feathertop soared just overhead, causing Glinda's coppery hair to flutter in the breeze of his broad wings.

"I'm still not entirely clear about who Mythra is," Locasta panted. "Besides being a hero of Oz, that is." She glanced at Shade. "Have you heard anything?"

"Only a whispered mention here and there," Shade replied. "It's said she was the king's Mystic, the one who ushered him to his place as rightful ruler. And because no one was more knowledgeable in the ways of Magic, it was she who trained the Regents Valiant to lead the four countries of Oz while Oz himself ruled from the Centerlands."

Glinda listened to Shade's insights and kept her eyes trained on the armory in the distance. The village was not far off, and in the center of it was Madam Mentir's Academy for Girls. As she hurried on, a plan began to form in her mind. She would commandeer the school as a base for the Foursworn Rebellion, and from there she would begin her search for Mythra, the Priestess Mysterious.

"Shade, please go to the academy," she instructed. "Find Madam Mentir, Misty Clarence, and any other faculty member who remains loyal to the Wicked regime. Until we can decide what to do with them, we'll hold them in the school's cellar."

"Like a dungeon?" Locasta let out a chuckle. "Impressive."

"Feathertop and I will help with that," Ben offered, and the three of them rushed ahead, disappearing into the falling twilight.

"Clumsy," she called, "go into the forest, and apprehend any Wicked sympathizer who might be attempting to flee."

The bear gave an affirmative wuffle-snuff, tripped over

his front paws, then righted himself and loped off toward the trees.

"Glinda!" Miss Gage shouted. "Please, wait . . . there's something you should know." Catching up at last, she clamped her hand around Glinda's arm and dragged her to a stop. "I'm sorry to have to say this, but no matter how hard you try, you will never find Mythra."

"Of course I will," said Glinda.

"No, you won't. You *can't* find her, Glinda. No one can."

Glinda's stomach clenched as the words sank in. "Why is that?"

"Because," the teacher whispered, lowering her eyes. "Mythra . . . is *dead*!"

2

TRUTH . . . ABOVE ALL

*D*ead.

The word was like a spell designed to strike Glinda senseless. Mythra was *dead*.

"I'm sorry," said Gage. "But the powerful Priestess Mysterious died the same night King Oz was defeated."

"I don't understand," said Glinda, recalling how Shade had listened to the stained-glass windows in King Oz's Reliquary to recount the events of that awful night. At the hands of the Wicked Witches, the Regents Valiant had been lost, and the king himself destroyed. But there had been no mention of a Mystic named Mythra falling victim to their attack. "The last thing my mother said before she left to follow the Road of Yellow Brick was 'Find Mythra.'"

"Maybe she was confused," ventured Locasta.

"My mother is a Grand Adept of the Foursworn," Glinda hissed. "She doesn't *get* confused!"

Locasta gave a little snort and planted her hands on her hips. "Parents *aren't* infallible, Glinda! Sometimes they let you down. Sometimes, like Tilda, they just disappear and never come ba—"

With a roar, Glinda yanked the sword from her sash and held the lethal tip to Locasta's throat.

Miss Gage gasped.

But Locasta simply grinned and whispered, "Go ahead, Protector. I dare you."

Glinda gripped the handle until her arm shook—she was holding a blade an inch from her best friend's throat, and the realization was so shameful she could barely breathe. But that didn't change the fact that Locasta was wrong. She *had to be* wrong!

Without removing her eyes from Locasta's, Glinda rasped, "Miss Gage . . . are you certain? The Mystic is dead?"

"I'm as certain as I can be," Gage answered glumly. "There hasn't been a sign of her in ages. If she had survived the Witches' attack, I'm sure she would have shown herself by now."

"But . . ." Glinda's mouth went dry; her sword arm trembled so terribly that ripples of cold light flashed under

Locasta's chin. "Why would my mother tell me to find someone who couldn't be found?"

"She probably just made a mistake," said Locasta. "After all, it's been a rather hectic few days." Her tone was uncharacteristically reasonable, likely owing to the fact that there was a Magical sword poised against her neck. "Did you ever wonder why I'm always humming that little counting song?"

Glinda shook her head.

"Sometimes my father, Thruff, and I would get separated from one another in the mines. And believe me, you don't know 'scary' until you find yourself alone in some deep, dark gash in the world. But Papa said that as long we could hear one another humming, we'd each know that the others were all right. And you know what? I believed him. I actually believed that some silly jumble of notes he'd put together in no particular key could keep us safe. But one day Papa's song went silent. Just like that. He was gone. He'd said the humming would keep us safe . . . but he was *mistaken*." Locasta placed her fingertip gingerly on Illumina's point, and slowly, carefully pushed the weapon away until Glinda's arm hung limp at her side. "Parents fail sometimes, Glin. They let you down. They don't mean to, but they do. Tilda was just *wrong* to tell you to find Mythra, and the sooner you accept that, the better."

Glinda returned the blade to her sash with a trembling

hand. "Locasta, I'm *so* sorry. About your father, about . . ." She trailed off, too ashamed to even say the words.

"The sword?" Locasta shrugged as if having a weapon aimed at her throat was an everyday occurrence. "You were upset. And besides, even if you wanted to hurt me— which you didn't—I think we both know Illumina would never have allowed it."

Glinda nodded. "But my mother told me to—what was it she said?—to ensure that the momentum of the rebellion was not lost. Surely she thought that finding Mythra had something to do with that. If she's dead, I don't know what else I can do."

"You'll think of something," Locasta assured her, draping an arm over Glinda's shoulder. "I mean, you figured out how to release Ember by sticking that stone in your sword. I'm sure you'll—"

Glinda's eyes widened and her heart fluttered in her chest. "Locasta, that's it!"

"What's it?"

"I vanquished one Witch, I can vanquish the others. All I have to do is find the Elemental Fairies and unleash them on the Witches of the North, East, and West! How's *that* for momentum?" Beaming, she started walking again, charging toward town with a spring in her step.

"Uh . . ." Locasta's eyebrows shot upward. "Were you and I *not* on the same quest? Because the way I remember it, just finding Ember was an extremely difficult thing to do . . . and you'd been living in the *same house* with *him* for the last thirteen years!'"

"Locasta's right," said Gage. "The secret of the Elemental Fairies is the most heavily guarded secret in Oz."

"I realize that," said Glinda. "But this time, all we have to do is ask a Grand Adept, three of whom we just met on the Road of Red Cobble. That little Munchkin lady, for instance, or the rugged gentleman from Gillikin with the purple beard. Or that dapper fellow from Winkie—you know, with the funny suit and the fancy pocket hankie—he seemed eager to help."

"Good plan," said Locasta. "Too bad you didn't come up with it *before* they all followed the red road out of Quadling."

"It might not have even mattered if she had," Gage noted with a heavy sigh. "When I said that *only* the Grand Adepts knew where the Fairies were hiding, I did not mean to imply that *every* Grand Adept was privy to such knowledge. In fact, only a select few were entrusted with it, and since Dally and the others might very well *not* be among that number, I fear that traveling to meet with them now would be too great a risk. You heard the Witches say they were doubling their border guards."

"But the Road of Red Cobble—" Glinda began.

"Is quirky," was Locasta's stern reminder. "You can't risk having it bottom out on you at the Munchkin border, or disappearing halfway through Winkie."

Much as Glinda wished she could argue with that, Locasta had a point.

"What about Magic? Miss Gage, can we use your scrying mirror? Or cast a summoning spell?"

"Under other circumstances, maybe," said Gage. "Though with so little to go on, it would be difficult to know where to start."

"But we have to try!"

"Let me see if I've got this straight," said Locasta, planting her hands on her hips. "You're proposing that we try to find the hidden Elemental Fairies, who—let's face it—could be *anywhere* in the entire Land of Oz . . . but before we can even begin to look for *them*, we have to track down one of a *very* small handful of Grand Adepts who actually *know* where the Fairies *are*, and who, by the way, could also be anywhere, and who—just sayin'—have successfully managed to keep their Foursworn status a complete and total secret not only from the Wickeds but from just about everybody else in Oz as well, since the night the king was defeated." She rolled her eyes. "I don't know about you, but to me that sounds like the *worst* game of hide-and-seek *ever*."

"Well, when you put it that way . . . ," Glinda muttered, and trudged on.

They walked in silence until they reached the town square, where they saw several Quadling citizens huddled in groups, discussing the fall of Aphidina. Some looked hopeful, others wary, as they tried to process their great change in circumstance.

At the apothecary shop, a crowd had gathered—storekeepers who'd been about on the day Master Squillicoat was removed from his shop. Under the illusion of Aphidina's rule, no one had found it the least bit alarming to see soldiers guiding an innocent tradesman away from his place of business. *This is Quadling and all is well,* they'd told themselves. Little had anyone known that the good chemist was being hauled off to be sewn into a Wicked tapestry as an enemy of the Witch.

One of the merchants, the chandler, waved Glinda over and invited her to say a few words about their absent comrade. Still reeling from the grim news about Mythra and the Elemental Fairies, she climbed the steps to the shop's front door to deliver an impromputu tribute to her fallen friend, who had given his life back in Maud's cottage.

"Abrahavel Squillicoat understood that Magic is in the air we breathe," she began. "The tears we cry, the thoughts we think. It's in the footsteps that carry us across the solid ground of Quadling Country. Aphidina told us a lie that made us forget that; she stole our right to Magic. But nonuse of rights does not destroy them! It's time for all of us to learn the long-forgotten secrets of Magic—" She stopped short, her eyes going wide, her heart racing at the unexpected wisdom of her own words. "To the *secrets* of Magic!" she cried.

Pushing past the cheering spectators, Locasta sidled up to Glinda and gave her a stern look. "Okay, what're you thinking? I can practically see the wheels turning in your head."

Glinda's reply was to shout to the crowd, "Let's begin by opening Squillicoat's shop!"

A carpenter clapped his hands and touched his nose; the boards that had been nailed over Squillicoat's windows turned to glittering kites and lifted away on a Quadling breeze. He was both surprised and delighted by his accomplishment. "It's most enjoyable, isn't it? To be who one is!"

"Indeed it is," said Glinda.

Next a seamstress stepped forward to place her hand upon the door handle. *"Magic brings Magic to find and explore . . . unlock, unlatch, unbolt this door!"*

There was a click and a clatter, and sure enough, the door swung open.

Now Glinda nodded to the chandler. "I will be in need of some candlelight within, sir, if you please."

Beaming, the chandler strode through the open door and snapped his fingers; suddenly fresh tapers appeared in every empty, wax-dribbled candlestick Squillicoat had left scattered around the shop. A wave of the chandler's hand brought flames to each wick. "Hah!" he laughed. "Never did that before!"

"Thank you," said Glinda, dipping a curtsy to the candle maker as he and the rest of the onlookers took their leave. "Thank you in most generous amounts!" Then she rushed into the tiny shop.

Navigating the maze of tables and towering shelves that sagged under the weight of the apothecary's wares, she went first to Squillicoat's battered desk in the corner. How many times had she seen the friendly chemist seated there, working out his recipes and formulas, never dreaming he would turn out to be a prominent member of a Magical rebel faction. Pulling open the top drawer, she began to rummage through it.

"What are we doing in here?" Locasta asked, picking up a small jar of glistening salve and sniffing its contents. "Have you suddenly developed a rash?"

"I've suddenly developed an idea," Glinda retorted. "Squillicoat was the one who told us about the Gifts of Oz, remember? Through the steam of the teakettle in Maud's cottage."

"Of course I remember." Locasta gave a droll little snort. "It was right before you nearly got yourself smoked into oblivion."

Glinda ignored the gibe and moved from the desk to an open cupboard filled with dusty bottles, flagons, and crockery pots. "Miss Gage, when the Wickeds took over, what became of . . . well, *everything*? Everything that had to do with Oz's reign—official documents, public records, works of art and literature—anything that pertained to King Oz's rule?"

"I'd always just assumed Aphidina destroyed those things," Gage replied with a dainty shrug. "Her goal was complete and total illusion, so anything that might have reminded her subjects of Oz's reign would have threatened her power."

Glinda considered this, her mind turning over the many possibilities. "All right . . . so what if Abrahavel managed to gather up the secrets of Oz's past before Aphidina did and create a kind of archive of Ozian history?" Glinda's eyes shone. "He wasn't a Grand Adept, but he did know of the king's Gifts. Maybe he knew because he had access to that secret and others like it in the form of records, writings, artifacts. . . ."

"But he only knew the Gifts existed," Locasta pointed out. "He didn't know where the Gifts were, and he wasn't aware that the Fairies had saved them."

"That doesn't mean the information wasn't recorded somewhere," Glinda countered. "It just means he hadn't come upon it yet."

"Seems far-fetched to me," Locasta huffed. "And even if a guy who brews wart remover and pinkeye potion for a living *did* have the foresight to gather up all evidence of Oz's true history, do you really think he'd just leave it lying around in his workshop?"

"Of course not," said Glinda. "He would have created an illusion of his own." Glancing around the messy shop, she knit her brow. "Which means what we're looking for could be anywhere, in any form."

She plucked a squat jar with a glass stopper from the shelf. Inside, slender tremors of light flickered and flashed, emitting a crackling glow. There was a label tied to the neck that read QUISH.

"As in Baloonda?" she murmured. A mere three days ago Glinda had watched poor Baloonda Quish declare improperly, only to be violently Youngified at the hands of Misty Clarence, the Dean of Disastrous Decisions. And, she suddenly recalled, although Squillicoat himself had been apprehended before the Declaration ceremony, his apprentice Wally Huntz had attended the festivities—despite the fact that Huntz did not have a daughter, or even a niece, graduating from Mentir's Academy. But as intriguing as this realization was, it brought Glinda no closer to finding the Elementals.

Nerves prickling, she continued to search the cluttered shop. Every inch of the place was brimming with chemist's tools and medical journals. She peered at scales and spoons, searching for encoded engravings that might hint at what she wished to learn; she dug through leather trunks and a sprawling chest with a hundred tiny drawers. But she found nothing that spoke of Oz in days gone by—no ancient records, no dusty tomes, no painted portraits celebrating the rightful king, or the rightful queen before him. Just a jumble of flasks and scales, shriveling plants and manuals for mixing medicines. When Glinda discovered a half-empty vial labeled FOR RELIEF FROM THE INSIDIOUS SPLOTCHES, TO BE TAKEN TWICE A DAY WITH MEALS, she was overcome with lonesomeness for her friend Ursie.

"Where would someone hide eons and eons' worth of Ozian truth?" Locasta grumbled. "I mean, that's what we're looking for, isn't it? The truth."

"Yes," Gage agreed. "Truth."

"Truth," Glinda repeated, then, out of habit, added, "Above All."

The familiar phrase struck all three of them at once, and three pairs of eyes were suddenly cast upward to the ceiling, where a scuttle hole had been cut out, presumably to allow the apothecary access to his attic.

"*Above* All!" they chorused.

"Maybe?" said Glinda.

"Possibly," Gage allowed.

"I still don't think you're going to find anything," Locasta huffed, but she was already piling wooden crates on a rickety chair to construct a makeshift ladder. Seconds later the two girls had clambered up to the attic to crouch beneath the rafters, blinking as their eyes adjusted to the dimness.

"Any luck?" Gage called from below. "What do you see?"

"Nothing," Locasta announced smugly.

The sloping space stretched out around them, containing nothing but a few cobwebs and a thick coating of dust.

But as Glinda gazed into the emptiness, it occurred to her how strange it was that the apothecary would have hindered himself with such an untidy work space when he had so much attic space available to clutter up instead.

"What aren't I seeing?" she wondered aloud. "What is it that eludes my vision?"

As she posed the question, the blade at her hip gave off a soft pulse of light; for the scantest of seconds, Illumina cast a shining pool on the splintery floorboards under Glinda's knees. At the same moment, she felt a phrase tickling the tip of her tongue and she heard herself whisper into the gloom, "Blade of brilliance forged of vision . . ."

Vision!

Heart racing, she drew her sword and let the unbidden words form Magically upon her lips:

> *"True light of this sword I invite you to glow,*
> *So I may see the unseen, and the unknown I may*
> *know."*

Illumina's blade burst into a brilliant column of light, a Magical gleam that touched every corner of the attic. In its glow, the pitched roof dissolved into nothingness and was replaced by an unimaginable expanse of space. Contained in the vastness were countless leather-bound volumes, and forgotten scrolls, shelves filled with jars and vials bubbling with colorful potions and tinctures. Glinda saw sculptures and artifacts, objects and implements, all of which were examples and evidence of an Oz that once was.

And any of which might lead her to the Elemental Fairies.

"Incredible," said Locasta, running a finger gently along the spine of a book entitled *The Nomes of the Underlands: A Complete Genealogy.*

"Miss Gage," Glinda called down through the scuttle hole. "Please summon the chandler, and the carpenter and the baker as well! Tell them to come quickly and bring their carts and barrows."

"May I tell them what for?"

"Tell them we're bringing the truth back to Mentir's Academy," said Glinda, smiling. "And we're going to need all the help we can get."

As Miss Gage hurried off to enlist the aid of the towns-folk, Glinda quickly collected items that looked the most promising. Then she made her way carefully down the makeshift ladder and through the clutter of the shop's first floor. Halfway to the door, she remembered some-thing and retraced her steps to the shelf where the jar marked QUISH sat. Not that she imagined the sparkles of lightning it contained would help her find the Elemental Fairies. But it was possible that the apothecary had come up with an antidote to Youngification. If he did, and if she ever saw Baloonda again, she might be able to return her childhood to her.

But for now, that would have to wait.

Because she was sure that somewhere in the Magical boundlessness of Squillicoat's attic collection was the answer to the mystery of the hidden Fairies.

All Glinda had to do was find it.

Eager to assist, the merchants filled their wheelbarrows and wagons near to overflowing. Other villagers arrived to offer a hand, taking as much as they could carry, balancing armloads of books atop ivory chests bound in chains. They toted gilt-framed paintings, and etchings on frayed canvases; they filled their pockets with medals, talismans, and amulets of all shapes and sizes. What a peculiar caravan they made, marching to Madam Mentir's Academy for Girls, where they deposited Squillicoat's treasures in the library. When the long, polished study tables began to creak under the weight of the apothecary's carefully curated collection, Glinda directed her helpers to bring the rest to the academy's opulent dining hall.

When Ben, Shade, and Feathertop appeared, blinking in amazement at such a vast array of historical writings, records, and artifacts scattered around the library, Glinda quickly told them her plan to find the Elementals.

"Wait a minute," said Ben, cocking his head. "I thought you were supposed to be looking for Mythra. What happened to her?"

"She stopped being alive, that's what happened,"

Locasta informed him. "We're looking for the Fairies now."
She rolled her eyes. "C'mon on, Earth boy. Try to keep up."

"We're hoping we'll find some clue to their whereabouts
in the artifacts the apothecary was hiding," Glinda clarified.

Ben let out a long whistle. "It must have been a colos-
sal, not to mention dangerous, undertaking to preserve so
much of Oz's history. Let's hope it wasn't all for naught."

Glinda was about to agree when a cheerful and familiar
voice rang out from the library doorway. "Well, if it isn't
Glinda Gavaria, Protector of Oz!"

Glinda turned in the direction of the greeting, and her
eyes lit as she ran to throw her arms around Ursie Blauf.

"I owe you my deepest thanks, Ursie," said Glinda.
"Luring that soldier away from my house was so brave. I
had no idea you were a Revo."

"Well, I wasn't officially until you and the Grand Adept
disappeared," Ursie explained. "Before that, Master Squillicoat and Miss Gage had been cautiously 'recruiting'
me. The apothecary said he saw my potential when we
first met—back when I came down with those Insidious
Splotches. I'm heartsick over his demise, but thanks to his
example, many are now willing to take up the cause." A
tiny smile tugged at the corners of Ursie's mouth. "In fact,
some of them might surprise you."

The sound of giggling—and a hiccup—came from
across the library, and the next thing Glinda knew, she

was caught in an exuberant hug between Trebly Nox and D'Lorp Twipple.

"Ursie told us what a nasty Blingle turned out to be," Trebly grumbled. "I feel silly that we ever wished to be friends with her!"

"So silly!" D'Lorp hiccuped emphatically.

Glinda quickly introduced her old friends to her new ones. She had to mention Shade's name three times before Ursie, D'Lorp, and Trebly even noticed she was there.

"We so verily wish to be of assistance to the Foursworn," Trebly vowed.

D'Lorp concurred. "We serve—*hic-hic-hic*—at your command!"

Glinda thanked them and sent them off to help unload the three additional carts that were rumbling up to the front door. Then she settled into a chair and examined the wealth of Magical materials before her.

"I'll stay here," Ursie offered. "And help with"—she eyed the sprawling collection of artifacts—"with whatever this is."

"This," said Feathertop, "is your old school chum attempting to unravel the best-kept secret in Ozian history."

"Ooh! Sounds like fun!" said Ursie, plopping herself into the chair next to Glinda. Ben and Shade sat across from them, while Miss Gage glided from table to table, inspecting a chapbook here, a piece of sculpture there.

With a deep breath, Glinda reached for the largest book she could find—an ancient-looking tome entitled *The Compendium of Archaic Ozian Legendencia*, written by a historian named Gabriel Gale. But just as she made to open it, Locasta lunged across the table and swatted her hand away.

"Wait! Don't open that!"

"Why not?"

"Because I just thought of something! Don't you remember what happened with the Makewright's zoetrope, and Maud's teakettle? Every time you came upon some new lesson, we were attacked by that disgusting black cloud."

"Yes," whispered Shade. "It was almost as though it were spying on us."

Glinda went cold, remembering how those glowing red eyes had glared at her from the smoke that cut short the zoetrope's tale, then again from the steam of the teapot. They'd appeared to her once more in the Reliquary window. With a stab of horror, she realized who those hideous eyes belonged to. "The fifth Witch," she said. "From my mother's vision!"

Miss Gage looked up from a collection of old coins, her face suddenly pale. "Did you say 'fifth' Witch?"

Glinda nodded. "The one to whom the others answer."

"But . . . that's not . . . *possible*," Gage stammered, swaying on her feet. "I've never heard of a *fifth* Witch!"

"Don't feel bad," said Glinda. "My mother didn't know

of her either. But it occurs to me now that this fifth Witch can sense when I'm learning something new. Not just any little thing, but profound things about Ozian history."

"Which is why this all goes back to the apothecary's," Locasta declared, slamming her hand down on the dusty book. "Now! We are *not* risking another visit from that Wicked fog."

"But I can't just stop learning," Glinda argued. "I'm a Sorceress. Sorceresses create Magic through intellect. How else am I going to vanquish the Witches?"

"You'll have to find another way," said Locasta, pinning Glinda with a look of pure purple warning.

Glinda knew Locasta was right, but that didn't stop her from feeling sick about it. All this information spread out before her . . . but thanks to Wickedness, she was powerless to access a word of it. It was like being a student at Madam Mentir's all over again.

Miss Gage came over to smooth a stray lock of red hair from Glinda's forehead. "It has been an exceedingly long and tiring day," she said softly. "We'll be much more likely to solve the problem of the smoke after a good night's sleep."

Glinda was ready to argue, but thought better of it when she saw that Ben was in the middle of an enormous yawn, Shade's eyelids were drooping, and Locasta looked ready to drop. Even Feathertop seemed to be fighting the urge to tuck his head under his wing and go to sleep. *And no wonder,* she realized. Today they'd made the long trek back from the Centerlands to Quadling, found an Elemental Fairy hidden in a stone in the Gavarias' plundered home, fooled Leef Dashingwood into escorting them to the Wicked Harvester's palace, suffered an attack by the world's most violent trees, vanquished Aphidina with the help of Ember and Nick Chopper (a boy made partially of tin), then rescued Tilda and Clumsy Bear from the belly of the castle, released King Oz's final thought, endured a much-too-close-for-comfort encounter with three more Wicked Witches, and ultimately discovered an intellectual treasure trove in the apothecary's attic.

No wonder they looked exhausted! "All right," she said, pushing *The Compendium of Archaic Ozian Legendencia* away. "Let's get some rest."

"There are couches in the Grand Drawing Room," said Gage. "You should all be comfortable there."

Moments later, they were curled up on various pieces of furniture in the room where Glinda had, just three days before, been the first student in academy history to receive a blank scroll. Feathertop claimed the ceremonial urn as his nest for the night; snuggling into his feathers, he promptly began to snore.

"Sleep tight," said Ben.

"Don't let the woggle-bugs bite," giggled Ursie.

Shade did not chime in, but Glinda was too preoccupied to wonder why. And although she was sure she would spend the next several hours fending off nightmares about missing Fairies, dead Mystics, and Wicked smoke, she wished the others a sincere, "Pleasant dreams."

"Can we all just shut up and go to sleep!"

"Good night to you, too, Locasta," Glinda murmured. But when she closed her eyes, her mind was filled with the urgent echo of her mother's voice: *You must find Mythra*.

If only she could.

3

ON THE ROAD OF YELLOW BRICK

The Road of Yellow Brick wound out of the Woebegone Wilderness to the Quadling border at Munchkin Country.

Tilda and Nick Chopper crept cautiously out of the newly freed land and into a blue-tinted meadow, only to spy a platoon of Ava's insect soldiers patrolling the borderline.

"I'd give my right arm for a flyswatter right now," Nick quipped.

"It seems my little girl has frightened the Wickeds enough so that they are increasing their protection." Tilda chuckled, her eyes shining with pride. "Looks like we'll be resting here for the night."

Nick eyed the yellow bricks of the road beneath his tin feet. "Couldn't we utilize the Magic of the Road of Red Cobble to get past these buggy brutes?"

"We could," said Tilda, "but for this quest, I'm afraid we must put ourselves on a collision course with the thing we hope to uncover. The safety of the red road leads Good fairyfolk to their destinations, but the protection it provides can prevent them from finding unexpected insight along the way. Unfortunately, insight is often a by-product of trouble."

Nick frowned. "So you're *hoping* to discover trouble?"

"Sometimes that is where the answers are," Tilda explained. "As a general rule, I don't recommend looking for danger, but my Magic is strong enough that in most instances, I am able to make trouble for the trouble."

"But only *sometimes*," Nick qualified with a gulp.

"That is the nature of discovery, and it is why the Road of Yellow Brick is not for everyone." She placed a motherly hand on his shoulder and squeezed. "I will happily deliver you to your home in Munchkin if—"

"No!" Nick interrupted firmly, punching his tin fist into his real one. "The yellow brick road is most definitely for me! As I told you before we left Quadling, I have a stout heart!"

"Yes, my friend, you do," Tilda agreed. "But even stout hearts need their rest, and it has been a very tiring journey; a journey that is far from over. So let's gather some firewood and settle in for the night."

They set up camp in a dense copse of towering blue spruce trees. The needles that fell in a Magical sprinkle when Tilda had whispered, "*Comfort, come here,*" were swept into two narrow piles to create a pair of passably cozy beds on which the travelers reclined gratefully beneath the starry sky.

"Is it my imagination, or is this fire brighter than any I've ever seen before?" asked Nick.

"You are not imagining it," Tilda assured him. "It is because Ember has come out of hiding at last. From now on, the fires in Oz will all be as bright as this one."

"A marked improvement," said Nick, noting how the flickering flames seemed to turn his tin to molten gold. Even the heat of the fire went beyond the mere sensation of warmth; it seemed to contain sparks of compassion, kindness, even love.

"Truly, it's a bit of a miracle that we had flames at all during those ages the Fire Fairy spent in hiding," Tilda remarked. "I daresay our world would not have been much of a world without cozy firesides to warm ourselves by."

"I hope you won't think me coldhearted if I say that before I met you and Glinda, I used to wonder if it *was* much of a world." Nick's heavy eyelids fluttered sleepily. "What with the Wickeds in charge and me turning to tin and all.

"I'm poor, you see. And poor is not what the girl wants."

"The girl?"

"Nimmie Amee is her name, and she says she can only love a lad with coins jangling in his pockets. A lad who can afford to build her a house."

"And you cannot?"

"Not anymore. We Choppers have always done very well for ourselves, thanks to our talent with an ax. But when Ava Munch saw how our coffers overflowed, she became greedy and placed a tax on all blade-sharpening services throughout Munchkin Country. The Ax Tax, it was called, though it applied to anything sharp—scissors, shaving implements, kitchen cutlery. There was even talk of taxing those who were said to possess a 'razor-sharp tongue' or a 'rapier wit.' Because of the Ax Tax, my father died penniless, leaving me only this ax." Nick yawned and curled deeper into his pine needles, clanking as he did. "Then, of course, the Witch went and cursed it at the request of Nimmie Amee's employer. And you've seen how that's turned out for me."

"I'm so sorry," Tilda whispered, wishing her Good Magic could undo the hex, but knowing that to even try might result in graver problems.

"It's not ideal, you understand, to have an ax that cuts off one's own limbs whenever one hacks into a tree branch," Nick mused, "but I look at it this way. Most folks rarely get to prove themselves, but I get to test my mettle—*and* my metal—every day. I'm just lucky Ku-Klip the tinsmith can fashion new parts for me whenever I require them."

"Lucky," Tilda agreed, though her heart broke to say it.

They fell silent for a moment, and the only sound was the crackle of the fire and the not-so-far-off drone of Ava Munch's insect soldiers buzzing watchfully at their posts. Tilda was beginning to think her young companion had dozed off, when he spoke again—softly, in a voice filled with longing.

"Mistress Gavaria, there is something about stout hearts that you might not know."

"What is that?"

"They can break."

Tilda looked at his somber face through the fire and waited for him to continue.

"You invited me to join you on this yellow road because you thought I had much still to discover, and I believe you are quite correct in that. I think perhaps it is time for me to discover whether or not this stout heart of mine can be mended."

"Perhaps it is," Tilda concurred.

"And since we now find ourselves in Munchkin Country, I was hoping you wouldn't mind if we went together, you and I, to pay a brief visit to Miss Amee at her place of employment so that I may discover once and for all if she is willing to love a boy of tin."

Tilda gave the idea some thought. "If that is what you wish, Nick Chopper," she said at last, "then I think it is exactly what you must do."

Across the flickering tips of the flames she saw him smile, his sleepy blue eyes dancing with hope. A moment later, the brokenhearted boy was fast asleep.

Confident that Nick Chopper would be safe, hidden there among the trees, Tilda decided she would spend these midnight hours making careful inquiries—dangerous ones, to be sure—regarding the fifth Witch and the ceremony she and Glinda had witnessed in Elucida's vision. Daylight, she knew, lent itself to certain kinds of knowledge, but as she'd once told her daughter . . . some answers could only be found in the shadows.

Throwing a few more twigs onto the fire, Tilda Gavaria, Grand Adept of the Foursworn, hitched up her skirts and crept silently away from the camp.

In search of knowledge.

In search of trouble.

She was, as always, prepared for both.

4

THE NAUTILUS SHELL

Glinda was too restless to sleep. Slipping silently off the couch, she tiptoed out of the Grand Drawing Room, took a candlestick from a hall table, and lit the taper by placing a quick kiss to the wick. It flared as though it were honored to be lighting her way.

For hours she wandered aimlessly along the corridors, many of which were lined with portraits of the school's most illustrious Declarants. Glinda had always been too swept up in rushing to her next class to pay much attention to them before, but tonight she took the time to study them. What she saw were scores of girls from years, decades, even centuries gone by, all sporting the same uniform of red ruffled dress and white pinafore, all blissfully engaged in the pointless endeavor of what passed for an education at Madam Mentir's Academy.

To Glinda's shock, one of the portraits appeared to be of Blingle Plunkett. Holding the candle closer to the canvas, she peered at the likeness through the faded paint. The hairstyle was different—an old-fashioned coiffure Glinda had never known Blingle to favor—but the eyes were the same; in a word, *mean*. What was strange was that Blingle couldn't possibly have had time to pose for it, having gone off the day after Declaration to trap Glinda in Maud's cottage. So clearly this wasn't Blingle, but perhaps an ancestor to whom she bore an uncanny resemblance.

With a shudder, Glinda walked on, heading toward the library and pausing in the doorway. *Maybe it wouldn't hurt if I opened just one book, or unrolled a single scroll. . . .*

But she knew that delving into even one book would be tempting the smoky wrath of the Wicked fifth Witch. What she needed was to put some distance between herself and Squillicoat's collection. Perhaps a walk in the fresh air would clear her head.

She made her way out to the back lawn, withdrew Illumina, and said, "*Blade of Brilliance, blaze me a trail.*" Instantly the metal dissolved into a slender pulse of light.

Following the sword's path, she soon found herself at the lake where only days ago she'd defeated Aphidina's

Lurcher during a Magical blizzard brought on by the Wards of Lurl.

On the opposite side stood the Maker's cabin, clearly visible in the moonlight. When she'd first spied it from this spot days ago, it had been obscured by thick vines and tall weeds. But as it was no longer necessary for the Goodness that dwelled there to conceal itself, the vines had all fallen away. What remained was a cozy little lodge, nestled in the woods.

With a jolt, Glinda realized that she'd left something very precious in that cabin: Haley Poppet. The thought of her beloved rag doll being lost was almost too much to bear, and it occurred to Glinda that this was probably the reason her sword had led her here—so she could retrieve her doll without Locasta around to poke fun at her. But when she took a step toward the cabin, Illumina's blade dimmed.

Glinda cocked an eyebrow in confusion. "Don't you want me to visit the Maker's lodge?"

The answer came with her next step, when Illumina's light vanished completely.

"All right, then," she said, resting her foot upon a large stone that jutted up from the shallows. "I'll just stand here and enjoy the gentle lapping of the water."

At this, the sword flared mightily, casting a bright glow across the lake. Glinda watched as the dark water rippled under the gleam; despite the absence of any breeze, the

water rose up into a ruffle of tiny whitecaps. One of these rolled toward the edge where Glinda stood; she managed to jerk her foot off the stone just before the little wave broke over it with a splash.

"Hey!" She frowned at Illumina. "That wasn't nice!"

As though in apology, the blade's light twinkled briefly upon the water. Then it gathered itself into a gentle glow, revealing a beautiful seashell balanced upon the stone beside Glinda's foot.

It had not been there a moment ago.

Glinda bent down and lifted the fragile object. Similar in shape to the Queryor's horns, it glistened with golden stripes against a lustrous background of aquamarine; it seemed to weigh less than if she were holding nothing at all.

Returning Illumina to her sash, she turned the shell over, and the beauty of it nearly took her breath away. A series of perfectly graduated spirals curled outward from the center, opening wider and wider as they went. It was motionless and yet filled with motion, ancient and infinite. To Glinda it resembled a swirling stairway, a spiral of steps that might lead to the future or the past, to above or below, nearer or farther away, depending on where one wished to go. More than anything, the graceful design reminded her of the way Locasta looked when she was twirling into a Magical dance.

"Strange, though," she murmured, "to find a *sea*shell in a lake."

Illumina flared again, throwing its light back toward the path on which Glinda had come.

"Time to go already?" she asked the sword, smiling. "Yes, I suppose it is. Someone might wake up and wonder where I am. And I don't want them to think I've had a run-in with the smoke."

Glinda turned to leave, but whirled back again when she glimpsed something out of the corner of her eye— something shiny and swift, flicking across the lake and disappearing.

Probably just Illumina's reflection, she decided. Slipping the pretty shell into her pocket, she headed back toward town.

From the door of the Makewright's cabin, a figure watched Glinda accept the shell . . . and smiled. At long last, the time had come to set the plan in motion, this complex and delicate scheme that had taken the better part of forever to compose. And the burgeoning Magic of the young Sorceress would be the key. Indeed, any hope of Goodness once again prevailing in Oz would depend entirely on what Glinda Gavaria did next.

This silent witness, more than anyone—more than even Glinda herself—knew the cost of finding oneself in possession of unimaginable power. And though he could have simply come to her (again) and *told* her and the others what he wanted them to know, he had learned over the ages that to know things too early could be just as disastrous as knowing them too late. The most he could do was to nudge her from outside of Time, communicating within those tiny spaces that swam between then and now and later. He hoped that with the suggestion in place, and with this token from his undersea friends, she would arrive at her own conclusions.

In her own Time.

He could easily take himself to the end result, if he wished to, by skipping over all that lay between. But as he began the long walk through the Woebegone Wilderness, he found that he was in that rare sort of mood in which he felt the need to experience the multitude of seconds as he passed through them. Because no moment was insignificant enough to overlook.

He'd learned that the hard way.

The lake was well behind her when Glinda felt the words of a whisper swirl around her.

"Time will tell," the whisper said.

And although she would not remember, she would indeed know (in the corner of her mind where promises were made and secrets were kept) that the voice she hadn't heard belonged to Eturnus, the Timeless Magician.

Hero of Oz.

It was nearly dawn when she got back to the academy. Her first stop was the Grand Drawing Room, where she slipped the nautilus shell into Ben's knapsack for safekeeping. But while her visit to the lake had calmed her, it had also made her ravenously hungry. Craving a honey bun with tamorna jelly, she and her growling tummy headed for the kitchen.

To get there, she would have to pass through the dining hall . . . where a good portion of Squillicoat's historical treasures still waited.

The academy dining hall was an immense room with gleaming floors, broad fireplaces, and four enormous chandeliers—but these lights were not wrought from iron or brass; rather they consisted of delicate silken nets studded at each knot with a tiny faceted crystal; caught inside the nets were millions upon millions of twinkling fireflies. Once, during a particularly boring dining period in Fledgling year, Ursie Blauf had stared at one of these nets for so long and with such intensity that all the knots that held it together split open at once. Thousands of infinitesimal crystals showered down upon the delighted academy girls as they enjoyed their noonday meal and witnessed what could only be described as a fantastical firefly exodus. Ursie Blauf was instantly promoted to an advanced placement class called No Nexus Can Perplex Us: A Girl's Guide to Knots, where she could be both carefully instructed and closely watched. At the time, the untying incident had been fluffed off as an unfortunate consequence of "overaggressive daydreaming." No one had called it Magic.

Tonight the dining hall was lit not by fireflies but by streamers of pale moonglow. This was the Moon Fairy Elucida's promise to Oz, and the thought of the Wickeds torturing her into permanent darkness as she had seen them do in Tilda's vision both terrified and enraged Glinda. Also terrifying was the fact that when the vision repeated itself in the Reliquary, Glinda had seen herself and her mother being held prisoner in the center of it all. There had been a third captive as well, but Glinda still had no idea who it was.

Indeed, the entire purpose of the moon ceremony still evaded her.

But it suddenly occurred to Glinda that there was a certain vile someone who just might be able to help her understand the Witches' plans for the moon—a Wicked affiliate with strong ties to the late Aphidina, Witch of the South. And as it happened, this someone was currently being held captive, right downstairs.

5

STATIC

In the North, the sky was a wash of dull indigo. In Gillikin Country, even the dawn looked as if it had been beaten black and blue.

In a castle of quartz, the Witch Marada sat upon her throne, dressed, as always, for battle in a steel breastplate and spaulders on her shoulders. On her feet she wore sturdy leather sandals adorned with vicious spurs, and on her hands a pair of Silver Gauntlets with jointed fingers, which still carried smudges of red soil from her visit to Quadling. This distressed her. What good was a thing of silver if it did not shine?

The Witch grunted at the grubby lad who stood humming

in the corner, and held out her gloves to him. He came forward and took them without so much as a quiver.

"A good buffing is wanted," she commanded. "Mind the crevices, and gentle with the joints. Should you return them to me with so much as a dent, I will happily inflict the same upon your skull."

The scamp said nothing, just retreated to his corner to begin the chore. Humming.

The boy was a recent addition to her court, a fresh little slave hauled in just over a fortnight before, and he'd been standing stoically in that corner ever since. She had barely fed him (he was likely used to that) or even spoken to him until just this moment when she'd given him this task. Ordinarily she would have simply turned him into a statue of stone, as was her custom with those who displeased her.

But she didn't need another statue. The grounds surrounding her castle were already littered with them, as well as the stony wreckage of the ones she'd crushed—pebbles formerly known as peasants.

Marada turned to gaze out a tall, arched window, a gash in the stones perfect for shooting arrows, something she longed to do. Through it she could observe her subjects as they trudged out to toil in her mines. It was grueling work, descending deep into the belly of Lurlia to pick and hack away at the world's innards. But the Gillikins were hers to do with as she wished, which was why she had long ago ordered they be clasped into shackles—crude metal manacles secured around their wrists. The dull clunking sound they made as the miners trekked to work was music to her ears.

The only thing Marada enjoyed more than seeing her subjects slog off to the mines was taking from them what little they had. She called this process Levying, and it was her favorite game to play.

Two weeks past, Marada had gone out at daybreak to entertain herself by tormenting the residents of a shabby little mining camp. The stomping of the soldiers' boots and the clanking of her own heavy armor had roused them from the piles of hay and rags on which they slept. Tromping through the sad little village of tents and shacks and lean-tos where the Gillikins were forced to reside was the closest she'd come in ages to mounting an invasion.

"Get up, you Gillikin prospectors," she boomed. "Come bow to your Witch and make your pathetic offerings to she who is so much greater than you. It is time for the Levying."

The Gillikins staggered out of their shelters in their tattered nightclothes, rubbing the crust from their eyes.

As she made her way down the path, she held out her hands, the palms of her gauntlets upturned. The sleepy, hungry Gillikins rushed to proffer whatever they had to give: the speckled shell of an Ork's egg; a whimsically whittled knick-knack, colorful stone chips unearthed from the mines. All useless nothings the Witch despised on sight. Most of these she threw back in their haunted faces, but such ingratitude did not discourage their neighbors from trying to please her with their own piteous remembrances—bent coins, mended stockings, little brushes fashioned of boar's bristles. Garbage, all of it! The Witch had expected as much.

She stopped at the threshold of a shack where a boy and his sister waited, groggy and barefoot. The girl wore a nightshift of lilac cotton; her hair was a long tangle of plum-colored curls. Marada had to look away quickly, for the girl was quite beautiful, and beauty made her queasy. The brother, who was younger, though not by much, had a thatch of thick brown hair streaked with purple, and a mouth that might have pouted if he were younger and less courageous. He stood with his shoulders pressed back and his chin up, though whether his intention was to emulate or mock the Witch's liveried guards, Marada could not be certain.

"Have you an offering for me?" she demanded of the girl.

The girl slid one hand into the pocket of her nightgown and closed her fingers tight around something Marada could not see; then she shook her head. The Witch slid her gaze to the brother and drawled, "Do you have something to bestow?"

The boy snapped his violet-blue eyes up to meet Marada's; there she saw a glint of something she could not quite identify. Defiance? Zeal? Stupidity? All of these, perhaps.

"Your offering?" she prompted.

"How could a thing that is demanded be offered?" the urchin challenged. "Anything we have to give you is already yours."

At this, the Witch lifted an eyebrow. "You are a precocious little dung beetle, aren't you?" she replied calmly, just before her gauntleted fist slammed into his jaw. Even as the boy staggered backward, his shoulders remained squared.

Beside him, his sister had glowered but kept mum.

And Marada walked on.

The urchin, whose name was Thruff, had watched her go.

He saw the Witch stop next at the tent of an old man whose spine was bent into a brittle arc.

"What gift do you offer, you crooked waste of skin?"

The man showed her his empty hands. "Most humble apologies, Your Militancy, but I have no token suitable for one so glorious as you."

"That is not entirely true," Marada snarled. "I see you have three or four teeth left in your ugly head. Perhaps I shall yank those out and string them together for a charm bracelet."

Thruff moved like mist, darting out of the doorway and into the street before his sister could even reach out to stop him. He slipped unnoticed through the legs of one guard to place himself in the shadow of an even larger one; he was so close he could see his own reflection in the shine on the soldier's boots.

Marada remained focused on the stooped man, pondering his apology. "Cut off his toes," she decided. "I shall add them to the teeth and fashion a necklace."

A cry rang up from the Gillikin miners (who were all wide awake now) as the guard behind whom Thruff crouched stepped forward to catch the old man by the front of his grungy nightshirt. Dragging the frail victim into the middle of the street, the soldier pushed him down and grabbed one of his filthy, calloused feet.

"How many?" the soldier asked the Witch.

Marada sighed, already bored with the spectacle. "All of them," she replied.

The guard smiled and reached for his blade.

But found his scabbard empty.

"Looking for this?"

Thruff had returned to his doorway, holding a lethal-looking dagger in his hand. The village fell silent, but for the faint clanking of the old man's shackles as he shook with fear.

Thruff twirled the knife between his fingers. "Seems I have a gift to give you after all."

Marada let out a roar of fury. She crooked her gauntleted finger at Thruff in a Magical command, forcing him to stumble forth involuntarily until he'd come toe to toe with her.

He held up the stolen knife. "For you, Your Ungratefulness."

He might have gotten away with his sauciness, if only he hadn't grinned.

There was the flash of a silver glove, an explosion of pain, and Thruff's world went black.

Marada's thin lips curled into something approaching a smile as she recalled the slap she'd given the scamp for his disrespect. She'd taken great pleasure in watching him crumple to the mud. In the end, she'd left the hunchback's toes where they were and had the child hauled to the castle, where she could hit him again the moment he awoke from his stupor. Which she had. But that had been several days ago, so perhaps he was due for another.

She studied him now with mild hostility and saw that he was perhaps a dozen years into his existence. He was possessed of obvious grit, and Marada had to admit, he was disgustingly well-formed, with eyes the color of a Gillikin midnight.

Without warning, the sky outside suddenly bruised over to an even darker shade of gloom. Marada felt the room rumble, as a slim fissure appeared in the purplish paving stones at her feet. In the next second, the floor had cleaved itself in two.

"A lurlquake," she murmured, reluctantly impressed, for she knew this was no ordinary tectonic shift. This was

Mombi, the Krumbic one, announcing her presence.

And she certainly knew how to make an entrance.

"Keep buffing," Marada told the boy, who did as he was told, even as the floor shook violently beneath him.

Chunks of the paving stones spilled into the widening crack, and a stench exploded from below. Was this what it was like for the mine workers, in the cavernous depths? Marada wondered. All steam and stank and gaseous belching? She certainly hoped it was.

"Greetings, Brash Warrior."

Immediately Marada dropped to her knees in a gesture of reverence. Her eyes shot to the corner, where the boy was still hard at work, spit-shining the silver gauntlets as though nothing even remotely unnerving was afoot. Brave little idiot.

Of the quake, she inquired, "To what do I owe the honor of this visitation?"

A belch of hot smoke exploded from the shattered floor. *"Marching orders! You will deploy your horned and hooved and woolly army to Quadling Country for the purpose of capturing the young Foursworn rebel Glinda Gavaria. It will be an aggressive campaign, as I have already issued this same command to your sisters-in-arms."*

"They are *not* my sisters," the Warrior growled, then choked out humbly, "but I will endeavor to tolerate the presence of Ava and Daspina and do my best to enjoy the war."

"*You misunderstand me,*" the lurlquake intoned in a way that made Marada feel as if it were wagging a finger at her. "*You will not be joining your cattle beasts for this attack.*" The expulsion of gassy odor that followed told Marada exactly what Mombi thought of her army of draft animals.

"But I am a Warrior," Marada protested. "That's what I do . . . I attack."

More gas rose from the broken floor, and cracks began to snake up the stone walls. "*Not this time you don't,*" the quake retorted. "*But you mustn't feel slighted. The Witches of the East and West will be sending their armies, but they too are forbidden to take part. I cannot risk you turning on one another in battle. If you'll recall, that is precisely what happened the last time I sent the three of you and your fallen sister to collect a prize, and you failed spectacularly.*"

Marada flinched, wishing she had her Silver Gauntlets back, if only to conceal the angry twitching of her fingers. It had been ages since the murder of King Oz, and she'd nearly succeeded in wiping the shameful recollection from her mind completely. But leave it to this Krumbic tremor to bring it all back—the vivid image of the moment in which the Warrior and the other three Wickeds had divested the fading king of his armor. In their selfish excitement, they had neglected to gather the Gifts they'd been sent for, and they had been paying for that mistake ever since.

"How unfortunate that you don't have an army of your

own to carry out this mission," Marada grumbled. "Then you would not have to rely on ours."

There was a vicious shudder as the fault line widened between the kneeling Witch's calloused knees; she struggled to straddle the chasm without falling in.

"*Oh, but I will have an army*," the quake retorted. "*And to that end, I require from you a particular trinket. A Golden Cap, which you bullied away from some simpering miner some time ago. Do you recall it?*"

Marada made a quick mental accounting of the offerings she'd collected from desperate Gillikins over the years and could not for the life of her imagine why Mombi would want that one. When she'd acquired the cap, Marada had wondered how the miner had come to be in possession of such a peculiar piece of headwear. She'd asked him that very question with a blade to his throat, and his answer was that he'd uncovered it deep in the northernmost mines of Gillikin. Her only motive for accepting it was that it had seemed quite precious to him and she liked robbing her slaves of the things they cherished most. Having no interest in it herself, however, she'd tossed it into a chest and promptly forgotten all about it.

Until now.

"It is an unsightly gemstone-studded bonnet made of velvet, the color of which puts one in mind of jaundice. Ridiculous earflaps, if memory serves. Oh, and some poetical nonsense inscribed on the underside. 'Ep Kak' something-or-other. In my estimation, it is not only hideous but monumentally useless as well."

It was at this point that the boy stepped out of the shadows and handed the Silver Gauntlets back to Marada as indifferently as if they were a handkerchief he'd borrowed and soiled with snot.

A murky cloud billowed up from the roiling guts of Lurlia, sweeping toward the boy for a closer look. *"Who have we here?"*

"Just some scruffy little pickpocket," Marada said, slipping the gauntlets on and clenching her fists inside them. "Gillikin garbage, nothing more."

"I am Thruff," the boy proclaimed. "Son of Norr."

The malodorous vapors took a moment to inspect the urchin, swirling around him as if he were a thing of great interest. *"How angry you are!"*

Thruff shrugged, as though he saw no reason to dispute it. For it was true; his rage all but crackled off him in sparks. Marada noticed her gauntlets had never looked better.

"What does this Golden Cap do?" he asked the quake.

Marada stiffened, fully expecting that in the next moment she'd be sweeping his bones off the floor. How dare he presume to question the fifth Witch! Didn't he know she could slay him with a blink of her eyes, or implode him by simply blowing him a kiss? Marada very much disliked the possibility of having Gillikin guts splattered across her throne room.

But to the Warrior's surprise, the quake seemed impressed by the urchin's nerve and went on to enlighten him with uncharacteristic patience:

"The cap is an ancient thing. A wedding gift that went awry—or so the legend goes. It grants the one who wears it the power to control a staggeringly unique army."

Marada's bloodshot eyes nearly popped out of her head. To think she'd had this remarkable item in her keeping all this time, and had never had so much as an inkling of its Magic. Had she not still been kneeling, she would have stomped her oversize feet in fury.

"Control is a great power indeed," Thruff noted, his mouth quirking up into a lopsided grin. "And who better to wield such might than you, quake?"

"You are a wise lad," the quake allowed.

The Warrior's guts clenched at the issuance of such praise for the little upstart who should have been, at that very moment, clinging to a fraying rope and being lowered into a deep hole in the world. She wanted to slap the insolence right out of him. Or kick him hard in his bony rib cage. Where did this malnourished little bumpkin get off exhibiting such gumption? Perhaps she should consider employing tighter, rustier manacles in the future.

"Thank you, Your Seismicness," the scamp replied.

Marada had had enough. "Shut up and go fetch the cap!" she boomed. "And be quick about it or I'll break you in half."

She told him harshly where he could find it, and he scurried off through the antechamber. When he was gone, she rose from her knees and lumbered across the broken room to her throne. Whatever brittle chunk of a thing it was that throbbed in the place where her heart should be was aching. To think, a battle—a real weapon-slinging, enemy-bashing, land-decimating battle—was forthcoming . . . and she was not invited.

And what of this silly yellow hat? Rightfully, it belonged to *her*. Shouldn't that count for something? Settling into her chair, she addressed the chasm in her floor. "So the cap commands an army, you say?"

"Not the cap itself, you witless Warrior. The one who wears it! If you had been sporting it when I arrived, that honor would be yours, and I would have been powerless to take it from you."

Marada sank in her stony chair. "Not even by brute force? Because that certainly seems like something you would do."

Another violent fault split open across the floor. Marada took that as a "no."

"Once the cap is donned, it cannot be taken by another, not by any means. The wearer is gifted with three opportunities to lead the most ruthless army in all of Oz. This right endures until the cap is removed by the wearer."

Marada scowled, wishing the quake would depart and leave her to regret her ignorance in private. But she knew this Krumbic upset would not go without her treasure.

"Where has that dirty-elbowed little yak turd got off to anyway?" she spat. "Thrufffffff of Gillikin! Demonstrate your miserable presence at once."

And so he did, returning instantaneously from where he had been listening in the antechamber. He flashed a triumphant smile.

Marada's eyes went wide as a commotion arose outside the narrow windows—fierce chattering, a frenzied flapping of giant wings, and hundreds upon hundreds of furry tails, whipping and snapping in the stormy sky.

The quake shook with fury, but even the quivering of the castle could not keep the hard line of Marada's mouth from bending into a vindictive grin.

Because Thruff, the eavesdropping, pickpocket scamp, had placed the Golden Cap upon his head.

And there was not a blasted thing the Krumbic one could do about it.

6

MEMORIES, AND KNOWLEDGE, AND WISHES GO BYE!

Glinda dashed to the Grand Drawing Room and shook Locasta awake.

For this she was rewarded with a very nasty glare. "This better be important, Glimpy. The sun is barely up!"

"It's *very* important," Glinda assured her, hurrying to where Ursie was curled in an overstuffed chair and shaking her, too. Ben was stretched out on the plush carpet, under a blanket, with his trusty knapsack at his side. "Wake up, Urs. Benjamin, Shade—" Her eyes scanned the large space. "Where's Shade?"

"Who knows?" Feathertop muttered sleepily from the

depths of the urn. "Out spying somewhere would be my guess."

Ben let out a great yawn. "What's all the commotion? It's barely daylight."

"We're going to the cellar."

Locasta was suddenly wide awake. "You mean the *dungeon*," she corrected, leaping up from the couch to begin strapping on her boots.

"Why?" asked Ursie, rubbing her eyes.

"Because we need to talk to Madam Mentir. She's the only one who might be able to tell me why the Witches are planning to steal the Moon Fairy. And if I ask her, it might be considered learning. So I need you to come and ask her for me."

This statement was met with three wide-eyed, slack-jawed stares.

Locasta stopped strapping. "What did you say?"

"I said I need you to ask Mentir—"

"Not that part. The other part . . . about *stealing the Moon Fairy*!"

"Oh, that." Glinda felt her face flush scarlet. "I guess I never did tell you *how* Aphidina discovered my mother was a Grand Adept, did I?"

"No," said Ben. "You didn't."

"But please," said Ursie, raising an eyebrow. "Do enlighten us."

"Yeah," said Locasta with a ferocious yank on her boot-strap. "Enlighten us. And fast."

"Well . . ." Glinda drew a deep breath. "The night before Declaration Day, my mother summoned a Magical vision with the help of Elucida, the Moon Fairy. The vision was of all four of the Wicked Witches working together in what my mother coined a 'confluence of evil.' They were standing together in a circle as though they were four points on some giant compass."

"Compass?" Locasta repeated, her voice catching.

Glinda nodded. "They seemed to be united in the performance of some Wicked ceremony . . . to steal Princess Elucida from the moon."

Ursie gasped. Ben went pale. In the urn, Feathertop gave a little chirp of disbelief.

"And you never thought to mention this vision before?" Locasta hissed. "Since it turns out it was the whole reason we went on the quest for the Fire Fairy in the first place?"

"I didn't see any pointing in scaring anyone," was Glinda's defensive reply. "More than we already were, that is."

"That's understandable," Ben conceded, slinging his knapsack across his chest. "But Glinda, if there's anything else we should know about this vision, now is the time to reveal it."

Glinda swallowed hard. "Not that I can think of," she hedged. Though of course, there was something else, something hugely significant—and that was the fact that she, her mother, and an unknown third party appeared to be unwilling participants in the Witches' dark Magic.

"All right, then," said Locasta with a nod. "To the dungeon."

Two former Quadling soldiers, now proud and loyal members of the Foursworn army, were guarding the door to a small, dank storage area in the academy basement.

"Allow me!" said Locasta. Pointing her foot at the door, she circled her ankle once to the right, then back to the left. Then she shook her shoulders and spun on her toes.

The door dissolved into a heap of shavings and splinters.

"Or you could have just used that," said Ben, indicating the iron key that hung from one of the soldiers' belts.

"I could have." Locasta grinned. "But what fun would that've been?"

Glinda peered through the doorway into the dimly lit space beyond. Recalling how the headmistress had summoned her on the morning of Declaration, she shouted in an icy tone, "Madam Mentir! *Approach!*"

From out of the shadows, Mentir rushed forward, forcing a friendly smile. "Glinda! My favorite student! How lovely your hair looks this morning! Whatever was I thinking when I asked you to braid it?"

Ursie giggled. "Someone's certainly changed her tune, hasn't she?"

"I want you to tell me what Aphidina and the others were planning to do with the Moon Fairy," Glinda commanded.

At this, Mentir looked astonished. "You know about that?"

Glinda's response was a slow nod.

"Well, I always knew you were one of the truly intelligent ones," Mentir gushed. "And I'll be happy to tell you everything I know about the Ritual of Endless Shadow if only—"

"Ritual of Endless Shadow?" Glinda echoed. The menacing name brought up goose bumps on her arms. "Is that what it's called?"

"Yes, yes, it is. But for ages, we Wickeds have feared that the ceremony would be impossible to execute, what with the death of she who had the Magic and the Elemental Fairies concealing themselves and all."

Glinda's heart crashed in her chest. "So the ceremony has something to do with Elementals?"

"Of course it has something to do with them," Mentir crooned, looking smug. "It has quite a lot to do with them, in fact. And if you'll just extend to me your official pardon and grant me immunity from punishment for a lifetime of Wicked wrongdoing, I will be happy to explain it all to you."

"Do you really think you're in a position to negotiate?" Locasta snarled, lunging for the headmistress and clamping her hands down on her shoulders.

Mentir recoiled from Locasta's touch. "Take your hands off me, you filthy Gillikin brat!"

"I will, when you tell Glinda what she wants to know."

"Very well, I'll tell her!" cried Mentir, composing herself. "The purpose of the Ritual of Endless Shadow is to—"

Her next words were drowned out by a wild screech from the far corner of the shadowy room as Misty Clarence, the Dean of Disastrous Decisions, came barreling out of the gloom.

"Traitor!" she wailed, pointing a trembling finger right at Mentir's forehead.

Glinda's gut seized because she recognized this gesture; she'd seen it too many times not to. This was how the dean had always begun the process of Youngifaction. "No! Don't!"

But Misty was already chanting in a voice like boiling oil:

"Old you are, but young you'll grow
And what you knew, you will not know
You shan't succeed in this betrayal
For Youngifaction does not fail."

One of the soldiers jumped forth to cover Misty's pointer finger, but it was too late. The headmistress's wrinkled skin was already pulling itself taut across her cheekbones, and in a violent series of jerks and creaks her whole body contracted, her waist cinching in so quickly it nearly choked the breath from her shrinking lungs. Smaller and smaller she grew, and less and less important she became. They watched as her power bled away with her adulthood until she stood before them a puny, pinch-faced little girl.

Ben looked stunned. "Um . . . what just happened?"

"She's been Youngified," Glinda choked as the Fledgling-size Mentir squirmed a tiny finger up into her nostril. "She's forgotten everything she ever knew."

"Like the rules about nose picking in public, for instance?" Locasta observed with disgust.

"Like what she was about to tell us about the Ritual of Endless Shadow," Glinda clarified, crushed.

"Where am I?" the mini Mentir demanded, sticking her pinky up her other nostril. "And why is my hair unbound? Where are my hair ribbons?"

"Now what do we do with her?" asked Ben.

"Well, we can't leave her in the dungeon," Glinda said with a sigh. "She's a child."

"I have an idea," said Ursie, turning to the soldiers. "Please bring the headmistress directly to the Hitherinyon homestead. She'll make a perfect little playmate for my young charge Gertzsplatch."

"And for the love of Oz," Locasta muttered, "somebody give her a handkerchief."

As Glinda watched the soldiers lead the mite-size Madam Mentir away by the hand, she noticed a most peculiar thing.

Shimmering around the child's head were several tiny, crackling flashes, like miniature lightning bolts.

Locasta saw them too. Whirling on Misty and narrowing her eyes, she asked, "What's with the fireworks?"

"That is the stuff of Mentir's youth," Misty replied haughtily. "Memories, and knowledge, and wishes, all reduced to static electricity, thanks to the power of my Wizardry."

"I never noticed any 'static' when you performed all those Youngifactions at Declaration Day ceremonies," Glinda challenged.

"That's because it was cloaked. All part of Aphidina's illusion. The static, like the memories, would have faded away eventually, but until they did, I couldn't have anyone getting ideas. . . ."

"What kind of ideas?" Locasta prompted, her hand curling into a fist.

"The kind of ideas Squillicoat had?" said Glinda, remembering the jar she'd taken from Squillicoat's shop. "Like the idea he sent his apprentice Wally Huntz to carry out!"

Misty averted her eyes, which told Glinda she'd guessed correctly. Her hope restored, she quickly stomped one foot into the pile of dusty splinters in the doorway. As they scattered and billowed, she cried out, "Door!" And a new one appeared, much thicker and heavier than the one Locasta had danced into dust. This one had four locks . . . and no keys, and Glinda took great pleasure in slamming it in Misty's face.

"Ursie," she said. "Go wake Miss Gage, please, and bring her to the library."

"All right. But why?"

Glinda didn't answer; she had already taken off at a run, heading for the cellar stairs.

Heading for Baloonda Quish's stolen—but thanks to the apothecary and his apprentice, lovingly salvaged—childhood.

7

THE ENTRUSTEDS

Bursting into the library with Ben and Locasta at her heels, Glinda set about searching the items from Squillicoat's shop until she found the jar with the glass stopper labeled QUISH.

Ursie arrived moments later, with Miss Gage gusting in behind her, tousled from sleep. Feathertop soared in above their heads.

"What's happening?" the teacher asked, sweeping her hair into a hasty topknot.

"I think I've figured out a way to outsmart the smoke," Glinda explained. "I'm going to create a cloud of intellectual interference by surrounding myself with a charged field that will block the fifth Witch from intercepting my learning."

"Of course," quipped Feathertop. "Why didn't I think of that?"

"For ages upon generations upon lifetimes," Glinda went on, "Misty Clarence has stolen away the personal histories of every girl who ever misdeclared here at Mentir's. According to Misty, all those thoughts and memories, hopes and wishes, simply faded away into the Ozian ether."

"Sad," said Ursie.

"Extremely," said Glinda. "But in Baloonda's case, Master Squillicoat's apprentice Wally managed to retrieve them! Preserve them!" She held up the jar in which hundreds of tiny, jagged flashes sparked like a small electrical storm. "I suppose he just couldn't bear to see one more childhood obliterated."

"A jar of hopes and wishes," mused Ben with a grin. "That's kind of poetic, isn't it?"

Locasta looked unconvinced. "You're going to use the residual static of Baloonda's Youngifaction to protect *your* thoughts from being tracked by certain malevolent forces? Do you really think a bunch of fuzzy tea party and hopscotch memories will be enough to protect you from Witch number five?"

"I'm not sure," Glinda admitted. "But it's worth trying. And wouldn't it be comforting to Baloonda to know that her wishes and dreams and memories were being put to good use?"

"I'm sure it would," said Miss Gage.

"Absolutely," said Ursie.

Ben nodded and even Feathertop flapped his wings in agreement.

Glinda quickly composed what she hoped would be an effective spell. Then she pulled the stopper from the jar to set the flashes of light free. As they encircled her, she recited:

> *"Hear not, know not, track not through time nor*
> *space.*
> *Whatever my mind absorbs henceforth, let*
> *Wicked never trace.*
> *Please, Magic, cloak these sparks so none will*
> *ever see*
> *That Good Miss Quish's thoughts and wishes are now*
> *protecting me."*

The sizzle and glare of the streaks as they zipped around Glinda's head caused her red hair to shine like fire. They hovered, burning brightly for only a heartbeat, then faded completely from view.

"Did it work?" asked Ben.

"There's only one way to find out." Glinda put down the jar, now empty of Baloonda's childhood, and pointed to a slender chapbook on the table. "Let's start with that."

"Wait," Locasta advised. "Maybe you should use something

as a buffer, to put a bit of distance between you and the knowledge to start. Just in case the smoke is still listening."

Glinda scanned the collection of artifacts. Choosing a wand carved from ice, which showed no signs of melting, she took the chilly item firmly into her grasp, aimed it at the book, and said:

> *"Pick a passage to which to turn,*
> *Find something—anything—for me to learn."*

The little trifolded pamphlet gave what sounded like a dusty cough and fluttered open.

With a deep breath, Glinda looked down at the words Magic had found for her. Written there in handsome calligraphy was the poem from Maud's sampler—the same verse King Oz's castle had written with fragments of itself across the Reliquary floor. "A hero is he who as in a myth rallies on fields of battle . . . ," she read.

"Nope." Locasta shook her head. "Doesn't count as learning something new, since you already solved that puzzle in the Reliquary."

"Try this," said Ursie, sliding a colorfully illustrated book across the table. The title was *Tales of Fairies, Not Fairy Tales: An Accurate Accounting of the Lesser-Known Fairy Phylum of Oz*. The cover featured an elaborate rendering of a water sprite whose broad wings and shimmering fins were suddenly shivering as though from extreme cold.

"I think that icy wand is giving her the chills," Ursie observed.

Glinda put down the wand and turned to Ben. "Can you help? Perhaps do something Maker-ish?"

Ben thought for a moment, then reached for a quill and quickly traced the outline of the sprite on the cover. To everyone's delight, the Fairy's image immediately lifted itself up from the drawing and began splashing about in the air. When she spoke, glistening little bubbles escaped from her gills.

"The Sea Fairies are a gaggle of underwater sprites who dwell in the liquid depths of Oz," she burbled sweetly. "We are known for giving magnificent and unexpected trinkets, and our bestowals often carry charms that may be used to open portals into other worlds. We are beloved by all except the Sea Devils, predators who squandered their own Magic long ago. These Devils hunt us, capture us, and ultimately feast on our fins and scales in order to acquire our Magical powers."

"Not the cheeriest of tales, is it?" Locasta muttered. "And besides, who cares about a bunch of Sea Fair—*hey!*"

The Fairy had flicked her magnificent tailfin, splashing a shower of seawater right into Locasta's face. With another graceful flap of her fins, she dove back into the book cover.

"That's not how I saw that going," Locasta groused, wiping the salt water from her cheeks. "But at least Glinda didn't get smoked out by the fifth Witch."

"Thanks to Baloonda," Ursie said, her voice catching slightly.

"Yes, thanks to Baloonda," said Glinda, "I can now safely search for information about the Elementals." She reached for a small parcel around which a piece of parchment had been folded and tied with knotted lengths of red, purple, blue, and yellow string. After struggling with the knots to no avail, she gave the string one last futile tug, then handed the lightweight package to Ursie. "Think you can untie this?"

Ursie grinned and set her nimble fingers to work.

"What we really need," said Locasta, "is a *map*! A map that says, '*You* are here, and the Elemental Fairies are right'"—she poked her finger against the tabletop to indicate a point on an invisible map—"'*here!*'"

It was at this precise moment that Ursie succeeded in releasing the knot in the colored string. At the same time, Miss Gage's topknot unwound and sent her hair tumbling down in waves. The laces of Ben's borrowed boots came undone; even the knots securing both Glinda's and Locasta's sashes slipped free, sending their belts sliding to the floor.

"Well, that was interesting," said Ben, bending down to tie his boots.

"I've always been sort of exceptional at untying things," Ursie explained, unfolding the parchment wrapping and laying it aside to examine the contents. "It's a map."

Locasta shot her a sideways look. "Really?"

"Yes," Ursie affirmed with a nod. "Though it's not typical by any means. The background is linen and the cartography is rendered in—"

"Needlepoint," said Glinda, recognizing the fine fabric and elegant needlework. It was the same map her mother had shown her on Declaration Day, with the four countries of Oz and their landmarks embroidered in colorful thread.

But even as they all gaped at the map, the Quadling region was changing before their eyes. The words marking APHIDINA'S PALACE vanished and were replaced by zigzagging green seams—to mark the place where Glinda had infused the ground with King Oz's final thought! Indeed, all over the red quadrant, where Tilda had stitched the name of a Wicked building or topographical feature, the letters had begun to pull loose. This brought a stab of sorrow to Glinda's heart, reminding her how Maud had bravely given her life in the unraveling of the trapestry. But she pushed aside her grief to focus on the changing stitches as they spelled out new names: the Perilous Pasture was rechristening itself the Pasture of Plentiful Provisions; the Woebegone Wilderness was now Good Fortune's Forest; Lurcher Lake became the Shallows of Sweet Success. Even the name of Madam Mentir's Academy for Girls had been vastly improved—it was now designated the Foursworn Stronghold of Truth.

"Incredible," breathed Ben.

What showed no signs of changing, however, was the lovely compass rose with its pretty amethyst accent stitched into the center of the map, exactly where King Oz's plateau would have been. Locasta seemed captivated by the detail of its asterisk shape and the finely wrought letters indicating the four cardinal points: *N, E, S, W.*

"Locasta?" Glinda prompted. "Is something wrong?"

Locasta shook her head. "It's just . . . I used to have a compass with an amethyst in the center." As her gaze lingered on the embroidery, she began to softly hum her father's song.

"Does the map happen to indicate where the Fairies are hidden?" asked Miss Gage.

Glinda was disappointed to see that it did not. Noting Locasta's ongoing fascination with the compass rose, she said, "You may have it if you'd like."

Locasta snapped her gaze up from the map. "Have it? You mean, like, *keep* it? But this map is priceless. The jewel in the center . . . it's probably worth a small fortune and—"

Glinda smiled. "It's yours. Consider it an apology for the sword incident."

"Hah!" Locasta gave her a faux scowl. "For that you'd need a much bigger map." But she returned the smile and went back to studying the map, humming softly as she did.

A small velvet pouch at the far end of the table caught Glinda's eye. When she picked it up and pulled at the gathered opening, four small stones—varying in shape and color but all rough and uncut—tumbled out to scatter across the polished surface of the tabletop, skittering their way onto the linen map. Locasta jumped back from her examination of it with a little yelp of surprise as an emerald rolled into the blue of Munchkin, slowed to pause there briefly, then rolled onward, over the border into the red of Quadling, where a rose quartz had already landed. An alabaster pebble slid onto the purple of Gillikin, and finally, a small chunk of white marble skidded to a halt at the yellow edge of Winkie.

"What are they?" asked Locasta, poking a finger at the alabaster one to send it spinning in place on the purple background.

"Gaming tokens?" guessed Ben. "There aren't enough pieces for draughts or Nine Man Morris, but I suppose they could be part of some Ozian dice-throwing game." He leaned in for a closer look. "There's emerald, alabaster, rose quartz, marble . . . hey, four of the hero statues in the Reliquary were carved from these same kinds of stones. That can't be a coincidence."

"No, it can't," Glinda agreed, eyeing the two pebbles that had fallen onto the south quadrant of the map. She reached first for the pink one, but changed her mind and picked up the emerald instead. As the rough stone lay upon her open palm, her skin began to tingle . . . and the stone began to change! "Can you see that?" she asked. "Can you see what's happening?"

"All I see is a lumpy green rock," Locasta retorted, staring at the craggy stone. "Why? What do *you* see?"

Glinda was too fascinated by the metamorphosis she was witnessing to reply. Before her eyes, the emerald pebble was becoming something else, something delicate yet pulsing with potential. Every tiny protrusion and hollow of the stone's surface was in motion, pushing upward here and outward there, transforming itself until it had become a miniature but magnificent city, resting in the palm of her hand.

"Look!" she cried. "A city. An *emerald* city."

"There's no such thing as an emerald city," said Locasta, swiping up the alabaster stone from the Gillikin quadrant. "So if you're thinking that rock is telling you to search for the Elemental Fairies there"—she tossed the white stone into the air and caught it—"you're wrong."

Glinda watched as the tiny green city disappeared and once again became an emerald in the rough. Her heart actually mourned the loss of it, for in those scant few seconds it had existed, it had contained more promise than anything she'd ever seen before.

"Games usually have instructions for play," Ben observed. Picking up the pouch, he peered inside and grinned. "And this one is no exception." He withdrew a tiny scroll and handed it to Glinda, who unrolled it.

Locasta peered over her shoulder. "Oh hey, here's a surprise. *Another* obscure and cryptic verse for us to decipher."

Ignoring the sarcasm, Glinda cleared her throat and read aloud:

"From present to future, from future to past
The deed is done, the die is cast
Great secrets, placed in trusted hands,
Are marked by where the hero lands.

Two bore witness, this much is so
One from above and one from below
And to only them and them alone
Are all four hiding places known

But no Entrusted must ever say
Where Fairy and Gift are tucked away
Unless they're forced to take that chance
In the face of dire circumstance.

These stiches reveal, but will not last
So those 'in search of' must act fast
Let threads and pebbles act as one
When the die is cast, the deed is done."

When she finished, five heads turned in unison to stare at the map.

"Could it be?" said Ben. "Do these stones mark the locations of the hidden Fairies?"

Glinda almost didn't dare to believe it. But the stones had rolled just like dice being cast. "The Entrusteds must be the four Grand Adepts into whose care the Fairies were placed," she surmised, scanning the verse again. "'Where the hero lands.' Ozma's hero statue in the Reliquary was made of pink quartz." She picked up the rosy pebble from the neatly embroidered field of red thread, and for a fleeting moment, a tiny stitched word shimmered on the map:

EMBER.

It vanished almost instantly, and two more came and went so quickly, Glinda might not have been able to read them if she hadn't already known what they were going to say.

TILDA'S PENDANT.

"Astounding," said Ben. "Although, strictly speaking, Ember no longer resides at that location. So I guess the map is giving us his last known address."

Glinda's fingers tingled with excitement as she returned the stone to the map, swapping it for the one perched near the embroidered edge of Winkie Country. She noted with a pang of frustration that it was a piece of white marble—Mythra's statue in the Reliquary had been carved from marble.

When she lifted the stone, the map stitched out the words POOLE, followed by DALLYBRUNGSTON'S POCKET SQUARE; a second later they had vanished.

"That makes perfect sense!" cried Glinda. "Dally was there on the night the Fairies went into hiding. I saw him in the zoetrope's tale! Of course I didn't know who he was at the time. But I recall he was sporting that handkerchief in his pocket!"

"Poole must be the Elemental Fairy of Water," Locasta guessed. "Surely he would have gathered up King Oz's final tear."

"And where else does a tear belong but in a hankie?" Ben chuckled. "How utterly appropriate!"

Miss Gage gave an indignant sniff. "So Dally is Poole's Entrusted? All this time, he never even let on!"

"Well, the poem *was* fairly specific about that," said Ursie. "'No Entrusted must ever say where Fairy and Gift are tucked away.'"

"But if that's true," said Glinda, "how would Maud have known where Ember was hidden? My mother said she was the one who could help me rescue her from Aphidina's castle, which means she must have shared the Entrusted secret with Maud."

"I guess she found it necessary to invoke the 'dire circumstances' clause," said Ben with a grimace.

Glinda did not want to speculate about what those dire circumstances might have been, especially because they were now one Elemental Fairy closer to vanquishing another Witch. "I'll go to Dally in the West right this minute and—"

"Uh-uh-uh," Locasta interrupted, wagging her finger. "Quirky cobbles, extra guards. Remember?"

"Then Shade can do it," said Glinda, glancing around for their gray-cloaked friend. "Shade?"

"Maybe she's made herself invisible again," said Ben. But after several moments had passed and Shade had not materialized, Feathertop fluffed up his feathers and pushed out his chest.

"I volunteer!" he squawked. "Send me."

Relieved and grateful, Glinda quickly told Feathertop the message she wanted him to relay to the Grand Adept of Winkie Country. Everyone wished the eagle luck in grandiose quantities; then, with a snap of her fingers, Miss Gage opened one of the towering library windows, and Feathertop soared through it, heading due west.

"Is it odd," Ben wondered, turning his attention back to the map, "that no stone landed in the blue country?"

"I'd say so," said Ursie. "And there were *two* in Quadling. The green one landed there, but Glinda picked it up."

"And the alabaster one was in Gillikin," Ben added. "But Locasta picked that one up."

Glinda gulped, knowing exactly what Ben and Ursie were thinking—because she was thinking the same thing herself: they'd taken the stones off the map, but because they hadn't known how the game worked, they hadn't consulted the vanishing stitches. Withdrawing the emerald from her pocket, she studied the map. "I'm almost certain it landed there, by Lurcher Lake—I mean, the Shallows of Sweet Success." She frowned, her eyes darting to a point further south. "Or was it here, closer to the town square?"

"Roll again and find out," Ursie suggested with a shrug.

Glinda tossed the green pebble. But this time it did not choose Quadling. Or Munchkin. Or anywhere else for that matter; it rolled right across the map and rattled off the table. Heart thudding, she picked it up and tried again. Again, it fell to the floor.

"Read the poem," Locasta grumbled. "When the die is cast, the deed is *done*. It doesn't say anything about do-overs!"

She was right, of course. The enchanted embroidery had come and gone, before they'd known to look for it.

"Now we have no way of finding out where the remaining two Fairies are hidden," Glinda concluded miserably.

"Actually," said Locasta, "while you were busy daydreaming about nonexistent emerald cities, I *was* paying attention to the map. At least enough to see and remember exactly where the Gillikin pebble landed."

Glinda felt a surge of hope. "You saw the words appear after you picked up the stone?"

"Didn't have to," Locasta answered sullenly. "Because I know every inch of the Gillikin landscape by heart. That's what happens when you spend your whole life looking for escape routes."

"Then you *do* know what spot the alabaster marked!" said Ben with a clap of his hands. "You know where the third Elemental Fairy is!"

"Yes," said Locasta. "That's the good news."

Miss Gage paled. "And the bad news . . . ?"

Locasta placed the pebble on the table as if it had been dusted with poison. "The stone landed on the castle grounds of the Brash Warrior Marada, Wicked Witch of the North."

Before anyone could react to that disturbing fact, a quivering Trebly Nox and a madly hiccuping D'Lorp Twipple charged into the library.

"We're under siege!" Trebly shrieked. "The armies of all three Witches are attacking."

"And there's a fourth army," cried D'Lorp. "Worse than all the others put together. A squadron of . . . *hic* . . . of . . . *hic*—"

"Of *what*?" Glinda prompted.

"Monkeys!" Trebly finished, wringing her hands. "Winged ones!"

8

TAKING THE LOST ONE IN HAND

hey were outnumbered.

Out-clawed, out-horned, out-fanged, and most assuredly out-winged.

Bursting through the academy doors onto the open lawn, Glinda gasped at the pandemonium—the campus was being attacked by the same horrific hybrid soldiers that had delivered Ava, Marada, and Daspina to the grounds of Aphidina's fallen palace the day before. Hissing and croaking they came, hopping and clomping, with slamming tails, thundering hooves, bared fangs, and darting tongues.

Immediately Ben picked up a large stick and disappeared into the fray. Locasta and Ursie were hot on his heels to join the Quadling soldiers (formerly conscripted by the Witch of the South, now loyal to the Foursworn), who fell bravely into line with muskets exploding and blades flashing. Glinda recognized the Revos she'd met at the Mingling. The Munchkin girl was wielding her saber with ferocious grace, while Samiratur and Fwibbins shouted instructions to the panicked townsfolk who came scrambling to join the defense effort, taking up whatever arms they could. Fiercely they fought, battling legions of giant toads, swatting at low-swooping wisp-wasps, and dodging a violent stampede of wild-eyed buffalopes.

But by far the worst of the mutant beasts were the Winged Monkeys.

Glinda couldn't begin to guess at their numbers—the sky all but blistered with them! Chattering, flapping, screeching, and soaring, they cast a writhing shadow over the campus grounds. Some had already touched down on the lawn, swaying under the weight of their own immense wings. She spied the little monkey who'd accompanied the Witches to Aphidina's grounds scampering to and fro, as though he were confused as to which side he should be fighting on.

Glinda made to thrust herself into the fray, but a scraggly hawk swooped down from the sky to cut her off. At the same time, the little monkey flung himself at her. She tried to shake him off, but he clung fast to her arm—though whether to throw her into the hawk's path or to pull her out of harm's way, even he didn't seem to know. After a bit of a tussle, Glinda managed to disentangle herself from the monkey and give the hawk a sound swatting; screeching, it flapped away and perched upon the pointed tip of one of the academy's red turrets, watching the battle with fierce eyes.

Already several of Glinda's Foursworn comrades lay wounded in the grass. The soldiers in their red velvet coats fought valiantly, but the Witches' armies and the Winged Monkeys were both aggressive and plentiful. Suddenly Ursie's voice ripped through the din. "Glinda! Watch out!"

Glinda spun to see an enormous spotted salamander lumbering toward her. She reached for her sword and held it aloft; it flared white, shocking the monstrous creature, which squirmed in retreat, its bulging eyes blinking away the heat lightning of Illumina's blade. Her respite was short-lived, however, for just as the salamander's tail swung out of sight, two Winged Monkeys appeared above her, cackling and hooting as they trained their yellow eyes mercilessly on Glinda.

One of them was carrying a boy on its back.

A boy with tufts of purple-streaked hair sticking out from under the flaps of an ugly Golden Cap.

Thruff! Locasta's turncoat brother.

The monkey gave a violent hoot as Thruff spurred him forward and down—heading directly for Glinda.

Trebly appeared, throwing herself between Glinda and

the monkey; she tugged the belt from her pinafore and flung it up in the air. "Weapon!" she shouted, and the belt obeyed, landing in her hands as a sturdy rock sling. Scooping a sharp stone from the ground, she loaded the sling's pouch and spun it above her head. Glinda could hear the measured *vwuhsh—vwuhsh—vwuhsh* of the whirling weapon stirring the air. Then, with a jerk of her shoulder and a flick of her wrist, Trebly sent the rock sailing—flying so fast that Glinda didn't even realize it had been fired until the monkey cried out in pain. The jagged rock had torn a whole clump of feathers off the tip of his right wing. Trebly repeated the motion with a second stone. This time the projectile zoomed right past the monkey—but a loud hiccup from D'Lorp sent it circling back to clip the rider in the middle of his forehead.

"Quick!" cried Trebly. "I need another—"

Glinda's hand was already closing around the emerald game piece in her pocket. This she pressed into Trebly's open palm. Eyes narrowed, mouth set, Trebly loaded the pouch once again and spiraled the ropes of the sling above her head in a blur of strength and motion.

It hit its mark, landing right between the monkey's eyes. The beast squealed in agony, pressing its leathery hands to its forehead as it tumbled through the air. Thruff cleaved to the creature for dear life, one arm wrapped around the monkey's neck, his other hand clutching the Golden Cap to his head, as though he were more afraid of losing that

ridiculous hat than he was of crashing headfirst to the hard ground of the academy lawn.

Noticing that many of the monkeys carried bows and arrows, Glinda pointed skyward and cried out, "Ursie! Look!"

"Way ahead of you!" Ursie called back. Aiming her hands at the furry archers, she splayed her fingers wide, then crooked each one in turn while twirling her thumbs. A series of loud *pings* and *snaps* filled the air as every knot in every bowstring broke free. With their weapons rendered useless, the archer monkeys hooted in anger.

Unfortunately, Ursie's skill could do nothing to stop the other furry beasts, who were armed with maces, clubs, and cudgels.

Glinda's eyes scanned the chaos: she saw Ben wrestling a gigantic frog; she watched Locasta lead an enormous yakityak on a frenzied chase, then dart out of his path in the nick of time so that the beast plowed straight into a tree, lodging his horns in the trunk. Even Miss Gage was fighting valiantly; she had accepted a broadsword from an injured Quadling soldier and was fending off an onslaught of giant squirming caterpillars—then she cried out, "Flutter!" and the caterpillars instantaneously morphed into a squadron of delightfully oversize and utterly harmless butterflies.

Satisfied that her friends could hold their own, Glinda swung her gaze across the battlefield in search of Thruff, hoping to find him sprawled unconscious in the grass. But that was not to be. He and his injured mount had landed without incident, and there he was, Golden Cap still firmly upon his head, striding through the violence and danger as though he knew nothing even akin to fear. Thruff's gait was every bit as purposeful and determined as his sister's as he eluded angry chuckwallas, giant spidergnats, and horrific humpbacked bison. He stomped past every one of them as if they didn't even exist, as if he were on a mission.

And he was heading straight for Glinda.

A snap of his fingers brought three more monkeys swooping out of the sky to surround her, the force of their fiercely beating wings whipping her hair across her eyes. Blindly, she drew Illumina and swung, but one of the winged monsters kicked the sword out of her grasp and sent it spinning out of reach.

And then Thruff was standing right in front of her, even younger-looking up close than he'd appeared at a distance. He was glowering at her with eyes so eerily like his sister's that Glinda shivered. Another monkey grabbed the neck of her tunic and hoisted her off the ground, holding her suspended so that the soles of her boots dangled above the trampled grass.

"Locasta!" she screamed.

From across the lawn, Locasta whirled in the direction of Glinda's voice. Seeing her friend in peril, she spun into a dance, her rhythmic Witchcraft re-igniting the Magic that lingered in the fabric of Glinda's apparel. The monkey cried out and released his grip, shaking his stinging fingers.

Glinda landed on her backside with a hard thud and found herself staring into the round, blinking eyes of the littlest monkey. To her surprise, he had fetched Illumina and was holding it out to her, his tiny head bobbing eagerly as if to say, *Take it! Take it!*

She snatched the sword and leaped to her feet. In her hand, the blade gave off a shower of light. The gems on Thruff's Golden Cap glimmered in the glow, but he did not flinch.

She knew she could take him down with one swoop of her sword; she could burn the Wickedness out of his heart with the heat of it. But this was Locasta's brother; the brother she had come to Quadling to save. And because of that, Glinda could not bring herself to deliver him so much as a scratch.

Instead she began to back away slowly, keeping the brilliance of Illumina squarely between her and her enemy. Thruff kept pace, stalking her step for step, squinting into the light of her sword.

"I am to bring you to the fifth Witch," he informed her. "Come willingly and you won't be hurt."

At this, Glinda let out a snort of disgust that was almost worthy of his sister. "I very much doubt that," she sneered, and twirled Illumina to send a swirl of light springing from the blade; the swirl wrapped itself around Thruff's knees, tripping him to the ground. He rolled and kicked until he had wrenched himself free of it. But before he could gain his feet, Glinda had advanced, pressing Illumina's glowing tip to his chest, pinning him to the grass. "You command these flying apes?" she demanded.

He glared up at her and grunted. *Yes.*

"Call them off."

"Never!" Thruff's eyes burned hotter than the sword as he ground his words out through his teeth. "Your cause is lost, Sorceress. Wicked holds all. No use in rebelling only to lose what you love, and die in the process."

Glinda quirked one eyebrow at the boy. "Is that what you think?" she asked, truly surprised. Lessening the force but keeping Illumina pressed lightly against his collarbone, she motioned for him to stand and appealed to him in as reasonable a tone as she could muster. "We have already beaten one Witch. We can do it again. And if you have even one drop of your sister's blood in your veins, I know you cannot truly have aligned yourself with the Wickeds. Join the Foursworn, Thruff. Join *us!*"

The hard line of Thruff's mouth softened and his eyes darted sideways, though with confusion or remorse, Glinda could not say. Only now did she notice that several yards off, another pair of monkeys had alighted. Over the spiky purple tips of Thruff's hair, she watched with growing fear as the beasts sought out their master. One of the Winged things pointed and hooted; another chattered madly and picked at his matted fur as they approached. Wings pulsing, arms swaying, they swaggered toward Thruff and Glinda on bowed legs.

Thruff had just opened his mouth to shout out a command when Locasta appeared, hurtling out of the fracas like a comet to tackle her brother back to the ground.

"Glinda, run!"

"What? No! I—"

"*Run!* It's you they want!"

But the thought of hiding while her friends fought made Glinda's skin crawl. "I will not abandon this battle just to save myself."

"*You* need to stay alive for whatever comes next!" Locasta snarled as Thruff, squirming beneath her weight, jerked his knee into her stomach. She growled out something about obnoxious little brothers, then landed an elbow to his midsection, effectively putting a stop to his squirming. As Thruff struggled to catch his breath, Ben came skidding over, his waistcoat torn, his britches dirty, the leather cord gone from where it once bound his hair at the nape of his neck.

"Well, well, well." Locasta crooked a grin at him, even as she pressed her hand over Thruff's face and good-naturedly ground the back of his head into the dirt. "Aren't you the seasoned warrior?"

Ben gave her a sideways smile. "My father would be proud."

"Mine wouldn't," Locasta muttered, scowling pointedly at her brother. Then she tossed her head in Glinda's direction. "Get her to safety. She's too stubborn—or maybe just too dense—to do it herself." Then she turned to roar at Glinda, "*Go!*"

Ben reached out to grab Glinda's hand, and together they took off at a frantic pace, fighting off bucking bulls and spiky lizards as they went.

The fury of the fight unfolded all around them in a blur of swinging clubs, soaring stones, and the clang of swords colliding. The dark essence of battle surrounded her, tangling in her hair, soiling her clothes, burning her eyes and her skin. She could taste it, the bitter sting of violence, combat, conflict—*war* . . . and all its hateful waste. Hopelessness pummeled her from all sides.

And then she saw him, the tiny Winged Monkey, his eyes wide, his tail trembling, frozen in terror in the path of a galloping buffalope.

Without pausing to think, Glinda dove to grab the monkey's paw, bundling the petrified little creature into her arms and spiriting him away from the crushing power of the animal's hooves. Whisking him to the relative safety of the side lawn, Glinda could feel his little heart racing in his chest as he pressed his soft face into her neck, stroking her cheek and chattering his thanks.

"Glinda, come on!" cried Ben as another squadron of monkeys swept out of the sky.

"Be careful, little one," Glinda whispered, placing the monkey on the grass. "No . . . be *good*."

"*Goo—oot-oot-oot?*" the creature echoed, blinking his big eyes. He tried again: "*Good!*"

But Glinda had already turned on her heel to run after Ben.

Which was why she did not see the little monkey tilt his diminutive head this way and that, contemplating her words and listening to his own thudding heart. She did not see him dash back into the mayhem to snatch up that which the angry boy had for some reason just thrown off his head and she did not see the little beast skimming above the fray on his monkey wings in search of the purple-haired girl. Nor did she hear him impart to Locasta in a yipping, hooting attempt at language something of monumental significance as Locasta bent low to listen and accept the Golden Cap he offered.

Glinda witnessed none of this; she knew nothing of any of it, not at all.

Because in those critical moments during which the little monkey made the choice to be Good, and to alter the course of Ozian history forevermore, Glinda had been running.

Running for the toolshed.

Running for her life.

9

IN THE TOOLSHED

Ben slammed the door and shoved a heavy workbench against it.

Amid the stacks of chipped flowerpots and racks of rusting garden tools, Glinda struggled to catch her breath. The walls of the tiny building did little to shut out the noise of the escalating battle without. The shrill voices of the Winged Monkeys—multiplied to many hundreds now— were an assault on Glinda's senses, and the shed's rickety frame shook with the force of the wind their wings stirred up. She could have sworn she heard bones breaking.

"Try to think of something else," Ben suggested.

"Something besides the fact that I'm hiding in here like a

coward," Glinda murmured, "while the Foursworn forces, such as they are, are getting positively trounced?"

"You're not a coward, Glinda. What you are is indispensable."

"*Everyone* is indispensable, Ben! *Everyone* matters!"

"That's true. But under the present circumstances, you happen to be the most indispensable among us."

Glinda fiddled with Illumina's hilt and said nothing.

"They came of their own accord," he reminded her. "You didn't force anyone to take up a weapon and charge into danger. This is their fight too. And war, I am sorry to tell you, is a mad contrivance made more complicated by loyalties, hierarchies, and responsibilities." He paused, a bemused look on his face. "My father has expressed that belief many times, but I never understood what it meant until now."

Outside, a voice rose above the tumult—Locasta barking desperate orders—and Glinda thought she sensed a faltering of the battle's energy, as though some dramatic shift had just occurred in the short period during which she'd turned her back to the chaos. It sounded as if Thruff's monkeys were fighting with renewed energy and zeal.

Slumping to the floor, she dropped her head in her hands.

Ben slid the strap of his knapsack off his shoulder, sat down beside her, and began to rifle through the bag.

"What are you looking for?" she asked, peeking between her fingers.

"Anything that might take your mind off—" He was interrupted by a loud crash as something—or some*one*—collided with the north wall of the toolshed. "Off *that*," he muttered, still digging. "It occurred to me back in the library when we read about the Entrusteds that there may be something in the Makewright's journal that can help us find the Elemental Fairies." He gave her a look. "Perhaps even Mythra."

Glinda looked at him as if he'd lost his mind.

"I know Miss Gage believes she's dead. But your mother *did* tell you to find her. So I'm willing to allow that it's *possible* she might still be out there somewhere. Alive."

"Do you really think so?" Glinda was afraid to even hope.

"I'm a boy from New York in a land called Oz, who just saw a sky filled with flying monkeys! I'm willing to believe *anything* is possible."

Glinda considered this as the sounds of the battle clattered on. "But does it even matter, Ben? Fairies or no Fairies, Mythra or no Mythra, we're done for."

"Don't say that! We don't know what's going to happen out there—"

He was interrupted by a hail of musket fire clattering down upon the roof; the Winged Monkeys let loose another spine-chilling cheer.

"Oh, I think we do," Glinda countered glumly. "I think we know *exactly* what's going to happen. We're going to lose. Unless I let them take me to save the others!" She leaped to her feet and started for the door, but Ben caught the back of her tunic and tugged her back.

"You can't!"

"But they're *losing*!" she wailed. "To those hoppy toads and yakityaks and Winged Monkey beasts! And once they've beaten our army, they'll come looking for me!"

"Then we have to get you out of here." With a look that did not invite argument, Ben offered her the knapsack. "Perhaps there's something in the Maker's journal that might help."

As Glinda took the bag, Magic, both new and ancient, tingled through her like a soft breeze in the leaves of the ruby maple; she wished with all her might that her mother were there to help her use it. In her mind's eye she saw a deck of beautifully etched cards depicting eight Ozian heroes, heard the faint strains of a precious lullaby, and savored the warmth of freshly baked popovers.

But another raucous chorus of monkey yowling jarred Glinda from her thoughts. Their shouts sounded disheart-eningly celebratory. Blocking out the clamor, she reached into the knapsack and rummaged through the contents for the little leather book. But her hand brushed against some-thing smooth and round instead.

The seashell.

Slipping it out of the bag, she again admired its gentle geometry.

"A nautilus," Ben remarked. "Where did this come from?"

"I found it when I went walking by the lake. I thought it was odd to find a seashell in a lake, but—"

"The Sea Fairies! What did we learn about them? Something about bestowing trinkets."

"Yes!" Glinda's eyes lit. "Trinkets that can become . . . *portals*. But how can we know where a Sea Fairy portal might take us?"

Outside, the battle was reaching a feverish crescendo. The lowing of oxen was growing louder, the droning of insects more frantic, and above this noise came the frenzied chitter-chatter of those wild Winged Monkeys.

"Does it matter?" Ben's voice was dark. "Those monkeys are winning. Anywhere has got to be better than where they are."

Glinda knew he was right. Holding the shell in her upturned palm, she waited for it to do what the Fairy's story had promised. But no sparkle of Magic burst forth, no wave of enchantment swept in to carry them out of the shed and away from danger. Frowning, Glinda turned the shell over so that the graduated spiral was now facing up . . . and she listened.

"Do you hear that?" she asked, cocking her head. "It sounds like water trickling. Or lapping." She lifted the nautilus to her ear; the trickling sound was coming from deep within the tiniest compartment of the delicate swirl.

But a sudden violent pounding on the shed door scared her so badly that the shell fell from her hand, landing spiral side up in the dirt.

"Monkeys?" she croaked.

"Hurry!" Ben advised as the pounding came again, threatening to bang the door from its hinges.

In Glinda's ear, the whisper of the water turned to words:

> *"If you should desire to open a door*
> *You need only to be unconditionally sure*
> *That who you must find, is who you will see*
> *And where you are headed is where you must be."*

Now the shell began to spin, pressing itself into the dirt floor. It moved slowly at first, then picked up speed, whirling into a widening gyre, growing larger and deeper with every turn. The graduated sections took on dimension, dropping away in succession until the shell had become a graceful spiral staircase unfurling downward into something clear and pale and blue.

Water.

A fathomless pool. Or perhaps a piece of the sea.

The pounding on the door raged again; the workbench rattled and bucked.

"Go!" Ben urged, nudging Glinda toward the stairs. "I'm right behind you."

Gripping Illumina's handle, she placed her foot on the

top step, then the next one, making her way carefully down the luminous staircase. Ben followed her, awed by the grandeur of the Magic. Lower and lower they went until they were up to their knees in the crystalline pool, which seemed to be made as much of light as it was of water.

High above them in the toolshed, a determined shoulder collided with the door, and Glinda knew it would be crashing open soon enough.

Taking a hungry breath to fill her lungs, she motioned for Ben to do the same.

Then she grabbed his arm and together they dove into the depths.

10

CONNECTION MAGIC

Somewhere, a portal had opened.

The jolt of realization brought Tilda to a standstill, her dusty slippers scuffing to a halt on the bricks of the winding yellow road.

A new door, or perhaps a very old one, had just availed itself to give passage. She felt the Magic surround her but understood that the experience was a borrowed one; she was seeing with another's eyes, feeling with another's touch, knowing with an awareness that was not her own. It was not a Magical pathway or even a skill, but a precious bond between one Magician and another.

And oh, how she had missed it!

But the sensation would be fleeting, she knew. So she stopped walking, closed her eyes, and let the Magic fill her.

Water. Deep, lulling, clear. Filled with purpose. A necessary departure to ensure a fateful meeting.

When she swayed on her feet, Nick Chopper reached out a hand to steady her. "Tilda, are you ill?"

On the contrary, the Sorceress Gavaria had not felt this hopeful in ages. Not since before King Oz had been vanquished and with him had gone so much that mattered. Many times she'd considered going in search of the Mysterious Priestess herself, but in the end, she had resisted, knowing that the world was not ready, nor steady enough to warrant such a prodigious risk. Now Tilda herself had urged Glinda to attempt what she herself had never dared.

A tender ache of pride filled her chest. How right that *Glinda* would be the one to discover what had so long seemed undiscoverable.

"Mistress Gavaria?"

"I'm perfectly well, Nick. In fact, I'm amazed. Amazed and happy." *And perhaps the tiniest bit terrified,* she added silently as the Magic of Connection whispered away. *Anything can happen now.*

But Nick didn't budge. He was looking downward with a puzzled expression on his face, to where the hem of Tilda's long skirt met the yellow bricks of the road. "The bottom of your dress . . . it's soaking wet."

Tilda let out a musical peal of laughter that rang over the azure-and-turquoise hillside of Munchkin Country. "Well, would you look at that!" she exclaimed. "It's positively drenched!" Gathering up the lower half of her skirt, she began to wring it out, laughing all the while as she squeezed the water from the fabric.

Nick could only blink in confusion, his gaze going from Tilda's sparkling eyes to the shimmering puddle forming on the yellow road. Then he smiled, turning his attention back to the pretty stone dwelling, set a ways back from the yellow brick road.

"Now then, young Chopper," said Tilda, shaking water from her fingertips. "What was it you were about to tell me, before the Connection Magic had its say?"

Nick pointed to the house. "This is where I last saw my Nimmie Amee. This is the domicile of her employer, the selfish old woman who bribed the Witch of the East to put a hex on my ax."

"Then it seems the yellow road is ready for you to make your discovery," said Tilda, lifting his pointed blue hat and smoothing his tousled hair.

"I find I am suddenly nervous," Nick confessed.

"That is to be expected."

"What if she does not welcome me back?"

"That would be a very poor decision on her part," Tilda replied. "But whatever the outcome, you must follow your heart." She gave him a nudge in the direction of the house.

"Be as brave as you can and as sweet as you are," she whispered. "And I will be here waiting in the shade of that tree when you return, eager to hear Miss Amee's answer."

"And then we shall be once again on our way," said Nick with a nod. Huffing a puff of breath onto his tin arm, he polished the joint with the sleeve of his shirt until it gleamed. A moment later he was clanking up the walk, his ax swinging cheerfully as he went.

Following his heart.

Neither Nick nor Tilda saw the *other* Munchkin lad, approaching the stone house from the opposite direction, carrying a nosegay tied with blue ribbons.

But the Munchkin lad saw them and knew instantly why Nick Chopper was there. The lad (who made his living playing the hurdy-gurdy in a Munchkin musical act known as the Five Little Fiddlers) became deeply troubled, for in Nick Chopper's absence, *he* had fallen in love with Nimmie Amee too. And though the lad did not recognize the red-haired woman in the soggy crimson skirt who seemed so delighted to be witnessing Nick's grand romantic gesture, he surmised from the color of her clothes that she was a Quadling, and therefore, a trespasser on the Witch's sovereign land.

Tossing the nosegay bitterly to the ground, the lad decided he was not about to lose Nimmie Amee to some shiny boy with a useless ax—a fugitive, no less!

He knew that Ava Munch would pay handsomely for news of Chopper's return. And surely there would be a reward for the Quadling as well.

Pausing only long enough to grind his blue-heeled boot into the discarded flowers, the hurdy-gurdy player crept away unnoticed to send word to the Royal Tyrant Ava Munch of what he had seen.

11

UNDERTOW

The water was delightfully warm and welcoming—a sensation very unlike the one Glinda had experienced in the icy lake the day she'd outsmarted Aphidina's Lurcher.

As she and Ben shimmied through patches of cool blue shadow and glided between streamers of incandescence that seemed to come from nowhere, Glinda felt her long hair floating all around her face, swelling and waving in slow time with the current. She imagined she looked like a wonderful, copper-colored sea plant.

It was a moment before she realized Ben was not beside her, and only when she turned to see him thumping his fist anxiously against his chest did she notice that her own lungs were beginning to ache. They'd stayed under much too long.

Ben pointed upward—*Let's go*—and shot toward the surface, propelling himself with a powerful fluttering of his legs. Glinda followed, but as the moments passed, a new panic tightened around her heart:

Where is the staircase?

Surely they should have reached the bottom step by now. Had it vanished? Curled back into its shell-size origins? Perhaps it hadn't been a gift from the Sea Fairies at all but some horrid, Wicked trap!

Glinda struggled to keep pace with the flurry of bubbles that showered down in Ben's wake, but even as she kicked harder, the distance between them widened. She realized this was because he was unencumbered by the weight of a sword.

Illumina was slowing her ascent.

The sting in her lungs increased to a terrible burning; her strokes grew weaker, her climb clumsier as she battled the heavy embrace of the pool. Above her, she could just make out the soles of Ben's boots disappearing from view. *Swim,* she told herself, but she was barely treading water now; Illumina had become like an anchor at her waist.

Squinting up through the wavering light, she saw Ben peering down from the safety of the bank, his face obscured by the wriggling ripples his exit had left on the pool's surface—that glistening filament separating her from her own breath. If only she could get there. But her strength was dwindling under the drag of the sword.

She knew what she had to do.

Jerking the sword from her sash, she allowed herself one last look at the graceful blade, the braided metal of the handle, and the colorful gemstones, winking in the pale glow of the pool. It was the most beautiful and most important thing she had ever owned.

But to save herself, she would have to let it go.

Drop it, she told herself.

Drop it . . . or die.

The pain in her muscles raged, eclipsed only by the agony in her heart as she uncurled her fingers from the sword's grip.

If only it weren't so heavy, she thought. *If only it were . . . light.*

And then, suddenly, it was.

Light, lighter than light; weightless and glowing in her hand. This time, it was not just the blade that had given over to luminescence; it was the whole of Illumina—guard, grip, pommel. Where the stone-and-metal hilt had been, there was now the ethereal suggestion of a handle in Glinda's grasp. Shedding its own mass, the sword had reimagined itself into a watery glow.

Relieved of its weight, she rose quickly, higher and higher until she broke the surface, gulping for air. Ben reached out and pulled her to the edge, where she clung, exhausted, resting her head on her arms, her legs still dangling in the pool.

For a long moment, the only sound was the lapping of the water and the rhythm of her grateful breathing.

Then, Ben's voice: "Are you all right?"

"I think so." The words came out muffled against her wet sleeve.

"Good," Ben replied. "Because you've *got* to see this."

Glinda swiped a dripping lock of hair out of her eyes and glanced around the toolshed.

But it wasn't the toolshed.

As she gaped in amazement, Ben crouched down to whisper warily in her ear.

"Glinda," he murmured, "I have a feeling we aren't in Quadling anymore."

They had dived out of one place and emerged into another.

No point in wondering *how*; the only explanation was and would ever be Magic.

Where, on the other hand, was a perfectly terrifying question, and the answer, Glinda was certain, had already been shown to her. When her mother had first given her the linen map, it had revealed a labyrinth of tunnels *beneath* Oz, another whole landscape, hiding in the Lurlian depths. Now the lagoon had deposited them into that great, yawning cavern where it was dark, and dank and dismal but for the shimmering reflection of the water playing upon its walls. A series of craggy archways rimmed the perimeter of the cave, opening into long, winding tunnels.

She did not like this underlayer of Oz at all. "Let's get out of here."

"Excellent idea," said Ben. "Except that there's no sign of the shell staircase." His voice tumbled over itself in a nervous echo to roll down the shadowy passages and fade away in the dark. "How are we going to get back to the academy?"

"There has to be a way," said Glinda, lifting herself to her elbows. "I think if we just—*ummppffff*!" She was suddenly underwater again, descending fast!

But *not* of her own volition.

Something had grabbed her, something slippery and quick. Two strong, scaly hands had wrapped around her ankles and were dragging her downward, faster than her mind could think, into the blue-green, watery-gray gloom. The warmth was above; down here there was just the bone-biting chill of dark water that had never known light.

"Glinda, come back!" Ben screamed, his voice following her into the depths, growing thicker, fainter, until all she could hear was the *swhiiiisshh* of the water speeding past her ears.

She willed her roiling stomach to make peace with the velocity as her eyes adjusted to the dimness and she saw through the whip of the water the thing that had stolen her.

Her first impression was of muscles—broad Fairy shoulders, arms as solid as the rock walls of the cave from which she'd just been snatched. Her captor's face had a sickly gray complexion and peculiar features: eyes that did not blink, and a nose that was not so much a nose as an oddly-placed pair of gills—two flap-like slashes where his nostrils should have been. It had no mouth and no chin; instead, the lower part of its face trailed off into a mass of slender, writhing tentacles. Its body tapered into a long fin covered in red and black scales. This fin split off into yet more undulating tentacles—the source of his speed. On his head he wore a curved shell, bristling with spikes.

The water hissed in her ears: *Ssssea Devilssss!* it warned.

Having no intention of being devoured by this nasty bottom dweller, she began to squirm, wresting one ankle free from its grasp. But it was too late; he had already swum her into chaos.

Before her loomed a whole horde of these devilish creatures, darting and diving, fists swinging, tentacles slapping as they pursued two of the most gorgeous beings Glinda had ever seen.

Ssssea Fairiessss, the lagoon told her.

Of course! Indeed, their beauty seemed to be an extension of the water itself. Wildly lovely, they were a sparkle of silken scales, part Fairy, part fish. They moved with the frantic motion of their translucent winglike fins, the same pearly colors as the pool. Their webbed feet churned through the water as they tried desperately to dodge their attackers. But everywhere they went, a Sea Devil blocked their path, wielding a spear carved from blinding white fish bone.

Glinda reached for Illumina, once again its solid self, but the Devil slapped her hand away with a ready tentacle, tightening his hold on her leg. The pain of his grip and the absence of air made her head spin.

Oh, how she wanted to breathe! The weight of the water pressed against her chest, squeezing out what little air she'd managed to inhale in the cave. Some small rivulet of consciousness told her to fight, but the thought drifted away before it could become action.

Liquid oblivion threatened to overtake her.

Then something swung in from the left, and another from the right, and the Devil was suddenly flanked by Fairy wings. There was a roar as the Devil fell away and her glittering saviors returned to the battle. But Glinda was still without the luxury of air. Now more bright wings approached, more soft ripples in the murky deep. A third Sea Fairy swam up behind her, taking hold of her tunic and pulling her far from the melee.

Flooded—quite literally—with relief, Glinda dropped her head onto the Fairy's shoulder and let the sprite's elegant arm wrap around her waist. But the reprieve was fleeting . . . because the Fairy was now placing her hand over Glinda's mouth and nose!

With what little strength she had left, she tried to shake

off this savior-turned-captor who seemed determined to drown her.

But the water whispered, *Ressscue,* and when the Fairy's hand came away, Glinda's lungs were filled with glorious breath. Faster than phosphorescence, the Fairy spun Glinda around and shook her pretty head, pressing her hand over her own mouth in a silent command.

Glinda understood: she must keep her mouth closed or the spell would be broken. She nodded her thanks, but the Fairy was already racing back to join her sisters in the fray.

They fought valiantly, but more Devils were darting out of the shadows, their bony lances raised. The Sea Fairies were surrounded.

Glinda jerked Illumina out of her sash but knew she could not possibly fight off so many beasts at once. With her lips tightly closed, she looked down at the braided metal handle and thought as loudly as she could:

"To these Wicked Devils we will not yield; be light . . . be might . . . become . . . a shield!"

The handle quivered in Glinda's palm and the interwoven strands of metal wrenched free, unwinding into three jagged ropes of energy that became six, then nine, then twelve. These pulled away from Illumina's hilt, twisting into a helix of power, a braided current of light that shot toward the Fairies, then uncoiled to surround them in a glowing protective bubble.

When the first spear flew, it bounced off the blue light

and spun backward, end over lethal end, impaling the very Devil that had thrown it. The beast let out a gurgling shriek. Enraged, a second Devil flung itself at the globe of light, then scuttled backward, its skin burned black and its scales charred brittle. The sight of him frightened his brothers into a frantic retreat.

As the Devils sped off into the darkness, the Magical field formed by Illumina's handle dissolved into sparks; these floated back to Glinda to once again take the shape of the sword's grip, solid in her grasp.

The Fairies rejoiced, their wings coaxing up columns of iridescent bubbles as they danced. Glinda was so delighted by their celebration that she didn't notice the last of the Devils swimming straight for her until it was too late. She tried to duck out of its path, but his slimy fist delivered a blow to her sword arm.

And the blade slipped from her grasp.

"Illumina!" As the name ripped from Glinda's throat, her mouth filled with cold briny water and the word was drowned in the sound of her choking. All she could do was watch, helpless, as her beloved sword sank to the distant bottom of the pool, its gemstones winking colorfully, as if to say good-bye.

Glinda listened for the soft thud of her sword hitting the sandy bottom of the pool. But no thud came. For all she knew, it would continue to tumble downward into the darkness forever.

Forever . . . Illumina would be gone from her.

Gone, like the precious breath the Fairy had Magically provided, but which Glinda had lost in shouting Illumina's name. Again, she felt her lungs seize and her mind begin to cloud over. She was vaguely aware of wings enfolding her, a fluttering of fins, then a swift upward thrust. The last thing she understood was that the water had grown light and warm once more, and then there was no water at all, just pebbly ground—the edge of the lagoon, firm and dry against her back.

She did not feel the smooth round jewel being slipped into her pocket, nor did she hear the grateful Sea Fairy whisper:

"Take with you our thanks
From this watery whirl
For your kindness and courage
We gift you this pearl."

Then, with a motherly hand, the Sea Fairy stroked the wet hair from Glinda's forehead. *"Rest now, Good hero, sweet Ozian child. And in your sleep shall strength return to you, so that you may resume your worthy quest."*

Resssst, Glinda, the water echoed.

And so she did, rolling over onto her side and sinking into a most wondrous slumber.

The wisp of her sleepy breath filled the cave, mingling

with the hushed *thwumff* of metal landing softly on the faraway bottom of the pool. At the same moment, from somewhere other and above, there came the splintery crash of a door slamming inward.

But Glinda did not hear that, either. And she did not hear the quickening swish of Fairy wings retrieving Illumina from the lagoon's sandy floor to be borne safely upward through countless fathoms of watery darkness.

Nor did she awaken to the happy cry of a Good Witch's voice ringing through the toolshed, calling out in triumph:

"Glinda! Ben! Where are you? Glinda . . . *we won*!"

12

BEACON OF FRIENDSHIP

Breeches torn, curls tangled, Locasta thundered around the tiny toolshed, flinging over crates and peering behind rickety shelves.

"Glinda?"

No reply. She took another step and tripped over something. Ben's knapsack, abandoned on the dirt floor.

"Ben?" Locasta felt a curl of panic in the pit of her stomach as she hitched the pack over her shoulder. "You can come out now. It's safe."

Now Ursie came skidding into the shed, rambling gleefully. "Glinda! Oh, Glinda, wait until you hear how we beat the Witches' armies! You'll never believe it, but all

Locasta had to do was put the cap on her head and say—"
Ursie cut off with a little gasp.

Because Locasta had come to an abrupt halt in her
searching and was teetering on the edge of an opening in
the floor.

"What in the name of Oz is *that*?" asked Ursie.

"I don't know," Locasta admitted, crouching beside the
edge. "Some kind of portal?"

Ursie tiptoed closer, taking in the spiral-shell staircase
with an expression of wonder. "That's promising, don't
you think?"

Locasta frowned into the gap in the floor; clearly Glinda
and Ben had disappeared into it, but there was no way of
knowing whether they'd done so willingly or by the force
of something Wicked. And this made Locasta tremble.

After all, she was the one who'd sent them here to hide.

From her brother.

Their violent encounter on the battlefield came back to
her in a rush. She'd just dispatched Glinda to the toolshed.
Thruff was sprawled on the ground, gripped in a headlock.
It was a maneuver she'd often tricked him with when they
were younger, playing together on the scrubby patch of
yard outside their shack, exhausted from a hard day of
mining but still delighted by each other's company. There
they learned to juggle small rocks, to box and wrestle (for
their world was harsh and unpredictable and their father
was determined that they learn to fight). Norr would watch

from the moldering stoop of their shack, humming softly, absently rattling a pair of small amethyst stones in his palm—good luck charms, he called them—one for Locasta and one for Thruff. Sometimes he'd get a peculiar look on his face, as if a thought or a feeling had struck him out of nowhere, and he'd quickly press one or the other of his good luck stones to his eye and hold it up to the sun, as if trying to see through it. Or into the depths of it. Then he'd slip them into his shirt pocket, pick up a stick, and begin scratching strange, cryptic letters and symbols into the dirt, still humming. Always humming.

But there had been no humming today when Locasta pinned her brother to the academy grass—only the clashing of swords and the shrieking cry of the monkeys, reminding her how very far from home they both were.

"How dare you sic these airborne apes on us!" she'd barked at him.

"Let go of me . . . *Lo-spaz-sta!*"

"I told you *not* to call me that . . . *Fluff!*" she grunted, tightening her hold. "By the way, nice hat! Didn't know earflaps were in style this season."

They tussled wildly, Thruff kicking up chunks of the lawn in his efforts to free himself. Locasta's grasp did not falter until she noticed the large welt swelling on his forehead— the result of Trebly's expertise with a rock sling, no doubt. At the sight of his injury, she unwittingly loosened her grip. And Thruff had taken immediate advantage of her sympathy, squirming out of her clutches and leaping to his feet. But he didn't get far—there was a flash of red and a flutter of ruffles as two hands clamped around his left arm, then two more around his right.

He was caught.

By two graduates of Madam Mentir's Academy! D'Lorp and Trebly had planted themselves on either side of Thruff, and for a couple of girls in pinafores, they looked surprisingly fierce. Locasta could only stare in disbelief as Ursie Blauf marched up to join them, prepared to fend off any hybrid who might attempt to interrupt this interrogation. Pushing her riot of curls out of her face, Locasta stood and addressed Thruff with a sneer.

"You have nowhere to go, brother," she snarled. "So you might as well talk."

"I came for the Quadling Sorceress," Thruff growled. "The one *you* just told to run away! I could have traded that that prissy little redhead to the fifth Witch for our freedom, sister—mine and yours."

Locasta grabbed the front of her brother's shirt and yanked him out of Trebly and D'Lorp's grasp. "So you've thrown your lot in with that smoky menace! How could you?"

"Because she's strong, Locasta, and formidable. The other ruling Witches bow to *her*. And so should we."

"Bow to Wickedness? Never!" Locasta shook her head hard, her purple curls whipping silver in the sun. With a snort, she shoved her brother away. "Have you no memory of our father at all? He bowed to no one!"

"And look where that got him."

Locasta was only able to meet his glinting eyes for a heartbeat. Then her face crumpled with grief and she turned away.

Thrusting his hand into his pocket, Thruff withdrew two purple ovals that shone on his open palm.

"Gemstones?" Trebly remarked, incredulous.

"Am-*hic*-ethyst," D'Lorp clarified.

Locasta whirled back around to gape at the glittering stones in Thruff's hand. "Where did you get those?"

"Papa left them behind," said Thruff. "I found them sewn into his pallet, hidden in the straw. No sign of his compass, though. Did you—?"

Without warning, Locasta had shot out one booted foot and connected with Thruff's ankle, bringing him down hard to his hands and knees.

She recalled now how Thruff had looked up at her, mystified. His eyes were as cold and purple as the stones, but they were also smart; and while he hadn't known for certain before, he surely knew now. She'd turned away from his angry gaze, just as the ground beneath them began to shake. A towering gray toad was hopping in their direction.

Trebly aimed her rock sling, but before she could send the stone sailing, the toad shot out its long tongue; it wound around her shins and jerked her off her feet.

D'Lorp and Ursie hurried to help, and together they managed to shove the squat, squishy beast off their friend. Scrambling to her feet, Trebly let her rock sling fly, clonking the warty toad right between its bulging eyes. It let out an agonized croak and bounded back in the direction from which it had come.

Unfortunately, those scant few seconds in which their attention was on the toad were all Thruff needed to make his escape. He ran, zigzagging desperately between spider-gnats and salamanders, bison and beetle bugs, pausing only once, to yank the hideous golden hat from his head and fling it to the ground as though he wished he'd never worn it at all. D'Lorp gave chase, but he'd put too much distance between them to be caught. Locasta kept her eyes on her brother until the melee swallowed him from sight— and just before he disappeared, she spied a twinkling of bright purple falling from his grasp.

D'Lorp stopped running and bent to scoop up the amethyst stones. Panting and hiccuping, she brought these back to Locasta, who shoved them into her own pocket with a grunt.

It was then that the little monkey touched down at her side. The beast was holding Thruff's ugly Golden Cap out to her and chattering excitedly, tugging at the hem of Locasta's tunic, shaking the cap at her.

"I think he wants you to put it on," said Trebly. "My little brother Obblish spent the whole of last autumn speaking nothing but monkey just to annoy us. So I know a smattering of the language. I believe he's telling you that if you don the silly hat, the tide of battle will turn."

"Because of a *hat*? That's ridiculous."

"No," said Ursie, a tiny grin turning up the edges of her mouth. "That's Magic."

The monkey bobbed his head eagerly, pointing from the hat to Locasta's curls. Still skeptical, Locasta took the velvet hat and, with a deep breath, pulled it down over her hair so that the long earflaps swung almost to her shoulders.

"It's not particularly fetching," D'Lorp observed.

"Now what?" Locasta had asked the monkey.

And there in the middle of the battle, her furry little ally had guided her through the incantation of the Golden Cap. First he had her stand on her left foot and chant, "*EP-PE, PEP-PE, KAK-KE.*" Then he made her switch to her right foot and hoot, "*HIL-LO, HOL-LO, HEL-LO.*" Finally he had her stand on both feet and shout out, "*ZIZ-ZY, ZUZ-ZY, ZIK!!!*"

What had happened next astounded her.

The monkeys, many in mid-flight, others in mid-attack, instantly ceased their pummeling of the Quadling forces and as one, turned their glaring yellow eyes to Locasta, awaiting her first order. For it was the cap and the cap alone that commanded their loyalty—temporary as it might be—and their obedience.

"Mercenaries!" Locasta had gasped with distaste.

But the little monkey had given her a look as if to excuse them: *It's not their fault.*

The Winged ones continued to stare at their new leader with ugly, expectant faces.

"Protect the Quadling forces!" Locasta shouted. "Defeat the Witches' armies!"

And so the monkeys had turned their aggressions on the multitude of hybrids. With those weird, wild, winged creatures on their side, the Foursworn army had been unbeatable. The insects retreated first, speeding eastward in a droning panic. Marada's herd soon followed, and when Locasta glimpsed Thruff lashed to the horns of a buffalope, she understood that because of his failure to capture Glinda, he was not being brought back to the Gillikin north a leader, but a prisoner.

It was while she'd been debating whether or not to facilitate Thruff's rescue that the giant toad returned, pouncing from behind and tackling her to the ground. Its weight had taken the wind out of her, and she'd recoiled at the feeling of its bumpy hide and the swampy rot of its breath as his tongue slapped mercilessly against the back of her neck.

The toad's attack on Locasta had terrified D'Lorp so badly that it sent her into a hiccuping fit—and how lucky that had been, since hiccuping, it seemed, brought on her Magic. With every involuntary squeak from D'Lorp's larynx, the toad assailant shrank in size until it was nothing but a bulging-eyed blob hopping up and down between Locasta's shoulder blades! Jumping to her feet, Locasta had yanked the Golden Cap off her head and flung it at the warty menace, catching the toad under it. It stunned the creature for only a second. Then everyone (except Locasta) had laughed at the sight of that ugly yellow hat "hopping" away, heading west with the rest of Daspina's slithering dragoons.

In truth, Locasta had not been overly disappointed to be rid of the cap. The battle was finished and the Foursworn had emerged victorious; she had no further use for those flying mercenaries.

And now here she was, in the toolshed.

But Glinda was gone.

And without Glinda to lead them, the whole fight had been for naught. Locasta hung her head, and a single tear slid down her cheek, falling into the hole in the floor. She did not hear the tiny *splish* of her sadness becoming a part of the water far below.

Glinda was lost, and that meant all was lost.

Suddenly the whisper of a thought seemed to fill the toolshed, as though the very walls and the dusty air and the dirt of the floor were all thinking it at once: *That moment in which all is lost is the same moment in which begins the battle to regain it.*

"Locasta?" came Ursie's worried voice. "Should I find Miss Gage? Should I let her know that Glinda is missing?"

"Yes." Locasta nodded. "Go, Ursie. Go now."

Ursie spun and bolted from the toolshed.

Locasta was about to follow when she heard a distant rushing sound. Peering over the rim of the hole, she saw that the water had begun to whirl in its depths, and the whirl was rising! Splashing and swirling it came, like a contained flood, climbing up the rocky sides, deepening until it had swallowed the upper part of the spiral staircase and lapped over the bank, sloshing into the dirt.

Locasta felt the knees of her breeches growing wet; the overflow seeped through her leather boots and soaked her rough cotton stockings underneath. In the crystal swell she sensed motion; a fast, upward glide and a beating of wing-like fins scattering the watery light. Then something broke the surface—an elegant head whipping back in a cascade of silvery-citrine hair, which threw off water droplets like a shower of diamonds.

The creature bobbed there for a moment, studying Locasta with bright, unreadable eyes.

A Sea Fairy. Not a pen-and-ink outline this time, but an actual Sea Fairy.

"Where are Glinda and Ben?" Locasta demanded. "These steps—where do they lead?"

The Sea Fairy only stared.

Locasta's heart raced. As she waited for an explanation, she tried desperately not to imagine her friends drowned in this mysterious pool. But the Fairy said nothing, just continued to gaze at her with a serene, inscrutable expression.

Growing irritated, Locasta pressed, "Are they safe? Will they . . . *can* they . . . come back?"

The Fairy remained silent.

"So it's a secret, then?" Locasta stood up and began tugging off her sodden boots.

The Fairy tilted her head; this sent the water rippling around her shoulders as if someone had tossed a pebble into the pool. But still, she said nothing.

"I guess you enjoy being utterly unhelpful," Locasta huffed, slamming one foot onto the top step of the spiral. She felt the water *squoosh* between her stocking-clad toes. "Say something!" she yelled at the Fairy.

In response, the Fairy lifted her arms from beneath the surface.

To Locasta's shock, she was cradling Illumina.

"Where did you get that?" Locasta choked, because she knew that nothing less than abject tragedy could have caused Glinda to part with her beloved sword. "Look, if you don't tell me, I'm just going to dive in and find out for myself. Don't you understand? She's my *friend*."

Silence.

"Fine." Locasta prepared to dive, but the Fairy blew a delicate breath across the pool; this brought up a thundering wave that crashed over Locasta, knocking her down. She landed on her backside with a splat, drenched and dripping on the muddy toolshed floor.

"Clever," Locasta ground out through gritted teeth.

"But if you want to keep me out of that pool, you're going to have to do better than a measly little bath."

To her surprise, the Fairy smiled. And when she finally spoke, her voice filled the shed with the sound of gently bursting bubbles: "I am sorry, but you who have not been called are not free to enter this portal."

"Oh yeah? Well, *I'm* sorry, but not being free to do something has never stopped me before." Locasta clambered to her feet and made to throw herself into the pool. But the Fairy's next words stopped her cold.

"You cannot help her, Locasta."

Locasta went pale. "Are you saying I'm not allowed? Or not qualified? Or can I not help her because she's beyond help . . . because she's already—?"

"Take the sword," the Fairy urged.

"Tell me!" Locasta roared. "Is Glinda alive?" Her next words were like barbed wire in her throat. "Or is she dead?"

A graceful swish of her tail brought the Fairy to the edge of the pool, where she placed Illumina reverently on the bank. "Would the answer to that question—whichever answer it might be—have any bearing on whether you continue the fight? Tell me, fiery child of Gillikin, if I were to give you one truth or the other, would it make you any less willing to do what you can do . . . what you *must* do . . . from this moment forward?"

Locasta glared at the Fairy, clenching her fists as the

tears welled up behind her eyes. "It would not."

"Very well, then." The Sea Fairy nodded and gestured to Illumina. "Consider this a beacon of friendship to light your way."

Locasta bent down and picked up the sword with trembling hands; then she watched as the Sea Fairy arched and dove, her luminous tail swinging up just long enough to flick once—a wave good-bye—then flipping down to disappear into the blue-green shadows. Her departure sent a scuttle of tiny whitecaps across the surface; Locasta took them for what they were: a wish for luck.

She was not surprised when the hole began to pull in on itself, closing over the steps and the water until all that was left was a pretty, curling shell, resting on a muddied patch of floor.

13

NOMES!

Glinda came awake slowly, groaning at the unpleasant sensation of the pebbly ground beneath her cheek. She reached for Illumina before she'd even opened her eyes, only to recall as her hand came away empty where she was and what had transpired. Since her clothes were merely damp, not wet, she surmised that she'd been asleep for some time. She was in a grotto similar to the one the Sea Devil had snatched her from, but much larger. "Ben?" she murmured.

"Kaliko, actually."

Glinda sat bolt upright on the bank and scanned her shadowy surroundings. "Who's there?" she demanded.

But all she saw were rocks, hundreds of them scattered

around the cavern floor. Her first thought was that she'd slept through an underground avalanche. But as her eyes adjusted to the dimness, she saw that the rocks were not rocks at all. On closer inspection, Glinda realized she'd awoken amid a gathering of rock fairies. And though they all looked as if they'd been chipped or gouged straight from the walls, they were very much alive, with arms and legs and curious faces. Collectively, their build could be described as "stout," but as in all populations, there were some notable variations—a few were tall and narrow, like monoliths, while others were flatter and smoother, like stepping-stones.

One of them, the tallest by far, stepped toward Glinda. She guessed from his bearing, as well as the thick silver chain and medal he wore around his neck, that he enjoyed a measure of authority over the others.

"Welcome to the Underlands," the obelisk-like creature pronounced. "I am chief steward to King Roquat, the ruler of the Nomes." He grinned, exposing teeth that looked like tiny rows of stalactites and stalagmites. Then he gave a haughty sniff and importantly waved the other Nomes away. The sound of the stony assemblage rolling off down the tunnels was nearly deafening.

"Did you have a nice swim?"

"Not particularly." Glinda frowned. "Do you happen to know what's become of my friend?"

"He's at the palace of King Roquat."

"Will you take me to him, please?"

"Soon enough," said Kaliko. "Did they give you a present?"

"Did who give me a present?"

"The Sea Fairies. I assume you encountered them."

"Oh, I encountered them, all right. As a matter of fact, I saved them. And lost my sword in the battle."

"All the more reason for them to give you a gift," Kaliko twittered. "Check your pockets."

Dipping her hand into her pocket, Glinda's fingers closed around something smooth and round. She withdrew it, squinting in the dim light of the cave. "It's a pearl."

"And a rather sizable one at that!" said Kaliko with an approving bob of his head. "Quite priceless, I assure you. Though not quite as precious as the stones we Nomes mine. See for yourself. " When the steward gave the heavy links of his chain a shake, several torches in sconces affixed to the walls burst into flame. The torchlight revealed countless piles of colorful stones scattered around the edges of the cave. They reminded Glinda of the emerald in the rough, and the miniature city that had come to life in her hand.

"Lovely," said Glinda.

"I especially like the way they twinkle in the firelight," the lanky steward remarked. "The flames are so much brighter now that Ember is free."

This caught Glinda entirely by surprise. "So . . . you are aware of what's been happening above, then?"

"Not usually," said Kaliko. "But something very strange and sinister happened in the North earlier today." He pointed one rocky finger upward. "Right above our heads, in fact."

Glinda followed his gesture to the cavern ceiling. "Am I in the North?"

"No, you are *under* the North. To be *in* the North you would have to travel vertically from here."

"But I was in the South," Glinda persisted, "in Quadling. How did I get all the way to the North?"

"The lagoon that delivered you here is vast," Kaliko explained with a disinterested wobble of his stony head. "There are currents, and riptides, and undertows, not to mention Sea Devils, and of course, Magic. Put it all together and here you are, deep below the Northern region. And if the water carried you all the way here, I suspect it had a good reason."

Glinda could only hope. "Go on, please, about the strange and sinister happening in Gillikin."

"A lurlquake! Brief but powerful, a unique seismic event in that it was localized to the *interior* of Marada's castle, of all places!"

"There was a lurlquake *in* the castle?"

"Hard to believe, isn't it? *We* were certainly shocked. In fact, we were *after*shocked."

Glinda considered this news with a grimace. "I'm guessing such an upheaval would be the 'fault' of the fifth Witch."

"Ha!" Kaliko grinned. "Good one, Oz child. Although I have never heard of a *fifth* Witch." He shrugged. "In any case, the lurlquake, whatever its cause, resulted in a fair amount of pebbly debris trickling down here into the Underlands. And pebbles, if you didn't know, can be quite chatty. They heard of your success in the South and were more than happy to gossip all about it. Roquat seemed pleased to hear of Aphidina's demise. Of course, he has no official loyalty to either side of this conflict, but I choose to believe that in his stony heart, he's rooting for the side of Good."

"That's nice to hear," said Glinda. "I look forward to meeting your king. And to that end, will you please take me to the palace now?"

"Oh, but you're already here," Kaliko informed her. "This is Roquat's throne room!"

Glinda looked around at the sloping dirt walls and sandy floor. An archway on the far side of the cavern was blocked by the impenetrable bars of a rusted iron gate. "I don't see any king," she said. "For that matter, I don't even see a throne. This isn't a palace, it's just a cave."

Kaliko grinned down at her from his teetering height. "Is it?" He gave his medal a little flick and the wall torches were extinguished, plunging Glinda into darkness. Without thinking, she reached for her sword and felt her heart plummet when she remembered it was gone.

Then, in a burst of magnificent golden light, the torches

flared back to life and Glinda found herself standing in an extravagant hall complete with marble floors and walls studded with diamonds, rubies, and sapphires. In the center of the room was a gilt throne adorned with grand carvings, and perched upon it was the Nome King. And standing beside him was . . .

"Ben!" Glinda ran to throw her arms around her friend. "I thought you were lost forever."

"I thought the same about you." Ben was almost giddy with excitement. "Glinda, there's incredible news. We were right to believe!"

"What do you mean?"

"Remember the seashell's spell? 'Who you must find, is who you will see'?"

"The Elementals? Here in the Underlands?"

"Guess again," said Ben, eyes twinkling.

Glinda's knees nearly buckled. "Mythra?"

"I told you anything was possible! And the Nome King has confirmed it. He's quite hospitable, actually. He gave me this." Ben held up a golden cylinder for Glinda to admire. It was both lovely and strange, engraved with elaborate etchings all around, tapering off at one end to accommodate an eyepiece, while the opposite end was covered with a sort of rounded glass cap. "He calls it a collide-o-scope."

Recalling that she was in Roquat's audience chamber, Glinda quickly turned toward the throne and dropped into a curtsy before the king. "Your Highness!" she said.

"I am most honored to make your acquaintance."

Roquat, like his steward, was a being of animated stone. His rough, gray-brown skin sparkled with shimmering flecks of mica, and he was dressed in a sumptuous velvet robe of sapphire blue. His hair was a luxurious mane of white, as was the long, flowing beard he stroked, as he studied the girl from above.

"Care to play a game?" he asked.

The request surprised Glinda. She was hardly in the mood for games, given what Ben had just told her about Mythra.

"Perhaps later," she said as politely as she could manage. "Is it true that Mythra is alive? Do you know where I can find her? Is she close?"

The Nome King smiled, resembling a friendly gargoyle. "My responses, in reverse order, are as follows: Yes; of course; absolutely; and . . . what do you mean, 'perhaps later'? When the King of the Underlands invites you to partake in a game, you do not defer his gratification with vague promises! You accept his gracious invitation!"

"But Your Highness . . . or is it your Lowness? Either way, I have been tasked with finding the Mystic, and if you can help—"

"Silence!" The king roared the word with such force that Glinda stumbled backward. "If you refuse to partake in my game, I shall be forced to keep you here as my captive. Just like your associate."

"You mean Ben? But he's not a captive, he's . . ." Glinda shot a panicked glance to where Ben had been standing just seconds before.

But all that remained on the place where he'd stood was the gilt cylinder with the bulbous glass end.

"Go ahead," the king said. "Have a gander."

Glinda suddenly felt very uneasy. But she picked up the collide-o-scope and pressed the smaller end to her eye. Inside, she saw the most spectacular array of colored stones. Through the lens of the collide-o-scope they seemed to be enormous, which was a very good thing since among them was Ben, surrounded by giant gems and jewels.

"Twist it," the king urged in a casual tone. "Give it a turn!"

With quivering fingers, Glinda rotated the cap, and as she did, a squeal escaped her, though whether her reaction was one of joy or horror, she could not say. For inside the glass topper of this strange little instrument, endless designs were coming to life, defying dimension as they opened and closed in and out of themselves, creating countless mirror images of their own ever-changing shapes and colors. Glinda could not even describe the beauty of it except to imagine that if geometry joined hands with art and invited poetry and light to join them in a dance, *this* would be the result.

And in the middle of it all was Ben, toppling over and under, this way and that.

Jerking the collide-o-scope away from her face, she glared at the king. "Is he all right?"

"Oh, he's quite well, I can promise you that. A little dizzy, perhaps, but that's not fatal. Well, hardly ever at least."

Glinda felt sick. "You mean he could die?"

"I would hope not." The king gave a stony shrug. "But it's hard to predict what might happen when one is forced to look at oneself from a multitude of angles."

"But why? Why would you put him in such an odd little prison? He posed no threat to you."

"This is true," Roquat concurred breezily. "But it is my opinion that your earth friend has much to learn. He does not yet recognize that ideas come in many colors, and when they are allowed—nay, *encouraged*—to collide, the results can be nothing short of dazzling! There are rainbows of purpose to be found, when one is willing to see the many colors that make up other schools of thought."

"You're mad!" said Glinda. "You're not making sense!"

The king heaved one stone eyebrow upward and glared at her. "I'd be careful, if I were you. There's room in there for two, you know." He reached out to wriggle his stony fingers at her. "Give it back now. It's not a toy."

Reluctantly, Glinda obliged, placing the collide-o-scope in his open palm.

"Selfish girl!" Roquat scolded. "Did you think Master Benjamin Clay was brought to Oz only to help *you*? Did you not dream, just a little, that perhaps he was delivered here because he too has a future, and in order to achieve it, he just might require a bit of an attitude adjustment?"

Embarrassed, Glinda looked down at her boots. "I did not dream that, no," she admitted.

"Well then . . ." Roquat's hearty laughter boomed through the audience chamber. "Perhaps I've taught you something too."

He lifted his hand in the air and the collide-o-scope disappeared in a puff of jewel-toned smoke. Glinda let out a little yelp at the sight of Ben's prison vanishing into thin air.

"Seems you now require two things of me," Roquat observed with a grin. "You need your friend back *and* you want to know the Mystic's whereabouts. Yes?"

Glinda nodded.

"Tell you what . . ." The king crossed his stone legs and tapped the tips of his rocky fingers together. "How about . . . *I play you for it?*"

"Play me for it? What do you mean?"

"Our game! Nothing too taxing, mind you, just a little linguistic challenge."

"A word game?"

"Precisely. If *you* win, I will send you off to the Mystic and give you back your buddy."

Glinda gulped. "And if *you* win?"

Roquat winked, and the collide-o-scope reappeared in

his grasp. "I guess you didn't hear me," he said, giving the gadget a gentle shake in her direction. "I said there's room for two in this little beauty."

Glinda narrowed her eyes at him. "How can I be sure you won't cheat at this game?"

"Oh, you can't be sure, you can't be sure at all." Roquat stroked his long white beard. "But you are between a rock and a hard place. Indeed, you've hit rock bottom."

"If Locasta were here, she'd give you a kick in *your* rock bottom," Glinda muttered. But because he was right, she lifted her chin, met his smirk with a steely gaze, and said, "All right, then, Your Highness. Game on."

14

THE GREATEST PRIZE TO EARN

Locasta Norr was no stranger to loneliness.

Her beloved mother and sisters had been ripped away from her at the hands of the Witch Marada. Her adoring father had disappeared one winter's night without a hint as to why he'd gone or if he was ever coming back. And most recently she'd been betrayed by her dunderhead brother, who believed he could barter a hero like Glinda in exchange for his own freedom.

But not until this very moment—seated in the opulent dining hall of the Foursworn Stronghold with Miss Gage, Ursie Blauf, and two Mentir alums, Trebly and D'Lorp (who'd proven themselves far braver than she'd ever imagined)—not until *this* moment, with Glinda, Ben, and Shade all gone and unaccounted for, had Locasta ever felt completely and utterly *alone*.

"Please, Locasta," Miss Gage was saying as she slid a fancy cup and saucer across the table. "Drink this."

"Yes, do—*hic*," said D'Lorp. "Razzleberry is good—*hic*—for calming the nerves."

How is it for healing the heart? Locasta wondered as her gaze wandered to Illumina on the tabletop. It hurt just to look at it, since without Glinda there to . . . well, to simply *be Glinda*, the sword had gone from being an instrument of light to nothing more than a cold slab of metal. Her spirit leaped with hope every time a shimmer skittered along the blade . . . until she remembered that the fleeting twinkle was only the reflection of the firefly chandeliers above.

"Did the Fairy say when they'd be back?" asked Trebly.

Locasta shook her head.

"Did she say if they were safe?" asked Miss Gage.

Locasta took a gulp of tea. "She really wasn't much of a conversationalist."

"But she *didn't* say they *weren't* safe," Ursie prodded. "Right? So perhaps that means—"

"Stop it!" Locasta barked, cutting her off. "I already told you that slimy little fishfairy didn't tell me anything that could be considered encouraging, promising, or even marginally useful. Ben's gone, Glinda's gone, and we're all just going to have to get used to it." Then she slammed the teacup down so ferociously into the saucer that they both shattered into a thousand tiny pieces.

The sound caused Ursie to let out a little squeal, and the next thing they knew, the chandelier nets had burst wide open, showering crystals down on them like glassy rain.

"Ursie," cried Trebly, "not *again*!"

D'Lorp was already running for the door, shouting for jars to catch the fireflies, which were running amok. Miss Gage lowered her eyes to her hands folded in her lap and pretended to ignore the clicking rhythm of the falling crystals ricocheting off Illumina's blade.

But Ursie Blauf (who had some prior experience with this sort of thing) was looking *up*.

Up toward the ceiling, where the fireflies were now going into a kind of interpretive dance. "Look!" she breathed. "Locasta, Miss Gage. *Look!*"

Gage tilted her head back and gasped. "My goodness!"

What had begun as bioluminescent pandemonium had turned to graceful choreography as the fireflies darted back and forth among themselves, skillfully spinning light into letters and using their brilliant backsides to spell out, in glittering penmanship, a phrase that made Locasta's breath catch in her throat:

Terra, Elemental Fairy of Lurl

The words twinkled briefly overhead. Then, like the stitches on Tilda's linen map, they began to disappear as the fireflies abandoned their calligraphy and fell into one long, single-file line, which was suddenly winging its way down from the ceiling and fluttering straight for Locasta. The glowing bug parade circled her once, inviting her to join them before continuing on their way.

"I think they want you to follow them!" cried Ursie, but Locasta had already grabbed Illumina and was dashing after the fiery fleet.

The glimmering procession led her (with Gage and Ursie running along after) directly to the library. Locasta slipped Illumina into her sash and reached into her pocket, gently wrapping her hand around the amethyst stones. *For good luck.*

Tilda's Magical linen map still lay on the table, but it was not the map over which the fireflies chose to hover. Instead they positioned themselves like a halo above the creased sheet of parchment the map had been wrapped in (before Ursie's triumph over the knotted string), and onto this they cast their pearly glow.

In the excitement of the stone game, they had all failed to notice that the parchment was inscribed: A HERO IS HE . . .

Here again, as in the chapbook Glinda had read from, and Maud's embroidered sampler, was the poem from the Reliquary floor. But as Locasta gazed at it, she was not surprised to see that the words had altered themselves:

> *So solemn is this affair yet errant souls*
> *Can soon return to those who yearn and there shall learn*

To welcome that which surpasses hurt;
That with which all wounds are as good as healed:
Forgiveness
The greatest prize to earn.

She ran a finger over the unfamiliar lines, and the gemstones in her hand suddenly began to shimmy and squirm. Opening her fist, she watched with wide eyes as the amethysts tumbled from her palm and landed on the parchment.

"Here we go again," sighed Ursie. "Another game! Honestly, can the Foursworn never be direct?"

But Locasta felt herself smiling for the first time since she'd burst into the toolshed and found it empty but for a reticent Sea Fairy and Glinda's sword. "Not if they wish to protect their secrets, they can't," said Locasta, and as if to confirm it, the purple stones flew into action.

In a Magical fervor, they began to roll from word to word, back and forth, up and down, sliding and spinning until they became a purple blur. Occasionally they would linger on a certain letter ever so briefly, then they'd be off again like a shot.

Locasta tried to keep up with them, her eyes darting wildly across the parchment. She wished she could glimpse the letters through the translucency of the stones, but they were moving much too fast for her to make sense of what, if anything, they were rushing to spell out. And once they'd rolled off a letter, it disappeared from the page without a trace.

"Slow down," Locasta commanded. "I can't keep up." But the stones continued to roll and pause, roll and pause, with the same lightning speed.

When at last her father's good luck charms fell still, she scooped them up and read the poem again:

So solemn is this af
Can soon return to those who yearn and there shall learn
To wel e that which sur es hurt;
That with which all wounds are as good :
Forgiveness
The greatest prize to earn.

"Af?" read Ursie. "Wel e? Sur es? It's gibberish."

"Maybe we're missing something," said Miss Gage.

Locasta stared at the remaining pieces of poetry, at first baffled, then furious. "We *are* missing something," she stormed. "A bunch of letters! The ones that vanished when the stones touched them."

"Maybe the stones accidentally erased the wrong ones," Ursie offered. "Maybe amethysts are just poor spellers."

But the stones had once again begun to rattle in Locasta's grip. Unfurling her fingers, she peered down at them and saw that something was different.

Deep inside each of the gems was a series of squiggly black flecks. No, not flecks . . .

"Letters! The stones didn't *erase* them, they *absorbed* them!"

"So the letters are *inside* the stones?" said Gage. "How in the world are you supposed to read them like that?"

Locasta's first instinct was to shake them hard, hoping she might be able to dislodge the secret words from where they were trapped inside the stone. Then, in a flash, she remembered her father, sitting on the stoop of their ramshackle little house back in Gillikin, holding the amethysts up to his eyes and aiming them toward the sun.

"I need light," she blurted.

Ursie lifted an eyebrow in the direction of the fireflies still floating above the table. "Won't that do?"

"I need *bright* light," Locasta clarified. "*Extremely* bright light, and lots of it." She reached for the sword at her hip and swung it high above her head. With her best friend's blade in one hand and her father's good luck charms in the other, she closed her eyes and pictured herself dropping Miss Gage's mirror outside the toolshed, and Glinda retrieving it from the grass. A chuckle escaped her when she saw herself shoving the girl in the silly ruffled dress up against a cherry tree.

Illumina gave a slight flicker, and Ursie gasped. "I think it's working," she cried. "Whatever you're doing, keep doing it."

Locasta squeezed her eyes tighter and imagined herself

hoisting Glinda up onto her shoulder to run from Bog's wagon into the Woebegone Wilderness. She could almost hear herself laughing at the sight of Haley Poppet poking out of Glinda's pocket; laughing so hard she could barely catch her breath.

Again Illumina gave off a faint glow; this time the light lasted a little longer, and shone a bit brighter.

"Good girl, Locasta!" cheered Gage. "Almost there!"

Finally Locasta let her mind return to the Reliquary, where she pictured Glinda lying silent and motionless on the tile floor, clutching the handle of her newly acquired sword. The panic of that moment came back to her in a cold rush, but in the next moment she felt the great relief of watching Glinda awake from that strange and sudden slumber.

I thought you were gone from us.

I thought I'd lost you, too.

Illumina flared, a bright beyond brilliant. And with trembling fingers, Locasta held the amethysts up as she'd seen her father do a hundred times before, backlit not by the sun but by a radiant sword. Illumina's light shone through the stones, magnifying the letters and making them glow from within.

"What do they say?" asked Ursie.

Locasta read the words that only she could see: "Fairy . . . Terra . . . Compass . . . As Healed."

The moment she'd uttered the final word, Illumina cooled back to metal in her grasp.

"I do believe we've just been given the exact hiding

place of an Elemental Fairy of Lurl," said Gage. "She's in a compass!"

"A compass in the Witch Marada's castle," Ursie added with a shudder.

"Yes," said Locasta. "Although I confess, I don't know what 'as healed' means."

"Perhaps the Entrusted is a physician?"

Locasta shook her head. "No. Not a physician."

"How can you be sure?"

"Because," said Locasta, slipping first the amethysts, then the linen map and the parchment it had been wrapped in, deep into her pocket, "I know exactly who was keeping Terra in a compass."

"Who?!" Miss Gage and Ursie cried in unison.

"Norr," Locasta answered softly. "My father."

"Locasta . . . *no!*" Miss Gage was shaking her head so hard her upsweep became a downsweep, and this time without any help from Ursie. "As you yourself told Glinda, traveling out of Quadling now is far too dangerous."

"That's right," Ursie chimed in. "I believe your exact words were, 'Uh-uh-uh.'" She waved her finger, mimicking Locasta's earlier gesture.

"Too dangerous for Glinda maybe," Locasta said, with forced calm. "But I'm much savvier than she is. And besides, I'll have a Road of Red Cobble and a sword of light. What could possibly go wrong?"

Miss Gage let out a strangled bark of laughter, though it was clear she did not find Locasta's aplomb in the least bit amusing. "You're going off alone to confront the Witch of the North! I doubt very much the red road will reward such recklessness by carrying you there. I understand you want to retrieve the Elemental Fairy, but now is the time to exercise caution."

"Caution was *Glinda's* specialty," Locasta said dully. "She was the careful one."

"*Is*," Ursie said pointedly. "Glinda *is* careful. And Good."

"So was my father," Locasta snapped. "He hummed songs, and taught us to fight, and fanned the fires of freedom, but in the end, it didn't stop him from leaving my brother and me—not to mention the Elemental Fairy of Lurl—completely in the lurch. Now it's up to me to fix it. And that means going home to Gillikin."

"You're absolutely sure the Witch has this compass?" asked Ursie.

"Yes," Locasta muttered, looking away. "I'm sure."

Gage let out a weary rush of breath. "Then we'll leave it up to the road. If the red cobbles come for you, I will not stand in your way. But if they don't . . ."

"If they don't," said Ursie, "we'll all wait for Glinda to return and devise a new plan." She turned a desperate look to Locasta. "All right?"

Locasta thought about it, then nodded and said, "All right."

To which Ursie gave a little squeal of joy, and Gage looked visibly relieved.

"And I'm sorry for being stubborn," Locasta added, her tone genuine. "I know you're just looking out for me."

"Shall we go to the kitchen and treat ourselves to a light supper?" Miss Gage suggested. "I think I saw some biscuits and a pot of quince jelly-jam in the larder."

"And pickles," cried Ursie. "Wouldn't pickles be lovely right now?"

"Thank you just the same." Locasta managed a sleepy smile. "But if you don't mind, I think I'll turn in. Between the monkey battle and the fireflies and discovering that my father was an Entrusted . . . well, I'm exhausted. In fact, I bet I'll sleep right through breakfast."

"Sleep as long as you need to," said Gage, smoothing Locasta's riot of purple curls. "When you're ready, we'll meet on the back lawn and see what the Road of Red Cobble decides."

"See you after breakfast," said Ursie, as Locasta turned and headed for the Grand Drawing Room.

But she had no intention of seeing Ursie after breakfast or meeting Miss Gage on the lawn.

Because she planned to be gone long before that.

Whether the Road of Red Cobble liked it or not.

15

WRITTEN IN STONE

When the Nome King clapped his rocky hands, the sound was almost deafening. Kaliko came rushing to do his bidding, carrying a shiny pail that rattled noisily as he ran. He had a large piece of slate tucked under his arm.

Glinda's eyes remained fixed on the collide-o-scope, which Roquat was now tossing lazily into the air, watching it turn end over end before catching it again. *Poor Ben.*

"Let's get on with it," she said. "What is the contest?"

"A simple little word game, actually. Tell me, have you much knowledge of rocks?"

"Only a passing familiarity," Glinda admitted. "I took an elective course at Mentir's called Geology for Girls,

Why Bother? The professor put far more emphasis on the 'why bother' portion than the geology part."

"Too bad for you, then," Kaliko chirped, grinning as he placed the slate on the floor. On it was scrawled a word puzzle in a standard fill-in-the-blanks format—a short paragraph interspersed with empty spaces in which the game player was expected to inscribe the proper answer.

"Supremely creative, isn't?" crowed Roquat, as Kaliko plunked the pail of rocks down beside the slate. "It's multiple choice. All that you'll need can be found in that bucket."

"There are just rocks in the bucket!" Glinda protested. "How am I supposed to write in the answers? This doesn't make any sense."

"Isn't that the job of a hero, dearie?" asked Roquat with a craggy chuckle. "To make sense out of that which does not make sense? To find the answers when there appear to be none?"

With a heavy sigh, Glinda crouched down beside the slate and read:

A HERO ON A JOURNEY MUST HAVE AN _____ FOR
ADVENTURE. YOU MUST TAKE NOTHING FOR _____.
TAKE NOTICE OF _____ SHINES YOU TOWARD THE
PATH YOU ARE TO FOLLOW. BUT FIRST, YOU MUST BE
BRAVE ENOUGH _____ THROUGH _____. BEYOND IT
YOU WILL FIND A DOOR; ITS COLOR IS A _____.

"This is impossible. I can't write with rocks!"

"You disappoint me," Roquat lamented; he was now spinning the collide-o-scope on the tip of his finger. "I would have imagined that you of all people would be able to think *outside* the rocks. But I'm feeling rather charitable today, so I'll give you a hint." He tapped the collide-o-scope on his knee, deciding how to phrase his generous clue. "Oh! All right . . . think of this: What do you fairyfolk say about a rule, or a decision that is unchangeable? Something that is nonnegotiable, if you will. Permanent. You say it is . . ." He made a coaxing gesture with the scope, indicating that she should complete his thought.

"Written in stone!" cried Glinda. "Something that is unchangeable is said to be written in stone."

"And there is your hint!" said the king, looking inordinately pleased with himself for helping.

"You may begin," said Kaliko.

Glinda immediately tipped out the contents of the pail. Hundreds of little rocks and stone chips skittered across the words and blanks, reminding her of the game pebbles scattered over the Magical map. She only hoped she could remember the scant bit of terminology her geology professor had halfheartedly imparted in class.

The first of the stones to catch her eye were the bright gemstones: a golden-hued topaz, a gleaming pink

tourmaline, a deep blue sapphire, a bloodred garnet. Mixed in with these were opal and onyx, apatite and amethyst, moonstone and malachite.

Picking up a random handful, she spoke the names aloud. "Shale, igneous, granite . . . Aha!"

With eager fingers, she placed the granite chip on one of the blanks in the puzzle.

From his throne, Roquat gave a little nod of approval.

Scooping up another bunch, Glinda quickly picked out an apatite and an agate to add to the paragraph, then continued to search by lining up several more stones and tapping each one in turn, as she said their names out loud.

"Gneiss, basalt, topaz, marble, tuff . . . oh, wait!" She walked her fingers back and chose the topaz, which she placed on what she hoped was the proper blank. "Yes! That's right. At least I think so. It's a bit of a pun, I think. Tricky, but it works."

Next she positioned a blazing blue sapphire, and lastly, a flat stone of dullish gray that bore the lovely name of howlite, which Glinda considered a complete misnomer, since there was no shine to it at all.

"There!" she cried, leaping up from the ground and pointing down at the slate. "I'm finished. I've filled them all in!" Indeed, where before the puzzle had been shot through with empty spaces, it was now dotted with stones of various sizes, shapes, and hues. "Now, please, release Ben and tell me how to get to the Mystic!"

"Not so fast, let me see," fussed Kaliko, bowing low over the slate on the floor.

Then he cleared his throat and recited what Glinda had, indeed, "written in stone."

"'A hero on a journey must have an *apatite* for adventure. You must take nothing for *granite*. Take notice of *howlite* shines you toward the path you are to follow. But first, you must be brave enough *topaz* through *agate*. Beyond it you will find a door; its color is a *sapphire*.'"

"Marvelous!" proclaimed the king. "Most excellent indeed!"

"So . . . I won!"

"No!" Roquat shook his head. "Oh no. No, no, no. You most certainly did not win. In fact, you lost. Failed miserably, I'm sorry to say. Well, not *that* sorry."

"But how could I have failed?" Glinda argued. "Look, I even got the tricky ones. Topaz—to pass—through 'a gate.' I even reasoned that granite would translate to 'granted' when read aloud."

"No one said your game play was not impressive," Roquat conceded. "It's just incomplete."

"No, it isn't! Look. I filled in every blank space."

"Turn it over," said the king smugly.

Kaliko tipped the slate, spilling off Glinda's carefully placed stones, then flipped it over. There on the back was one final sentence, ending in a blank.

"That's not fair!" said Glinda. "You didn't say there was more on the back."

"And I didn't say there wasn't. You might have checked, mightn't you? It wouldn't have been against the rules. You just assumed that the entire puzzle was there before you, when in fact, there was more to see, if only you had been looking."

Glinda clenched her fists, and her face turned the color of rubies. "Cheater!"

"I prefer 'winner,'" said Roquat. "But there's no need to be such a spoilsport. You have your consolation prize right there! The part of the puzzle you did solve is the key to finding Mythra—assuming you can interpret it."

"What about Ben?"

"Good question." Roquat uncrossed his thunderous stone legs, then crossed them again. "How about this: if you do happen to locate your missing Mystic, there is something she has that I would very much like for myself. A belt."

Glinda was sure she'd heard him wrong. "Did you say 'belt'?"

"Oh, it's not just any belt," Roquat assured her. "It's all studded with gemstones and—unless I miss my guess—loaded with Magic of the highest quality." He patted his boulder-like tummy. "And besides, I occasionally have trouble keeping my robe closed, so . . . there's that."

"Fine," said Glinda. "I will bring you Mythra's belt—"

"*If* you can find her," Kaliko cut in ominously.

He's lucky I lost my sword, thought Glinda. "And you will give Ben back to me!"

"Yes, yes, contingent of course on whether you survive your dealings with Mythra, as she is known to be very, very—" He snapped his fingers, and the stone Glinda had earlier identified as tuff appeared in his hand; he tossed it to Glinda, who caught it.

"She's *tough*," said Glinda. "I get it."

"Aren't you even curious," Kaliko asked, "about the final line of the game? You know, the one you got wrong?"

"I didn't get it wrong, I just missed it," Glinda returned sharply. But she *was* curious, so she nodded, and Kaliko read the question scratched onto the back of the slate.

"'When shadows fall, for light you'll call, to make it right, use . . . . . . *blank*!'" The steward flashed his stony teeth. "It's a difficult one. I doubt you would have solved it anyway."

"Off with you now," said Roquat.

Luckily, Glinda was able to recall which stones she had placed on which blanks in the game. Ignoring the inspirational preamble, she focused on the part that seemed to be the directions. Looking around the throne room, she noticed that the iron fence blocking the archway was flanked by two flaming torches and saw instantly "how light" shone on the rusted bars. She marched straight to it and gave it a little push. It swung open on creaky hinges. The sound was ominous, and the corridor it led to foreboding, but according to the puzzle, she must be brave enough "to pass" through "a gate."

And so she did, only to find herself confronted with three doors.

Glinda studied them, wondering what might become of her if she chose the wrong one. Each was painted in a brilliant shade. The first was a dazzling blue, the second a brilliant orange, the third a pale pink. "Its color is a *sapphire*," she said, remembering the last line of the word game. "Why, it's almost too easy. The most common and popular color of sapphires is blue." Her hand reached for the silver knob of the blue door. But she drew it back quickly, realizing how unlike Roquat it would be to make this challenge so unchallenging. Closing her eyes, she pictured the words on the slate: ITS COLOR IS A SAPPHIRE.

Not just *sapphire* but *a* sapphire. Or, if one were clever: *as . . . a . . . pphire.*

Its color is *as a fire*! And after her experience with the Elemental Fairy Ember, she certainly knew what color that was.

Heart racing, she reached for the diamond-like knob and opened the flame-colored door.

16

Tin Again, Begin Again

Shade had been tramping along the Road of Red Cobble for miles, taking full advantage of its Magic when it presented itself, and employing her stealth methods when it did not. It was on those occasions when the road, for its own unknowable reasons, had disappeared, that Shade had been forced to tread the yellow bricks. These were the times when she'd had to dodge Witch minions out on their military rounds, or disappear into crowds. She took every opportunity to listen in unfamiliar doorways or read over unsuspecting shoulders in her attempt to glean information about Tilda and Nick. It was not until she'd stumbled upon a quintet of fiddlers that she'd learned something useful.

The band had just come to an earsplitting halt, mid-tune, so that the leader could scold the hurdy-gurdy player, who (even Shade could tell) was not playing the instrument so much as torturing it. The hurdy-gurdy player took offense, blaming his sour notes on the fact that he was in a bit of romantic turmoil at the moment, having seen that hatchet-holding heartthrob Nick Chopper on his sweetheart Nimmie Amee's doorstep.

So Shade set out again, and it wasn't long before she heard shouts of alarm.

With her cape whipping around her, she ran until she skidded to a halt in front of a little stone house. A pretty Munchkin girl stood on the front porch, wringing her hands, watching in terror as the black cloud, so familiar to Shade, came swirling up from the roots of a tall tree.

Tilda and Nick were caught right in the middle of it. It was circling them as though to bind them to the trunk like a rope. Shade bolted for them, bringing the red road with her; she reached out to grab Nick by his tin arm and jerked him onto the Magical path. The smoke gave no indication that it had noticed the abrupt disappearance of the young woodcutter. Indeed, it seemed concerned only with enveloping Tilda.

"Mistress Gavaria!" screamed Shade, reaching beyond the edge of the road as far as she dared. "Give me your hand."

But the smoke had grown so dense so quickly that Shade could no longer see Tilda in its depths.

"If only I had some manner of long stick for her to cling onto," said Nick, his eyes taking in the low-hanging branches of the tree.

"No, Woodcutter," Shade commanded. "You *can't*."

But Nick had already flung himself off the red road and was chopping with all his might, hacking at every bough he could reach, swinging his ax over and over again, until he had chopped clean through one of the longest branches. As it broke away from the trunk, the girl on the porch let out a wail of pure anguish. Because Nick's cursed ax was not finished yet.

Shade had never witnessed such a horrible sight as that of Nick's own ax slicing through his shoulder and removing him of his last real limb. Out of the corner of her eye, she saw the girl leap from the porch and sprint off toward town. How Nick Chopper could fall for such a coward, Shade could not imagine. For she was sure there was no Munchkin braver than the woodcutter who even now, with his arm severed clean off, refused to give up the fight.

Dropping his ax, he used his arm of tin to pick up the fallen bough, which he thrust into the smoke, calling out, "Sorceress, take hold!"

But the bough, too heavy for him to support in one hand, wobbled and nearly fell from his grasp. Mindless of the peril, Shade jumped off the road to help him, and together they steadied the branch and extended it into the darkness.

When the smoke saw what the tin boy and the cloaked girl were about, it rolled away from Tilda and swept toward them instead. In a flash of gleaming metal, Nick planted his tin foot on Shade's back and gave her a good hard push, away from the approaching cloud and back onto the red road. A moment later he was enshrouded in darkness!

Shade whipped her head around to Tilda, who was glowering at the enemy haze.

"Run, mistress!" she cried, flapping her cape madly, beckoning the Sorceress to the safety of the red cobbles.

But Tilda did not obey Shade's plea. Instead she roared, "Take *me*, smoke! I am the one you came for. Take me and leave the boy of tin."

And so it did.

With one raging swirl, the smoke of the fifth Witch surrounded Tilda as though it would happily suffocate her in its depths. Then it lifted itself from the yard of the stone house to billow skyward and away, with Tilda obscured within, its prisoner.

Shade did not wait for the cobblestones to sink into the blue Munchkin dirt. Dropping to her knees beside Nick, she bunched up a section of her cape and held it to the place where his arm should have been, applying gentle pressure.

"Why did you chop that branch?" she asked softly. "You knew the ax would slip; you knew it would remove you of another limb."

"Indeed I did," said Nick with a nod and a grimace.

"But in that moment, I did not care one splinter about that darned curse! All that mattered was saving Tilda."

Shade whirled at the sound of footsteps rushing in their direction. It was the girl from the porch, and she was practically dragging someone along with her. A Munchkin man in a thick leather apron, carrying an armful of tools.

The girl crouched down beside Nick and smoothed his hair from his forehead.

"Nimmie Amee," he whispered, and even his excruciating pain did not stop him from blushing at her nearness. "You brought Ku-Klip. How kind. And how necessary. I'm thankful he is here to lend his expertise to my current tribulation."

The tinsmith set about his work, and suddenly the air was filled with the clanking, banging, and creaking of the tinsmith's "expertise." Silvery sparks flew from the speed with which he hacksawed and hammered.

Shade adjusted the compress and was rewarded with a strained smile from Nick.

"What brought you here, my spy-ish friend?" he asked. "Is there news from Quadling?"

"Only that Mythra is dead." She looked up from under her lashes at Nimmie, who was gazing at Nick adoringly and looking quite troubled by his pain. While she no longer thought the girl cowardly, Shade still wasn't sure she trusted the stranger enough to say much more.

"Dead," Nick repeated. "That's rather tragic, isn't it?

And now Tilda has been taken captive. It's more than my heart can bear!"

"Who in Oz's name are you nattering to, Chopper?" Ku-Klip asked, looking up from the tin he was molding. When he saw Shade, he seemed surprised to find that someone other than Nimmie Amee was present. With a shake of his head, he went back to his smithing. Nick gritted his teeth as Ku-Klip continued the agonizing process of attaching the new arm to the old torso.

"I'm sorry, spy," said Nick. "I did all that I could, but it was still not enough. Please tell Glinda that I did my best, will you?"

"I shall tell her you were dauntless," Shade assured him in her softest voice.

She stayed by the woodcutter's side until the last rivet was secured. Then she leaned down, placed a kiss on his cheek, and rose to her feet. Pulling her gray hood up over her head, she was about to step onto the red cobblestones, but Nick's voice stopped her.

"Girl in the cloak?"

She turned back to face him. "Yes, woodcutter?"

"If you ever find the Sorceress—and I pray that you do—would you kindly pass on a message from me to her?"

"Of course," said Shade. "What would you have me tell her?"

"Tell her that she will forever and always hold a very special place in this tin woodman's heart."

17

DEBUNKING MYTHRA

The orange door opened on a flight of tightly coiled steps carved into stone—a far less delicate version of the nautilus spiral that had taken Glinda from the toolshed into the pool. The glow spilling from Roquat's chamber lit the stairwell only as far as the first curve; the rest of the way was swallowed up by shadow.

Glinda all but leaped onto the top step, continuing downward at a near gallop until the borrowed light was spent and she was forced to slow down. Descending into darkness, she felt for each step with the toe of her boot. The only sound was the scuff of her heels as they scattered a thick coating of pebbly dust. It was clear that no one had used this stairway in ages; even the air felt lonely, having gone far too long without someone there to breathe it.

The already snug staircase grew more narrow with every step, chasing itself in an ever-tighter circle; the walls were now brushing against Glinda's shoulders, snagging at the fabric of her sleeves. If the stairs did not deposit her somewhere soon, she would find herself wedged in like sap clogged in a flower stem. She briefly considered turning around and going back up, but the thought was immediately dismissed; she *had* to find Mythra—everything that meant anything to her, to Oz, was riding on this meeting. And besides, even if she were willing to give up and reverse direction, the dimensions of the stairwell would not allow it. She wondered how many of the world's heroes had actually become heroes not only because they possessed the unwavering courage and commitment to sally forth, but because their circumstances had simply left them no other choice but to see it through.

When at last she reached the bottom, she had to angle herself sideways and squeeze through a slender doorway. She was not surprised to see that she'd arrived in yet another cave. It was undoubtedly a dwelling place, lit by the struggling flame of a single candle stub. But unlike Roquat's lavish audience chamber, this place offered no frills, no luxuries, no comfort at all. The dampness was already clinging to her skin, the chill burrowing into her bones. The only furnishings she could make out were a rough-hewn wooden table flanked by two hard chairs, and a straw pallet on the floor for someone to sleep on. A lumpy burlap sack slouched in one cobwebbed corner, where it appeared to have been flung and promptly forgotten.

Glinda was beginning to fear that the Nome King had, indeed, cheated and tricked her into going through that door and down those spiraling steps. Reaching for the candlestick, she swung the feeble light into each distant corner of the hovel.

"Mythra?" she called softly. "Mythra, please . . . if you are here, do show yourself. My name is Glinda. I come from Oz and I know you are not expecting me—" Her gaze fell upon the rumpled bed linens, the collection of food-encrusted wooden bowls and horn cups scattered across the table. "Or anyone else, it seems—but I urgently require your help, good Mystic. I need it in abundant amounts. So if you could please just reveal yourself, I would very much appreciate it."

Out of the silence came a scuffling sound; a ripple in the stillness that became the hunched figure of a woman tiptoeing out of the shadows. Glinda tried to shine the candlelight on her, but her face was hidden under a hooded shawl. It was clear from the shambling approach and the stoop of the shoulders that she was very old; her form was frail, and her hands poking out from beneath the shawl were wrinkled and gnarled with age.

Impossible, Glinda thought. The Mythra she'd seen in the statue had been tall and strong, thrumming with Magical confidence. She refused to believe that a Fairy of such might could have diminished this dramatically.

Glinda swallowed hard and summoned her courage. "Are you the Mystic?"

After a moment's hesitation, a reply rattled out from the depths of the hood. "I am not."

"Beg your pardon, mistress," she ventured, "but do you happen to know where the Mystic is? It's crucial that I find her because—"

"If she wanted to be found, you would have found her," the stranger interrupted in a voice like settling dust.

"I don't think you understand the magnitude of this visit," Glinda persisted. "I was instructed to find Mythra by a very powerful Sorceress of Quadling Country."

"Then you have traveled long and far for nothing," the crone informed her.

It was all Glinda could do to keep from crumbling under the crushing weight of her disappointment. *Find Mythra,* her mother had instructed. But instead, all she'd succeed in doing was losing her sword, endangering Ben, and making the useless acquaintance of some hobbling old hag. "You can't help me locate her?"

"Not 'can't,'" the crone rasped, turning her back on Glinda. "*Won't.*"

Won't? Glinda felt a flash of anger such as she'd never known before. "Why in the world *not*?"

"BECAUSE YOU ARE NOT SUPPOSED TO BE HERE!"

Without warning, the old woman let loose a holler that shook the walls of the cave, and spun back around to lunge at Glinda. Glinda leaped back, dropping the candlestick and snuffing out what little light there was in the cave. In the next instant, the enemy pounced and Glinda found herself pinned to the floor, struggling blindly.

"Get *off* me! Let me go!"

But the crone only gripped her tighter. "What are you really doing here?" she demanded, the creak of her ancient voice even more unsettling in the dark.

"I told you," Glinda wheezed. "I was *sent* here to find Mythra."

"That's a lie!" She gave Glinda a bone-rattling shake. "You could not possibly have been *sent* here, for there is not a Fairy, living or dead, in all of Oz who could have directed you to the Underlands to find Mythra! Other than that Nome King, nobody knows where she is!"

"Well *somebody* knows," Glinda hurled back, her shock at being taken down by an old woman hardening into indignant fury. "Because *somebody* went to a great deal of trouble to get me down here."

"Liar!"

"No! I'm telling the truth—" Glinda sucked in a painful

breath as a knee slammed into her solar plexus, then gasped out the rest of the phrase. "*The Truth . . . Above All!*"

The hag froze, her hands still anchored at the base of Glinda's throat as the motto trembled in the damp air around them.

"You're Foursworn?"

When Glinda nodded, the back of her head scraped painfully against the rocky floor. The hag rolled off Glinda and bounded lithely to her feet. Since she did not make any attempt to help her visitor do the same, Glinda was forced to scramble up from the floor on her own, brushing the dirt from her backside.

The crone uttered a hasty spell and the candlewick bloomed, casting a clear, soft light. But Glinda no longer had any interest in looking into the face of this madwoman. "I'm sorry to have imposed on you," she huffed. "Clearly, I've made a mistake, so I'll just see myself out." But when she turned to where the stairwell should have been, she saw nothing but a solid rock wall. The doorway leading to the narrow staircase that would carry her back to King Roquat's palace was gone.

"It seems you're not meant to be leaving just yet," said the crone, reaching up to grasp the edges of her hood with smooth, limber fingers—fingers that had been wrinkled and crooked just moments before. With a gentle sweep, she pushed the hood back so that it pooled softly at her no-longer-stooped shoulders, revealing a tousled mane of

silvery hair, shining hazel eyes, and a face of fierce, ageless, and unmistakable beauty.

In fact, in her long, flowing white dress cinched with a gem-studded silver belt, she looked almost exactly as she had the first time Glinda had seen her.

Of course, that time she'd been carved from marble.

And she'd been offering Glinda a sword.

18

TALL TALES, SMALL FAILS

"Now who's a liar?" Glinda challenged. "You *are* Mythra!"

"And you are here without an invitation."

"I apologize," said Glinda. "But as I told you, I was *sent*. I almost gave up, but I'm glad I listened to Ben, since you are obviously not quite as dead as everyone believes."

Mythra raised one elegant eyebrow and stared at Glinda, studying her for such a long time that Glinda had to fight the urge to squirm under her scrutiny. Then, abruptly, the Mystic withdrew her gaze, strode to the darkest corner of the cave, and once again turned her back on Glinda as she fumbled in the burlap bag.

In the silence that followed, Glinda allowed herself a

more thorough examination of the Mystic's cave. It would be wrong to call it humble. It was whatever came *before* humble, a good notch or two below spare; perhaps more in the range of dismal. And, frankly, a mess. Though in Mythra's defense, she did live alone in the belly of the world, and Glinda *had* arrived unannounced. The ceiling was high, and dripping with stalactites that looked like fangs. In a far corner was what could only be described as a murky puddle, and scattered throughout were rocks and stones of all sizes.

The quiet stretched on for so long that Glinda was unable to remain still a moment more. Marching to the table, she began to clear away the dirty bowls and cups, only to find that there was no logical place to put them— no sideboard, basin, or cupboard, just shallow, shelflike niches dug into the stony walls, which held books, vials, quills, and inkpots. She gave up on the dishes and moved on to the pitiful straw bed. As she straightened the scratchy linens and threadbare blanket into some semblance of tidiness, she tried not to wonder how many fleazils and louse-mites had taken up residence in Mythra's bedding.

Priestess Mysterious? she thought wryly, smoothing the covers and fluffing the sagging feather bolster. *Priestess* Mess-*sterious more like it!*

A chuckle came from across the cave. "Clever."

Glinda whirled and saw that the Mystic was emerging from the corner at last. "Did you just read my mind?"

"Not exactly."

"But you knew what I was thinking."

"Not knew. *Sensed*."

"How?"

"Honestly, I don't know. It has proven itself to be a rare and untamable kind of Magic, which is to say it cannot be employed at will. It happens when it wants to, and I've yet to find a way to convince it to do otherwise. Then again, when you are given such a wonderful power, you do well to accept it without questioning."

"And what is the name of this Magic?" Glinda asked.

Mythra lifted one shoulder in an offhanded shrug. "It did not have one when it availed itself to me, so I coined it Connection. It is not a conversation, rather a sharing of sensation, of observation. A melding of awareness."

"I think perhaps someone has been connecting with *me*," Glinda realized, moving back to the table and using her sleeve to wipe at the heavy layer of grime. "I felt a voice in the lagoon. And then, of course, there was that shell—"

"*Why* exactly were you sent here?" the Mystic asked coolly. "Surely it was not to clean up after me?"

"I'm not entirely sure," Glinda confessed, wondering the same thing herself. "Except that it must have something to do with the fact that the Foursworn Revolution has begun, though quite by accident. You see, it was all the fault of the vision and—" Suddenly everything Shade had told her about Mythra and her role in King Oz's court came back to her. "Perhaps I'm here because you trained the king and his Regents! Perhaps I was sent so you could train *me*, too. As it happens, I'm quite new to Magic, so—"

Mythra drew a sharp breath. "You *dare* to equate yourself with one as revered and distinguished as King Oz? Are you so bold as to compare yourself to his most noble and courageous Regents Valiant?"

"No, no . . . I did not mean to imply that," Glinda amended hurriedly.

"And how is it that you are, as you say, 'new'?" Mythra's hazel eyes sparked with interest and surprise. "You are twelve summers at least. How is it your sense of your own power is still so unfamiliar to you?"

"Because there is—has long been, in fact—a strictly enforced Magical Embargo," Glinda explained.

"Embargo? Enforced by whom?"

"The four Witches who have been ruling Oz for ages now. Only the Wickeds and those in their employ are allowed to use Magic."

Mythra looked incredulous. "My apologies, fairychild, but did you say . . . *ages*?"

Glinda nodded.

Now the Priestess looked thoroughly waylaid. "If it has taken this long for the Foursworn to rise up, things in Oz must be dire indeed." With a furrowed brow and a pale complexion, she asked, "Precisely how long have I been gone, child?"

Glinda had no idea. She shrugged. "How long do you *think* you've been away?"

"In truth, I cannot say. Without sunsets or moonrises to tally, the days and nights begin to run together." The Mystic let out a weary breath. "Time has become a bit of a blur, which I suppose is the lot that one who feigns her own demise and exiles herself to a place of utter secrecy must endure. There is very little point in keeping track of the passage of seasons, the onward march of Time, when everyone I considered a friend or comrade believes me dead."

"Not everyone," Glinda reminded her. "As I told you, I was sent by a powerful Sorceress, a former associate of yours in fact, and I now believe it was so that you could mentor me in the ways of Sorcery. I am in profound need of your expertise."

"Need does not always guarantee aptitude," Mythra drawled. "Do you believe you are worthy?"

"I do."

"And what evidence can you offer for such a claim?"

"The Road of Red Cobble came for me in the Woebegone."

"Red road?' Mythra looked mildly puzzled. "I've never heard of such a thoroughfare."

"It's new . . . *ish*," Glinda improvised. "It's how the Foursworn travel around Oz these days. But it only makes itself visible to those who possess a rebel's spirit, and it's made itself visible to me many times."

Mythra considered this, then leaned down close enough for her warm breath to ruffle Glinda's eyelashes. "If you truly desire my assistance, I would have you tell me—*right now*, without mulling it over—ten significant things about yourself that will aid me in bringing you into your Magic."

"Ten *things*?" Glinda repeated. "What kinds of things?"

"I believe my directive was quite clear," Mythra sniped. *"Ten significant things about yourself."*

Glinda frowned. It had never occurred to her that she would be required to present credentials. But if that was what the Mystic wanted, so be it. Beads of perspiration had begun to form on her brow, and her knees felt like they were made of soup. Indeed, if the staircase hadn't disappeared on her, she might very well have turned and fled.

"All right," she began shakily. "Ten things. Significant thing number one is that I have always been an excellent student. Best in my class at Madam Mentir's, in fact."

"Who, pray tell, is Madam Mentir?'" scoffed Mythra, then quickly gave a dismissive wave of her hand. "Never mind. I doubt very much that it matters. Continue."

"The second thing is that I saved Clumsy Bear from the Field Waifs, which took, as Locasta might say, *guts*, and three: I gave him my hair ribbons, even though I knew it would get me into horrific trouble with the headmistress."

She looked up at the Mystic, whose expression was disturbingly bland.

"Four," Glinda went on, "I solved the Queryor's puzzle

with relative ease." This revelation had Glinda smiling. She was fittingly proud of how she'd handled the entire Queryor encounter, and in the end he'd actually bowed to *her*, which was hardly an everyday occurrence! As she recalled the experience, she suddenly had the strange sensation that she was growing taller. Much taller.

"Um . . . significant things number five and six: I figured out that the Elemental Fairy of Fire, Ember, was hidden in a red beryl pendant, and I also determined that to release him from the stone, it had to be united with the sword." She gave Mythra a hopeful look. "*Your* sword, actually. Which, come to think of it, is another significant thing . . . I correctly chose your statue from the Arc of Heroes in King Oz's Reliquary."

Again she felt herself growing in size and found that it was not an unpleasant feeling at all. It was almost as if her body were expanding to contain her increasing confidence. "How many is that? Seven? Yes, I believe it is. Which brings us to significant thing number eight . . ."

Her voice was louder now, though she was not aware of consciously raising it; in fact, it was louder *and* deeper and it filled the cave like thunder. Stranger still was that Mythra, who (once she'd quit pretending to be a hunchback) had been two feet taller than Glinda at least, was now looking *up* at her. Way up.

". . . I fooled Leef Dashingwood by making him think I was swooning over his affections, when in reality I was just using him to secure an audience with Aphidina!" Glinda was enjoying this immensely—rattling off her list of grand heroic accomplishments and growing taller and taller in the bargain!

"Thing nine," she said, and the boom of her voice was so loud she made her own ears ring. *"I VANQUISHED THE WICKED WITCH OF THE SOUTH AND FREED THE FINAL THOUGHT OF THE KING!"*

Her head bumped against the ceiling, though now she was gigantic enough that it didn't hurt in the slightest. She was so large she could have pulverized Mythra by grinding her under the heel of her gigantic boot.

"And finally," she bellowed, "thing ten! I rescued my mother from the dungeon of the Haunting Harvester." Here, to her surprise, she heard a catch of emotion in her giant voice. An enormous tear slipped from her enormous eye as she added, "And then I watched her go off with a tin boy into a dark wilderness, leaving me behind to carry the weight of all of Oz's hopes and dreams on my shoulders."

Glinda suddenly felt herself growing small again, so quickly and so violently that she thought she might be sick; she found herself cut back down to her normal size before the echo of her last word had even faded into silence. And still the shrinking did not stop. Littler and littler she became, tinier, punier, until she was less substantial than a grain of sand.

The ground beneath her minuscule boots had gone from

solid and rough to soft and smooth, and there were five tall columns rising up around her, five fleshy pillars.

No, not pillars. *Fingers!*

She had gone from towering over the Mystic to standing in the palm of her hand!

And judging from the way those tremendous fingers were curling slowly toward her, she had no doubt that she was about to be crushed in the Mystic's gigantic fist!

As the fingers loomed closer, Glinda's mind began to flash back to other moments.

She saw herself cowering before Madam Mentir, trembling and apologizing, all for want of a couple of braids. How subservient she'd been; how unaware! She'd been a fool to let Mentir treat her so viciously.

And she remembered watching Abrahavel Squillicoat get hauled away from his apothecary shop by two of Aphidina's soldiers, watching but not acting—*not even thinking to act*—even when she knew deep in her heart that he deserved no such punishment and that something was horribly wrong.

Above her, Mythra's curling fingers suddenly looked smaller, less threating. But still, Glinda could not stop the thoughts that assaulted her. She imagined her own fingers pinching loose that first bleached knot of the Wicked trapestry, and pulling . . . pulling the thread until she had unraveled her beloved Maud right out of existence! Oh, why hadn't she tried harder to save her mother's friend?

The memory of Maud dissolved, giving way to an image of the Queryor bowing, but along with it spun a new thought—how could she have been so cavalier as to just walk away, full of her own success but without even trying to help the poor Searchers trapped in his Conundrum? She could have made a plea for their release; she could have reasoned with the gentle beast to give them another chance. But she'd simply left the Queryor's lair, victorious, and hadn't bothered to look back.

But by far the worst realization of all was the one that came thundering into her head now, like a storm on a dark night—it was the memory of how she'd spent the better part of her quest bickering and arguing with Locasta at every turn! True, the girl was headstrong, impulsive, and sarcastic, but she was also loyal, brave, and willing to fight for what she believed in.

And yesterday Glinda had *pulled a sword on her*!

It was this gut-wrenching thought that brought Glinda to her knees—only to find that she was no longer caught in Mythra's grasp; rather, she was back on the solid ground of the cave, kneeling at Mythra's feet.

She had returned to her normal size. But she'd never felt smaller in her life. "Why did you do that to me?" she whispered, keeping her head bowed, her eyes low.

"You did it to yourself," was Mythra's sharp reply. "I asked you to tell me ten things about yourself that would help me train you in the use of your Good Magic. Yet somehow, you took that as an invitation to boast, to brag, to rattle off a list of your most stellar accomplishments."

"But they were all true!"

"Yet they were not the whole truth, were they? Though I am pleased to say you corrected your error on your own, as evidenced by the fact that you are restored to your appropriate proportions."

"I saved myself by thinking all those miserable, humiliating thoughts?"

"You *redeemed* yourself," Mythra countered. "The 'saving' of oneself, I feel obliged to tell you, is hardly a onetime occurrence. It is an ongoing quest that takes many forms throughout the whole of one's life. And for the record, humil*ity* is not the same as humiliation."

Even with her eyes on the ground, Glinda could feel the Mystic shaking her head.

"Drew a sword on your friend, did you?"

Glinda snapped her gaze up to meet Mythra's glittering eyes. "How could you possibly know—?" She stopped short. "Connection Magic?"

Mythra nodded. "Tell me . . . did it not occur to you, while you were ticking off your victories, that it might also be useful to inform me of at least one of your failures?"

Glinda hesitated, then shook her head.

"There you have it, then. The reason you grew so incredibly *tall* was because you refused to admit to any *short*comings at all."

"Miss Gage would call that a metaphor."

"Miss Gage, whoever she is, would be right." Mythra surprised Glinda by offering her a hand up. "Your strengths will not need nearly as much coaxing as your weaknesses will need mending. But Magic, the caliber of which you are hoping to master, will not tolerate arrogance, ever. Confidence, yes, but *over*confidence? Never!"

"I understand."

"Good. Now then, Zephyr, let the training begin." The Mystic motioned to one of the chairs. "Sit."

Glinda sat.

"There is more to learning than just acquiring and improving one's skills. It requires a shifting from one state of being to the next, a step forward from the you of just a moment ago, toward the you of *this* moment. Being is becoming, Glinda. It is time for you to shed."

Glinda's mouth dropped open. *"Shed?"*

"Don't look so squeamish!" Mythra admonished, lowering herself gracefully into the chair across from Glinda. "I won't be requiring you to peel away large patches of skin, or cast off limbs or anything quite so grotesque as that. A symbolic shedding is all that's required."

"Does clothing count?" asked Glinda, her fingers toying with the tail of her red sash. "In the Makewright's lodge, I shed my old school uniform and replaced it with these new clothes that Locasta made for me, which is why there aren't any ruffles on them."

Mythra curled her lip as she eyed Glinda's outfit. "I suppose a wardrobe change will suffice."

But the Mystic's earlier allusion to shedding limbs had Glinda thinking about poor Nick Chopper, with his tin arm and legs. She felt for the Munchkin boy and was glad he was currently off on the yellow brick road of Discovery in the safe company of her mother.

Without warning, Mythra gasped and pressed her hand to her heart. "You were just thinking of someone."

"Yes. I was thinking of Nick Chopper, the Munchkin woodcutter."

"No! Someone else."

"Oh." Glinda swallowed hard. "My mother."

Mythra sprang up so quickly she nearly knocked over her chair. "*Who* is your mother?"

"I—" Glinda was confused. "I thought I told you. She is a very powerful Sorceress from Quadling."

Mythra seemed to be trying very hard to remain in control of herself. Her next question came out in a voice that was both anxious and hushed. "But what is her *name*?"

"Tilda! Her name is Tilda."

For several seconds, Mythra stared at Glinda, her hazel eyes wide, her handsome face slack-jawed in profound surprise. "You are Tilda's daughter?" she whispered at last. "Truly?"

When Glinda nodded, Mythra's expression softened by an almost imperceptible degree. "How very, very . . . *unexpected*."

"But I told you the Sorceress who sent me to you was a former associate of yours. Tilda *was* your associate, wasn't she?"

"That is one way to put it," Mythra mused with a far-away look in her eyes. "What is your father's name?"

"Sir Stanton of Another Place."

At this, Mythra's face lit with a broad smile. "Of course! And how is he? Is he well?"

"He's . . ." Glinda's voice broke. "Gone." To Mythra's credit, she looked as sad to hear it as Glinda was to say it. "May I ask why you're so surprised to learn that Tilda is my mother?"

"Because . . . ," said Mythra, leaning down to slip her thumb beneath Glinda's chin and lift her face so their gazes met, "*I* am Tilda's mother. Which means that *you*, young Sorceress in training . . . are my granddaughter."

19

IN THE DUNGEON

The hawk was delicious.

As tender and succulent as any the Krumbic one had ever tasted. *It helps to eat them alive,* she thought. *And stuffed . . . not with nuts or cornbread dressing, but with news of the enemy.* As this bird had been.

Earlier, the hawk had presented himself to Mombi. He told her of the battle in the South, which he had watched from the top of a red spire. And being that he had no particular affiliation to any of the three Wickeds, his account of their failure was both unbiased and reliable. Especially with regard to the scamp who had stolen her Golden Cap.

The hawk had told her that while Glinda Gavaria had

not been captured—in fact, she had disappeared without a trace—there was another who took part in the fray who just might be of interest.

According to the bird, Glinda was in the company of a plummy-haired girl called Locasta, a Gillikin with a feisty nature. Marada confirmed that the brat with purple curls was the sister of the scamp, Thruff.

Mombi had not needed to listen to the hawk anymore after that. She'd used her teeth to sever the bird's talons first (succulent), and had then bitten off his head (juicy).

All in all a delightful meal, though the feathers had tickled going down.

And now it was time to visit Marada's dungeon to confer with the little bumpkin. It would not do to greet him in her own form, for her appearance tended to distract, and she was extremely mindful of her mystery. So she slipped herself into the bulky body of the Brash Warrior Witch (whose innards were as cold as Mombi had expected) to impose herself upon the scamp as his sovereign.

He was being held in the Warrior's moldering dungeon, where he'd been tossed after his shameful performance at the academy battle. He was not alone. There was another captive seated beside him on the cold stone of the floor. When the clanking of Marada's armor filled the gloomy passage that led to their cell, the second prisoner gave Thruff a gentle nudge.

He awoke from his stupor, displeased but not surprised to find himself chained to a wall.

"Do not be afraid," the second prisoner whispered close to his ear. "She will sense it and it will only cause her to be more dreadful."

"I'm not afraid," the boy whispered back, eyeing the heavy chains around his cellmate's wrists. "And who are you?"

The prisoner smiled, and every memory Thruff had of his mother came slamming back into his heart.

"I am Tilda," she said, and the name sounded like springtime. "I am Glinda's mother."

At this, Thruff looked mildly amused. "You're supposed to be powerful. How is it you're caught?"

"My capture was the result of a difficult choice," the Sorceress said on a sigh. "The lesser of two evils, you could say."

"I didn't know evil could be anything less than what it was," Thruff observed.

"You are a bright lad," said Tilda, "so listen to me carefully: the one who is approaching will only *look* like the Witch of the North. But her form will be inhabited by one who is far more despicable and cruel."

To Tilda's amazement, the boy grinned. "She who became the quake? Don't worry. I know how to handle her. I've already—"

It was then that the body of Marada came clomping

into the cell, and he was silenced by a kick of her spurred sandal. The order came swiftly and eerily:

"*Bring me your sister,*" said Mombi with Marada's mouth.

Thruff appraised her with eyes like jewels. Her movements were puppetlike; her tongue had turned to a clot of dirt, and when the Warrior's mouth opened to speak another's commands, instead of spittle, pebbles spewed out. Her irises were the dull, lifeless gray of stones.

"Why is it you cannot get her for yourself?" he asked.

Mombi did not like to be questioned, and worse, she detested admitting to her shortcomings (few that they were). Marada's reflexes itched to attack, and Mombi's own instincts agreed. But if she tore the boy to pieces, how would he do her bidding? And so she answered:

"*I could not scry for her, even with a dark mirror, for unlike Glinda's natural gifts, which I traced effortlessly, your sister's Magic is too raw to track. But I believe you can get close to her.*"

"What do you want with her?" Thruff demanded. "She'll never turn to your side. Believe me, I've asked her."

"*I do not wish to recruit her, you audacious little imbecile. She will be bait and nothing more.*"

"Bait," Thruff repeated. "For Glinda."

Mombi nodded with Marada's head; the gesture was so weird and unnatural that Thruff felt his stomach turn a little. "Why do you need Locasta to lure her?" he asked, as though he didn't really care. "Won't her mother be bait enough?" Then he turned an apologetic expression to Tilda and whispered, "No offense."

Marada's body jerked forward so that her lifeless eyes were level with his. *"Because her mother's presence here is a secret."*

Thruff did not like the sound of that. It would annoy him greatly if the Krumbic fifth Witch did away with this Tilda. There was something warm about her eyes. Hazel, he thought the color might be called. His mother's had been lavender blue. At least, that's what Locasta had told him.

"And Glinda?" he pressed. "What of her?"

"Perhaps I shall roast you on a spit and serve you to her as her last meal."

"So she is to perish?"

This time, the Witch inside the Witch did not seem to feel the need to answer him. Beside Thruff, Tilda had gone cold, not with fear, but with fury.

"There is something I believe the Witch Marada has that I would very much like," Thruff announced. "If you think with her brain for a moment, I believe you will know what it is."

Mombi let Marada's thoughts ooze to the surface. Then she nodded.

"If I bring you my sister, will you give it to me?"

Mombi's irritation at this request turned Marada's eyes

darker than midnight in a mineshaft. *"Are you under the impression that this is a* negotiation, *you insolent little dragon dropping?"*

"Isn't it?" the dragon dropping challenged. "You wouldn't be here if you did not require my assistance, and since there is nothing you can do to me that could be worse than my life so far, well, *yes*, I do think I am in a position to bargain." He shrugged. "The rawness of Locasta's Magic is not an obstacle for *me*."

Mombi felt Marada's hands clench; the Warrior's foot ached to kick the boy between his eyes. But it was not Marada's impulses that counted. Marada was not in charge. Mombi was.

"Very well," she said. *"The item you desire shall be traded to you upon delivery of your sister."*

"Locasta is strong and cunning, and treacherous with her fists, not to mention fairly good with what little Magic she has. What if she will not come with me?"

"If she wants to fight you, you must say these words: Zizzle. Umph-scutch. Wurdlin. Dink. They will enchant you into something quite menacing. Your sister will have no hope of beating you then."

You don't know Locasta, thought Thruff, but he repeated the words back to the Witch. *"Zizzle. Umph-scutch. Wurdlin. Dink."* It sounded the opposite of menacing to him. It sounded ridiculous. But then again, the incantation to ignite the Golden Cap had been laughable too, and that spell had certainly done its job.

Mombi again leaned down with her borrowed body to where Thruff crouched upon the rushes rotting on the dungeon floor. After a few graceless jerks and twists of Marada's burly arms and stubby fingers, Thruff's chains were unlocked. Mombi would have preferred to blow the cuffs to bits with her Magic, but given her agitated state, she could not trust herself to resist aiming for the boy's skull instead. Marada certainly would have enjoyed that. But Mombi understood consequences. She could not destroy Thruff of Gillikin.

At least not until after he had delivered Locasta, who would in turn lure Glinda.

And when that time came, the Krumbic one would take immense satisfaction in crushing this insolent pup, his mutinous sister, the daughter of the Sorceress, and whoever else happened to get in her Krumbic way.

When he stood up, his chains jangled to the floor. "Show it to me," he said. "The thing I've requested. So I know that it will be waiting for me upon my return."

The Witch made a jerky dance twirl (which caused the joints of her armor to grind) and then extended an open hand to the boy. In Marada's calloused palm lay a round golden case with a clasp. Thruff felt his chest tighten at the sight of it, and it took all the willpower he could muster to keep from shooting out his grubby hand to nab it right before her eyes.

"*If you succeed in this task,*" said the Witch, closing the fingers of Marada's gauntlets loosely around his prize, "*you will have played a part in something more Wicked than anyone of your piteous ilk could even dream.*"

Thruff looked bored. "You don't know what I dream," he said. Then, in a thoroughly uncharacteristic gesture, he threw his arms around the Witch and hugged her. "Thank you," he said, his voice husky with gratitude, "for trusting me with such an important chore."

Marada's body recoiled from the embrace as though such a show of affection might prove to be poisonous. Mombi, burrowed there among her guts, actually found this quite funny. "*Begone now; go look for your sister.*"

They didn't see him slip the stolen item into his pocket. Sauntering across the cell, Thruff tossed a hank of purple hair out of his eyes and called over his shoulder, "You have greater need of me than you know, Witches."

Mombi let out a Marada-esque grunt. "*Meaning?*"

"Meaning that *I* do not have to *look* for Locasta. I just have to listen . . . for the humming."

20

Time Shall Unfurl

Dawn had not yet broken when Locasta crept out the back door of Madam Mentir's with Tilda's Magical map in her grasp.

"Road?" she whispered, wiggling her toes, then digging in her heels.

But as Miss Gage had predicted, the red cobblestones did not appear.

In truth, she didn't blame them. This was a risky journey she was embarking on. Her only consolation was that her passage through Quadling would be safe. It was what might happen when she got to the Centerlands that worried her, and the Gillikin border, where surely Marada's soldiers would be grazing watchfully, ready for a fight.

She might be able to dance them into a temporary trance, or bribe them with her father's amethysts. The thought of losing those precious stones was loathsome, but growing up in Gillikin, she'd learned that sometimes, an ugly bargain must be made.

As she ran across the back lawn of the academy, she averted her eyes from the toolshed. She couldn't look at it, not yet. It was the place where her best friend had vanished, so for Locasta, the shed had become nothing but a bad memory.

Make that *another* bad memory. And she had plenty.

As her boots hit the dirt road, the worst one of them all came somersaulting into her mind like a cruel acrobat. She was very small, standing on the stoop of her shack, watching her mother and sisters being chained together—wrist, to wrist, to wrist—by Marada's soldiers, then marched off toward the castle.

Thruff, wrapped in a flimsy purple blanket, had toddled after them for as long as his little legs would hold him. Then he fell down on his rump in the mud, poked his thumb in his mouth, and murmured, "Mama? Swisters? Mama?" over and over. It was perhaps his first stab at Magic—a singsong spell designed to bring his mother back to him, so she could sweep him into her arms and hum him off to sleep.

It hadn't worked.

And since Papa had already gone to the mines and would not return until dark, it had been skinny little Locasta who'd squished her way down the stinking, muddy lane to lift her brother and carry him back to the shack, where she fed him a meager porridge and told him in her best brave voice that Mama and the big girls—the *swisters* as he so sweetly called them then—were all with the Witch now, where they would likely remain forever. And if he were smart (which he was, even then—dauntless and daring but *smart*), he would just forget about them.

Because Locasta had known, even at that tender age, what the Witch could do to them. But she didn't tell Thruff. All she'd said was, "Mama is with the Witch."

It occurred to her now that it might be her own fault that he'd decided to skew Wicked. Maybe by telling him that Mama and the swisters were "with the witch," she'd unwittingly implied that they had *aligned with* Marada of their own accord; that they had volunteered themselves in the name of Wickedness. Maybe all this time he'd just been waiting to grow big enough to run off and become Wicked too.

As Locasta tramped through the Woebegone Wilderness— correction: Good Fortune's Forest, according to the linen map in her hand—her dark recollection of Mama's departure melted into another memory of another dawn, just as wretched but much more recent.

The day of her last Levying. The day before she'd fled

Gillikin in search of the teacher-Sorceress and the Grand Adept, Tilda Gavaria.

How could a thing that is demanded be offered? Anything we have to give you is already yours.

Locasta could still hear Thruff sassing the Witch, and she could still see the flash of silver as Marada's mighty gauntlet came down on the back of his head. But despite the pain it must have caused him, his sister knew it was exactly what he'd been hoping for. That had been his way *in*; an invitation (for an invitation from Marada could never be anything but violent) to the castle, where he would use his angry charm to win a place in the court of the Warrior.

She could still hear the shrieks and cries of her neighbors echoing through the little shantytown as the soldier whose dagger Thruff had stolen threw the unconscious boy over his shoulder and began marching back toward the castle.

"Wait! Stop! *Wait!*" The words felt as if they were being torn from her throat.

The Witch had stopped dead in her tracks. "You dare to give me an order?"

"Not an order, Your Maliciousness," Locasta had said, hastily adjusting her tone. "A most reverent request." Then she'd dropped to her knees, ignoring the malodorous muck seeping through the lilac cotton of her nightshirt. "If I offer you something, will you give him back?" Withdrawing a treasure from her pocket, she held it up for the Witch to admire, and forced down the lump rising in her throat. "He's my brother. He's all I have."

"He is not *all* you have, clearly, if you are in possession of this fine bauble," the Witch had countered. "It's gold. *Solid gold.*" She examined the thing as though she were trying to decide if the brightness of the gold would clash with—or worse, outshine—the silver of her gauntlets. "Where did you get it? Did you steal it?"

Locasta shook her head.

"Too bad. I'd be impressed if you had."

Locasta had extended the treasure a little farther toward the Witch. "Take it," she persisted, looking at Thruff dangling from the guard's shoulder; his eyelids fluttered open to meet hers briefly before closing again. "Take it in exchange for my brother, and I vow he will never bother you again."

"Very well," said the Witch, plucking the object from Locasta's palm with her thick forefinger and stubby thumb. "I shall accept your levy offering."

"And give me back my brother," Locasta clarified. "Right?"

"Wrong, dung beetle. Very, very wrong."

"But—"

Marada had laughed then, and it was a sound like rust and rot. "Did you think I would deign to barter with a mine-rat like you?" she'd roared. "I am the Wicked Warrior Witch of the North and your brother is a spoil of war!"

With that, she had turned her back on Locasta and

tromped off down the path, the spurs of her sandals spewing muck.

Locasta had remained on her knees in the mud long after the Witch and her soldiers had disappeared from view; long after her neighbors had retreated into their tents and shacks and lean-tos, slightly more broken than they had been the day before, slightly less of who they might have become if the Witch had never come to rule Gillikin in the wake of Good King Oz's passing.

She'd kept her eyes on the castle in the distance until she heard the faint clatter and clunk of the portcullis closing. It was then she knew that Thruff had accomplished exactly what he'd set out to do. He was with the Witch.

He had gotten his wish.

And the Witch had gotten their father's compass.

Locasta had surrendered it for nothing, without knowing how truly, incomparably valuable it was.

It had taken all she had not to curl up in a tight little ball right there on the path and weep. But Locasta—who was the daughter of Norr, who was the Entrusted of Terra (though at the time she hadn't known that, either)—did not curl nor cry.

She got to her feet. And with steady strides on sturdy legs, she stomped back to her miserable little house. There she'd tugged off her soiled nightdress, put on her mining clothes—patched purple overalls and a threadbare shirt—and set out for Quadling Country.

Her father had once told her—almost in passing, almost as if it didn't matter much at all—that if she ever found herself in trouble, she should make her way as cautiously as possible to the South, where she should seek a pretty young teacher-Sorceress who would bring her to the Grand Adept. Locasta hadn't really understood at the time; she'd been too preoccupied with admiring the amethyst stones he'd been holding in his hands. The same stones she carried in her pocket now.

For luck.

On that trek from Gillikin to Quadling she'd traveled under cover of darkness, napping during the daylight hours in the thick shadows of tamorna trees, and waking at dusk to feast on the delicious tamorna fruit that dropped from their branches like gifts from the Land of Oz itself.

It was from one of these naps that she awoke to find she'd somehow shed her shabby mining clothes and that they had been inexplicably replaced by a most terrific sort of warrior's garb—a hooded tunic of pale violet with leather knee breeches tucked into tall, strapped boots. Discouragingly, her manacles had not vanished with her overalls (that had not happened until Tilda Gavaria had turned them to gold), but there was no denying that the tunic and trousers were a great improvement. And despite the fact that she could not explain it, all in all it had been a most restful and productive sleep.

Sleep. The mere thought of it brought forth a huge yawn. And no wonder; she'd barely dozed at all last night, planning her stealthy exit. Consulting Tilda's embroidered landscape, she determined that she had already traversed several miles of Quadling terrain.

Ahead she spied a small patch of poppies, which the map identified as the Dreaming Field. *Sounds like an exceptional place to rest,* she thought, and was instantly overcome with the urge to close her eyes. But it was not all the fault of the poppies. It was also the work of someone else. Someone who was leaning down to tickle her cheek with one of the bright red flowers, which he'd yanked up by the roots.

With a start, Locasta opened her eyes. Then she jumped to her feet and pulled Glinda's sword from her sash. "Who are you?" she demanded.

"Look closely," the stranger said. "Don't I look familiar to you?"

Locasta studied him through narrowed eyes.

"Picture me less animated," he advised, flashing what he had once described to the owner of the sword she was wielding as his *disarmingly crooked smile.* "Imagine me carved in stone. And make it obsidian; I always did look fabulous in black."

Warily, Locasta continued her examination of the stranger in his strange garb—he wore fitted gray trousers and a tight shirt that seemed to glow from within, as if he'd ventured too close to the stars and some of their light had rubbed off on him.

And he was carrying a scepter.

"You look a bit like the Timeless Magician from the Arc of Heroes," said Locasta.

Eturnus beamed. "And with good reason. I'm him." He gestured to the blade she was aiming at him. "I helped your friend forge this little beauty, you know. She doesn't remember meeting me, of course. And neither do you. If you did, you'd be thanking me for that fashionable-yet-battle-ready ensemble you're sporting."

Locasta looked down at her clothing, then back up at the Timeless one. "You did this?"

"I did, the last time you decided to go traipsing about through unwelcoming countrysides unescorted. And since *you're* up to your old tricks, *I* might as well be up to mine."

Locasta narrowed her eyes. "What's that supposed to mean?"

"It means I've come to escort you."

"To where?"

"To a place where only I can take you," Eturnus replied with a wink. "To a place that is farther than you can imagine and closer than you think." With that, he took Locasta's hand.

"Lurl Ly Lee, Listen and Be
Lurl Ly Lo, Question and Know

Lee Lily Lurl, Time Shall Unfurl
Lee Lolly Lawl, Truth Above All!"

Then he waved his scepter in the air. "To the past!"

"So much for my nap," Locasta muttered, and Eturnus let out a jovial crack of laughter.

It was the last thing she heard before everything went light.

21

THE PARAGON CHEST

For a long time, Glinda sat on the hard chair in Mythra's cave, unable to form words.

The Mystic—her *grandmother*—made excellent use of the silence, clearing the untidy table of its crusty bowls and sticky cups by simply employing a grand flourish of her arm. Where the clutter disappeared to was anyone's guess. Then she removed the shawl from her shoulders, twirled it once over her head, and brought it down in a billow—not of itchy wool but of sheer, sparkling gossamer. This she draped over the scarred wood of the tabletop.

That done, she closed her eyes and recited a simple incantation:

*"Magic work at my request
Bring to me the Paragon Chest."*

The musty air seemed to gather itself together as though the cave were drawing a deep, dank breath. A moment later the cave exhaled, and this became a solid object. An exquisite wooden chest, sitting upon the gossamer cloth in the center of the table. Both were almost exact replicas of the ones Tilda had used when she'd presented Glinda's Magic to her on Declaration Day.

Well, thought Glinda, *I see my mother comes by her traditions honestly.*

"Yes, she does," said Mythra, addressing the unspoken observation. "The tamorna doesn't fall far from the tree."

"So you're really and truly my grandmother?" Glinda's voice was a mix of astonishment and glee.

"I am."

Unable to contain herself, Glinda jumped up from her chair and threw her arms around the Priestess. "This is so wonderful! Wonderful in large amounts. I have always wished for a grandmother!" Looking up at Mythra's face, she wondered how she hadn't seen it immediately; of course this revered Mystic was her mother's mother. They had the same eyes—that lovely shade of greenish gold, crackling with intelligence. "What shall I call you?" Glinda blurted.

"Call me?"

"Well, 'Grandmother' seems terribly formal. 'Nana,' perhaps? Or maybe that's too precious."

Mythra was looking at her with an expression of startled disdain.

"Oh! I have just the name!" Glinda cried, throwing herself back into the hug. "It's perfect! Dignified yet affectionate. Sophisticated but sweet. Yes! I shall call you . . . 'Grand-mamá'! What do you think of 'Grand-mamá,' Grand-mamá?"

Extracting herself from the embrace, Mythra fixed Glinda with a stern glare. "Do I *look* like someone's *Grand-mamá*?" she demanded in an icy voice. "No. I most certainly do not. You may call me Mythra, or Priestess. One or the other, both if you wish, but never, *ever* Grand-mamá. Is that understood?"

Glinda managed a nod and the subject of endearments was closed.

Now Mythra swept her hand over the chest. "Do you know what a paragon is?"

"Someone or something that is regarded as a perfect or quintessential example of some worthy quality," was Glinda's prompt reply. "At least, that's the definition I was taught in a class called Approved Vocabulary for Girls."

"That is a ridiculous name for a course of academic study," Mythra opined tartly. "But you are correct." She tapped the lid of the trunk. "Inside this chest you will find four Magical Paragons. Items that will become exemplary representations of the craft of Good Sorcery."

Glinda nodded to indicate she understood the importance.

"As a Sorceress-in-training, you have more to learn than you can even begin to imagine. And the timing could not be worse, what with *everything* else with which you have to concern yourself. Think of *all* the things weighing on you at this moment."

Glinda hardly needed to be reminded of her distress: Oz's future, her mother's safety, her friends in the aftermath of the monkey battle, which she was certain they had lost. Each of these on its own was upsetting; combined, they were almost too much to bear, and suddenly she could think of nothing else but her worries. Panic swooped down on her; misery rose from the pit of her stomach.

"Now," barked Mythra, "open the chest!"

The Sorceress-in-training did as she was told, and the next order came in a shout so harsh that Glinda nearly jumped out of her seat.

"EMPTY IT!"

With a yelp, Glinda reached into the trunk. Her hand immediately clunked against something large. Shaking the sting from her knuckles, she gave the thing a yank, then winced when a bolt of pain shot through her shoulder. She gave another tug but the object, whatever it was, did not budge.

"Problem, Zephyr?"

"It's much too heavy."

Mythra's nostrils flared with disgust.

Biting back her embarrassment, Glinda made a third attempt; this time she climbed onto the chair, reached down into the chest with both hands, and gave a mighty heave. But again, the weighty object remained where it was.

"I suppose it never occurred to you to use a spell?"

"I didn't realize that was allowed."

"You are undertaking your *Magical* training, yet you did not imagine that *Magic* would be permitted?"

Glinda's cheeks flushed. "I suppose not. But you said yourself I've got a lot on my mind. I'm worried about my friends. I'm scared for Oz."

The Priestess let out an impatient sigh and dipped her hand into the chest. When she withdrew it again, there was an enormous rectangular shield balancing on the tip of her pinky finger. She let it drop to the ground, where it made a hollow clunk that practically rattled Glinda's teeth.

The shield appeared to be made of lead, which to Glinda's way of thinking seemed thoroughly illogical. The face of it was dull gray and unadorned, except for a small round indentation in the exact center, about the size of the glass cap on Roquat's collide-o-scope.

Ben. Trapped and spinning, with no hope of rescue.

"Lift it," Mythra commanded.

But the memory of Ben set Glinda's mind roiling with

other images: *Locasta left behind to fend off those horrid monkeys; Shade, unseen and unheard from; Tilda, a fugitive from the Wicked fifth Witch.* Glinda hunched down in front of the shield and wrapped her arms around it. Now that she knew she could use Magic, she quickly composed a spell:

"Grant me a gift, the gift of a lift!" Then she heaved.

And *heaved*.

To no avail.

Ignoring Mythra's scowl, Glinda stepped back to examine the shield from the other side and saw that there was a handle—a rod bolted across the upper half. She slid her fingers under it, grasped tightly, and tried to lift again, shouting out the command, *"Shield, YIELD!"*

But the ridiculous hunk of lead remained on the ground.

"Imagine that you are engaged in battle," Mythra prompted. "Tell me, who is your opponent? Right here and now, who is your foe?"

"The fifth Witch," Glinda replied automatically, grunting the words as she tried yet again to pick up the leaden shield.

"But the fifth Witch isn't here," Mythra retorted. "So who exactly are you fighting? And if you wish for this training to continue, I strongly advise you not to identify *me* as your enemy."

Glinda was glad for the warning, as that was to be her next answer.

"*Time* is my enemy," she guessed, squeezing the handle

tighter and giving it another good hoist. "I am racing against time to defeat the Witches."

"Nice try, but Time is *everyone's* enemy," Mythra sneered. "It is also our dearest friend. Now, lift again, and whatever you do, do *not* imagine the guilt you will be forced to endure should you fail in your quest to bring down the Wicked reign."

Well, thanks for bringing that *up!* thought Glinda, for she could suddenly imagine nothing else. She jerked on the shield as hard as she could, but still it would not move.

"Think, Glinda!" Mythra was circling her now, like a vulture. "You're engaged in a battle and you don't even know who you're fighting! Think! Who do you need to shield yourself *from*?"

Glinda huffed. "I need to shield myself from . . ." She wheezed. "From . . ."

She didn't know! The name of her enemy evaded her! Probably because she could no longer think of anything beyond the crushing thoughts of danger and loss that pummeled her. Her breath came in shallow gasps, and her eyes were welling with tears, even as she planted her feet on either side of the infernal shield and pulled, desperate to raise it even a fraction of an inch off the ground. But the weight of her emotion bearing down on her made the shield even heavier.

And in that moment, she understood; the answer exploded from her like thunder.

"I must shield myself from my own *fear*! I am my own enemy because I am afraid! Afraid, and sad, and guilty and anxious."

To her supreme shock and unbridled relief, the shield rose slightly in her grasp.

"Yes!" said Mythra. "It's true that you are in the midst of great internal turmoil, but when has a hero ever been free from such distress? You fight *because* you are afraid, because there is so much to be lost. A hero fights when the stakes are at their highest, so naturally she comes to the battle with a tortured mind and tormented heart. But you must find a way to carry the fear with you into the fray, without allowing it to distract you from your goal."

Glinda groaned, still straining under the weight of the lead. "How can I do that when all I can think of is what might be taken from me if I lose?"

"Give your fears to the shield, and it will protect you from them. Give voice to that which threatens to hold you down as if *you* were made of lead and let the shield bear it into battle for you. Shield yourself from yourself, Zephyr. Now . . . start talking!"

Glinda gritted her teeth; her muscles were trembling, but she did not let go. "I'm afraid my friends were lost in the monkey battle. I'm afraid the Foursworn Stronghold of Truth has been burned to the ground or, worse, has fallen into the hands of the fifth Witch."

As she spoke, the shield grew lighter. She lifted it as high as her knees. "What if I can't rescue Ben from the Nome King's collide-o-scope? What if even after I have been taught all the Magic I can learn, I still cannot defeat the Witches?"

With every fear she named, she lifted the rectangle of lead a little higher—it was taking on the weight of her worry, but growing lighter at the same time; lighter and lighter until it was almost weightless and she was finally holding it at proper shoulder height.

She smiled, awaiting Mythra's praise.

But the praise did not come.

Just a quick, curt nod as Glinda laid the shield on the table beside the Paragon Chest.

"Now then," said the Mystic, lighting more candles. "Shall we see what else this trunk contains?"

22

GOOD NIGHT, GOOD KNIGHTS

The Timeless Magician's laughter was still ringing in Locasta's ears when the air fell in on her, crashing forth from all sides—from above like a waterfall, from below like a geyser, from left and right like rain in the wind. The sky spun overhead, while a yawning cavity of light opened up beneath her feet. But she did not fall into the past; history rose up from its depths to surround her, claiming her into its passage. She felt the tickle of days, the caress of months, the sturdiness of years as these fragments of eternity melded together to whisk her backward through Time. She was engulfed in a silence so profound it became a noise all its own. Ages and eons sidestepped themselves, allowing her to pass through the enormously minuscule space that divided then from now. There was no dimension, but all dimension; Locasta thickened into it and dissolved out of it as she traveled to what was.

At last she felt solid ground beneath her boots. Around her the atmosphere faltered, as though it were still piecing itself together.

"Give it a moment to catch up," the Timeless one advised, materializing at her side. "I trust you recognize the place. You were here just the other day."

Indeed, she had been. "It's King Oz's Reliquary!" she said. "The ruins are unmistakable. Although they look far more . . . fresh . . . than they did when I first saw them."

"That is because we have arrived on the very night of the unveiling party," Eturnus clarified, "not long after the king's tragedy. His home has only just destroyed itself in an act of grief and solidarity."

Locasta felt a pang of loss as the dust of the demolished castle continued to settle around her. "Why am I here?" she asked.

"To see," Eturnus answered. "To know. Not all, but enough. I tried to accomplish this earlier, via the zoetrope and the teakettle, but I hadn't counted on being interrupted."

"The zoetrope?" Locasta was shocked. "That was *you*?"

Eturnus grinned. "I hope you're okay with coming into this tale *in medias res*. Which is to say, with the action already in progress."

"It's history," Locasta pointed out. "How else would I come into it?"

"Good point. And I'll be forced to skip around a bit. So how about you just think of this as your own personal highlight reel, hmm?"

"Whatever that is," Locasta muttered.

"Now watch." Eturnus twirled his scepter toward the Reliquary terrace.

As Locasta stared, the past caught up to itself. Time brought forth a glimmering, which became a young groundskeeper making his way onto the Reliquary terrace. Pulling his cap low over his eyes, he examined the broken pieces of the castle—bits of shattered glass, chunks of stone, even a large rectangle of lead that had broken away from the roof. He struggled to lift the heavy remnant.

"Did you catch that?" Eturnus asked.

"Catch what? All I saw was a gardener picking up a piece of lead."

"Exactly!" The Magician abruptly moved the scepter to his other hand and began to turn himself in a slow circle, then another, and another. To Locasta's shock, the atmosphere spun with him and as it did, the groundskeeper, the roof tile, and the terrace all began to blur, to *smear*, like a painting left out in the rain. But rather than dripping downward in a wash, everything was blurring sideways— or perhaps forward—toward whatever event would—or was it *had*?—come next.

Completing his rotation, Eturnus rested the scepter on his shoulder and gave Locasta a lopsided smile. "And that is why I am called E-*turn*-us," he boasted. "Because that is the trick I am able to perpetrate on Time. I turn eternity to my will."

Now a second scene wavered out of the blur. Locasta watched as a tall, handsome figure stepped out of and into a moment he had never left—the precise moment where she and Eturnus now waited.

A knight.

"Sir Stanton of Another Place!" Locasta cried, running toward him.

But he made no sign of acknowledgment, and when Locasta reached the knight, she ran right through him as if he were no more than a morning mist.

"We can't be seen or heard here," Eturnus explained as Locasta made her way back to him. "We are trespassing, you and I, on a portion of history to which we have no chronological right."

She scowled at him. "Is this dark Magic, then?"

"Time Magic occupies a bit of a gray area in the craft hierarchy," was his cagey reply. "Now, pay attention. You'll need to know this stuff."

The knight had just spied a piece of something silver lying on the ground, and he strode across the terrace to retrieve it. Locasta realized he was already holding three similar chunks of silver in his arms.

"What are those?" Locasta asked.

"King Oz was not the only brave soul to be destroyed this night," Eturnus reminded her. "His beloved Regents were defeated in their attempts to defend him, and those scraps are what's left of their armor, all that remains of the Archduke of Munch-Kindred, Lord Quadle, the Viscount Gilli, and Sir Wink. Now listen. I think you'll like how Glinda's father pays tribute to those Good knights."

Gathering the four pieces of armor close against his heart, Sir Stanton whispered over them in a voice like velvet:

> *"Let this immortal Night of knights*
> *Be hidden among celestial lights,*
> *As orbits spin, and worlds collide*
> *In darkness these four knights shall hide*
> *Till once again, they'll show their worth*
> *On the night of Princess Ozma's birth*
> *Let Magic do what Magic does*
> *Let Ozma be what Oz once was*
> *For all that's true, and all that's right*
> *Depends upon this hidden night."*

With that, he flung each broken piece of armor into the sky, where they tumbled upward toward the moon. Locasta flinched, certain they would fall back down to the terrace with a crash . . . until she saw several tiny Fairy arms reaching out from the blue-black blanket of the night

to catch them. She gasped with relief and delight.

"We have Mythra to thank for that," Eturnus said, smiling. "When she saw the Elementals go into hiding, she wisely dispatched several lesser Fairies to stand in for them in their absence—an absence she had hoped would be far more temporary than it's turned out to be. Even so, this is why the sky over Oz and all its lakes and rivers are still filled with the Magic of Fairy spirits. The ground teems with them; some have taken themselves into the fires, though the flames did not burn at full brightness until you and Glinda set Ember free. As long as Poole, Ria, and Terra continue to hide, the streams will not splash as freely, the breezes will not blow as sweetly, and the Ozian ground will not feel truly solid beneath our feet."

Locasta watched the brigade of Fairies lift the pieces of armor higher and higher, and soon the silver objects had been set in place around the moon. Four new celestial bodies, more substantial than planets and brighter than stars, now formed a sparkling constellation of courage, forever to be held aloft in the cradling arms of the air Fairies. Locasta watched as ever so slowly, they began to fade to do as Sir Stanton had decreed: *hide*.

"Time to fast-forward again," Eturnus announced.

"Fast *what*?"

The Timeless Magician switched the scepter to his other hand and repeated his turning Magic until they were once again looking at the groundskeeper. Locasta understood that a small swath of Time had passed since her first glimpse of him—and it was clear that whatever had occurred in the interim had not been good. He was facing away from her now, his shoulders hunched with sadness, his cap lost, and he was holding the lead roof tile, which had somehow become a shield. Locasta thought she noticed a small round dent in the center of it. So intrigued was she by this detail that it was a moment before she realized the groundskeeper was looking down at a figure dressed in white. She was sprawled on the ground . . . and pinned beneath the heavy emerald statue of King Oz!

"Who is that?" Locasta cried. "She's hurt. Dying, perhaps."

"Is she?" Eturnus waggled his eyebrows and grinned. "Or is she wise beyond wise, brave beyond brave, and—oh, let's just call it what it is—unbelievably *sneaky*?"

"But who are they?" Locasta demanded. "And what does any of this mean?"

If he gave her an answer, it was drowned out by the crashing in of the atmosphere, which was again breathing Locasta in, pulling her into Time and out of Time. The Magic enfolded her and the silence had its say. . . .

In the space of a lifetime divided by a heartbeat, Locasta felt herself falling out of a dream and back into a gentle sleep.

She would not be aware until she awoke that the

Timeless Magician had saved her the treacherous trip through the Centerlands by delivering her right to the Gillikin border, where she would sleep in the purplish grass, forgetting all that she had learned until the time came for her to know.

Eturnus could only hope that that time would come soon.

23

A How, a Why, and a When

Breathless from her experience with the shield, Glinda again reached into the Paragon Chest. She removed the remaining three items, which were a coil of rope, a beautiful ring of rosy gold, and finally a glimmering pearl of inordinate size.

The pearl the Sea Fairies had given her.

"This is mine!"

Mythra looked down her nose. "So it is."

"You took it from my pocket?"

"I did."

"But how? When? Why?"

"Your first question should not even require a response,

but I shall give you one anyway. The answer is Magic. In this case, a simple sleight of hand, when you weren't paying attention."

"So this is a lesson about paying attention?"

"Do you *need* a lesson in paying attention?"

Glinda frowned; if Locasta were there, she would have rolled her eyes.

"As to when," the Mystic went on, "well, what exactly did you think I was doing in that corner earlier? Fixing my hair?"

Glinda eyed Mythra's tousled silver mane and made a little face. "Obviously not."

Before she'd even gotten the words out, Mythra's eyes flared and Glinda found herself gently but firmly pinned against the far wall of the cave.

"I will be requiring an apology," said Mythra tautly. "In my world, Zephyr, you will treat the mentor as you would the Magic—with respect."

Glinda murmured, "I'm sorry," and the Magic released her. Chastised, she returned her attention to the rope, the ring, and the pearl.

On closer inspection, she saw that the ring's pinkish gold band was adorned with careful cutouts—a filigree design just like Miss Gage's silver scrying mirror. The setting held a large pink tourmaline blazing with facets, which caught the light from Mythra's candles.

"What does it do?"

"It goes on one's finger."

"No, I mean what sort of Magic does it do?"

"It's a ring, Glinda. It does not do Magic. However, a Sorceress may breathe Magic into it and use it for Magical purpose."

"Breathe Magic into it," Glinda echoed thoughtfully. She slid a glance at the Mystic and briefly considered blowing a puff of air at the ring. But she knew it could not be that easy.

"Sorcery is first and foremost an enchanting art form. And before you misconstrue, I do not mean 'enchanting' as in 'delightful.' It often *is* delightful, but that is not the point of this exercise. A Sorceress is a Magician who enchants, and enchantment relies heavily on wisdom and intellect."

"Yes, my mother told me that."

"The best Sorceress realizes that intelligence is her greatest tool, and prefers to express her intellect and her Magic through useful things. A Witch will dance or use gestures to bring forth Magic. A Wizard employs great Magical illusions. A Makewright will put Magic into a thing, then set it free to live on its own, often with no further participation from him. But a Sorceress assembles a fine and mighty collection of instruments to which she gives her Magic, and unlike the Maker, she keeps these Magicated items close at hand. Occasionally she finds cause to bestow one on a needful being in her sphere of concern, but typically they belong to she who forged them."

"'Magicated' sounds like 'educated,'" Glinda observed. "The Sorceress imparts her Magical wisdom to an item to make it capable of more than it was before. She Magicates it."

Mythra seemed to be resisting the urge to smile. "There are many ways to 'Magicate' an implement. One is to invoke power from another source and invite it to share itself with the object. Another is to recite an incantation. Sometimes it is a combination of both. For a Sorceress with great natural talent, it is possible to simply hold an object in her hands and command it to take on the Magic that is required."

She closed the lid of the chest, rested both elbows upon it, and wiggled her fingers. Then she rolled her hands over each other three times and slapped them flat against either side of the trunk. "And then . . . there are potions."

The next thing Glinda knew, the wooden chest had become a sturdy iron cauldron resting between Mythra's hands.

"To make this ring useful, you must coat it, or 'plate' it with Magic, as a goldsmith might plate a charger or a chalice. I will guide you in creating the potion, as it must be properly blended in order to work."

She handed the cauldron to Glinda and gestured to the murky puddle on the floor. "Fetch just enough water to cover the bottom."

Glinda did, wrinkling her nose against the odor as she

scooped the stagnant water into the cauldron. When she returned to the table, there were no less than one hundred different vials, jars, flagons, and bowls arranged upon it, each containing a different powder or a liquid in an array of colors such as Glinda had never seen before.

"What's the first ingredient?" she asked eagerly.

To which her mentor replied without hesitation, "Something only you can provide." With that, Mythra reached into the folds of her white gown and withdrew a gleaming dagger.

"What are you going to do with *that*?"

"What do you think I'm going to do with it?"

"I d-d-don't know," Glinda stammered. "You said the potion called for something only *I* could provide."

Mythra stepped closer. "And you immediately thought a section of a finger, perhaps the tip of your tongue?" The point of the blade was now hovering between Glinda's eyebrows; she had to cross her eyes upward just to see its lethal edge.

"No!" Glinda shrieked, covering her face. "Please!"

Mythra promptly lowered the dagger and as she did, a satisfied smirk appeared on her face.

"Why would you frighten me like that?" Glinda rasped, her heart still pounding thunderously.

"Because I want you to *remember* how it feels to face a foe whose only goal is to do you harm. Monumental harm. For while I may be frightening, I am *nothing* compared to those vile Witches, who would gladly remove the flesh from your fingers, the tongue from your mouth, and, depending on how much they fear you, THE HEAD FROM YOUR BODY!" Then, like lightning, Mythra's hand shot out and wrapped around a lock of Glinda's coppery hair. Glinda squealed as the blade sliced through it.

The moment the task was complete, the dagger vanished in a sizzle of silver dust and Glinda nearly crumpled with relief. "So the potion requires a lock of my hair?"

"No, I just thought your bangs could use a trim," Mythra replied drolly, handing the section of beautiful red hair to Glinda. "*Yes*, it requires your hair! Now add it to the cauldron."

Glinda dropped the wispy handful into the depths of the pot. The minute it hit the water, there was a loud *pop* and a stinking splat of brown slime erupted from the cauldron to spatter in her face.

Mythra folded her arms across her chest and made a tutting sound.

"Uhhhhhcccch!" Glinda moaned, wiping the goo from her eyes. "What did I do wrong? You said put it in. I put it in."

"But did I say how to put it in?"

Glinda frowned. "There's a 'how'?"

"There is always a how!" Mythra bellowed. "And a why and a when! This is a Magical plating potion you're preparing, not a root vegetable stew!"

"I'm sorry," said Glinda. "I didn't know."

"Of course you didn't know," Mythra said impatiently.

Then she tapped her left elbow and the dagger reappeared. In a flash, she'd cut off another clump of Glinda's hair.

If she keeps this up, I'm going to be bald, thought Glinda as she held the handful of hair over the cauldron. "*How* do I put it in?" she asked obediently.

Mythra gave a small nod of approval. "One strand at a time."

So Glinda painstakingly divided each copper filament from the lock and let it flutter into the cauldron one strand at a time. As she did so, Mythra strutted around the cave.

"Now, stir."

Glinda glanced around the table for a spoon and saw a long wooden one lying between a bowl of pink powder and a flagon of lilac liquid.

She reached for it and got burned, not badly, but just enough to hurt. "You could have warned me!" she said, bringing her scorched finger to her lips

Mythra kept strutting. "I would have, if you had asked for my help with the stirring."

"Who needs help stirring?" Glinda challenged.

"You, apparently. Now think: What did I just tell you?"

Glinda continued to suck on the burn, which was swiftly swelling into a blister. *There is always a how, a why, and a when.* "*Why* did the spoon burn me?"

"Because I enchanted it so that only I can command it. Would you like my assistance?"

"Yes," Glinda muttered.

"Then ask for it!"

Glinda clenched her fists. "Will you please help me with the stirring?"

Mythra nodded, then spun her finger in the air in a stirring motion. Glinda watched as the spoon rose from the table and dipped itself into the cauldron, where it waited, perfectly still.

Copying Mythra's motion, Glinda circled her finger and the spoon began to stir.

That done, she eyed the collection of fluids and powders spread out before her. "How shall I proceed?"

"The potion calls for the following: half a dram of Eniarrol extract, seven scruples of Trebla concentrate, a quarter pint of Nootski juice, a paste made from equal parts Serolod solution and Kire powder, and twenty-five Ūndpicky seeds. Have a care with those, for they are exceedingly rare and surprisingly powerful."

Glinda hurried to read the inscriptions on the containers, selecting the ones that Mythra had named. Popping the cork on the Eniarrol extract, she tipped it over the edge of the cauldron.

Just before the first drop splashed over the lip of the vial, Mythra stopped strutting. Glinda jerked her hand back. "*When* do I add them?" she asked.

"You pour the Nootski juice now."

Glinda put down the extract, picked up the juice, and poured it in.

"Wait for it to come to a bubbling sparkle," Mythra went on, "then add the rest, but always exactly three seconds apart and in this sequence. . . ."

As Mythra recited the order in which the ingredients were to be added, Glinda lined up their containers. When the cauldron began to bubble, she waited three seconds, then picked up the Trebla powder.

"How?" she asked in a reverent tone.

"With your left hand, by tossing it over your right shoulder."

Three seconds later she prepared to add the Serolod-and-Kire paste. "How?"

"With your eyes closed."

Glinda did as she was told.

The extract went in next and had to be dribbled into the mixture in a counterclockwise circle. Lastly the Ūndpicky seeds had to be sprinkled in with her right hand while she stood on her right foot, touching the tip of her nose with her left thumb.

The potion simmered in the cauldron (which Glinda found quite marvelous, since there was no fire beneath it). Finally Mythra said, "Pick up the ring. Use the pinky of your right hand. Very good. Now, immerse it. And when the plating is complete, the power it will contain will be the power of the lesson you have just learned. Do you know what that lesson is?"

Glinda thought for a moment, then gave her mentor

a confident grin. "To ask for help when I need it."

Mythra's hazel eyes twinkled. "This ring will carry the power to summon help whenever you most require it. It is as simple as giving the band one full turn to the right, then back around to the left." She nodded to the cauldron. "Remove it."

"Why?"

"Because it is ready."

"How?"

"With both hands, for it is precious."

"When?"

"As soon as I finish my incantation." The Priestess closed her eyes, extended her hands toward the cauldron, and to Glinda's great joy, sang a version of Maud's counting song:

> *"Count by one and count by two, with Sorcery I*
> * now imbue*
> *Count by three and count by four, a summoning*
> * ring forevermore*
> *A turn to the right in the dead of the night*
> *A turn to the left, when lost or bereft*
> *Whosoever can help you shall swiftly bring aid*
> *As I decree, so it is made."*

24

OH, BROTHER

Something smelled wonderful. Sweet and lush; a tempting aroma strong enough to tickle Locasta out of a deep and dreamy sleep.

Her eyes came open slowly, clouded with fleeting images—*an emerald statue, a heavy shield, four new stars around the moon.*

Sitting up, she shook away the dream and blinked into the shade of a tall, leafy tree. All around her lay at least a peck's worth of plump, deliciously scented tamornas.

Smiling, Locasta reached over Illumina lying beside her in the grass and snatched up one of the soft, shiny fruits. And as she did, she realized with a start that she was surrounded by the dry indigo grasses and purple-tinted ground of Gillikin Country.

"How did I get to Gillikin?" she asked aloud, biting into the squashy, ripe tamorna and wiping the juice from her chin on the sleeve of her tunic.

No, not her tunic. Her old purple mining shirt.

"*What?!*"

She jumped to her feet, frantically examining her altered clothing; her stomach nearly rejected the fruit when she realized her bold purple garments had once again become a pair of faded lilac overalls and a tattered top. Even her high strapped boots had been replaced by her old worn ones with their broken laces and patched soles.

Worst of all, the golden cuffs Tilda had conjured for her were gone and the tight rusted manacles had returned to her wrists. Locasta nearly wept for the loss, but her shock and disappointment soon gave way to understanding: it would not do to be strolling through Marada's country clad in leather breeches and lovely bangles—she would be spotted immediately and arrested. And that would be only the beginning, for Marada had a very particular way of dealing with those who displeased her. So Magic had interceded in the face of her homecoming, adjusting her wardrobe for her own safety.

With a heavy sigh, she slid Illumina into a belt loop. Taking another bite of fruit, she began to hum the melody of her father's song.

"Greetings, Locasta," came a familiar voice from behind her.

Locasta turned. Dark hair, gray cloak, an aura of absence . . .

"Shade!"

From inside the cloak's hood, the spy cocked her head. "What are you doing in Gillikin?"

"I could ask you the same question," Locasta said, and took another bite of the drippy fruit.

"I went to find the Grand Adept on the Road of Yellow Brick," said Shade, "to ask about the Elemental Fairies." She shook her head, her hair swinging silently inside her charcoal hood. "On that front, the news is not good, I'm afraid. . . ." In her clipped and quiet way, she relayed what had happened to both Nick Chopper and Tilda.

Locasta felt a shiver at the thought of Tilda being captured a second time, this time by the fifth Witch. Tossing the tamorna pit into the grass, she told Shade everything that had taken place in her absence—the dice game, the monkey battle, Glinda's heart-wrenching disappearance, the dance of the fireflies, and finally, how the altered poem had revealed Norr's compass (which she herself had stupidly surrendered to Marada) to be the hiding place of Terra.

"And your plan is to return to Gillikin to retrieve it?" said Shade, incredulous. "All by yourself?"

Locasta was about to answer, but another voice—also

familiar—filled the space between the question and its answer. Not with words. But with humming.

And Locasta found herself looking at her brother, Thruff, bruised and dirtier than usual, approaching at a jaunty clip with a scowl on his face.

"Hello, brother," Locasta said, her voice as tight and scratchy as the manacles around her wrists. "No longer a glorified monkey trainer, I see."

"I could say the same to you," Thruff retorted.

There was a glint of something dark and desperate in his eyes that was not quite malice, but a shade away from safe. Locasta's hand went to the sword, and she let out a quick spank of laughter. "Come to battle me again, brother? To capture another of my friends, perhaps? Though that didn't work out too well for you last time, did it?"

Thruff glowered but said nothing.

"I've seen this boy before," said Shade. "This past winter, when I found myself in Gillikin. He was on his way to the Witch's castle. He'd asked an old miner, who told him your mother and sisters were being held captive there."

"Because *you* wouldn't tell me!" Thruff interjected, glowering at Locasta.

"Because I didn't wish for you to be *hurt*!" Locasta hurled back.

"*Hnh*," Thruff grunted, kicking at a stone in the road. "Didn't work."

Locasta sighed and nodded for Shade to continue.

"I followed him. He was small and alone, and I thought I could help him if he found danger."

"And how does he repay that kindness?" Locasta seethed. "By attacking us with monkeys, that's how!" She dove for him, but he dodged her attack.

"Wait!" he cried, reaching into his pocket. "I have something—"

"I want *nothing* from you!"

Locasta lunged again and Thruff let out a roar of outrage. Then he screamed the strangest thing:

"ZIZZLE. UMPH-SCUTCH. WURDLIN. DINK!"

And suddenly Locasta wasn't looking at her brother anymore.

25

GOING TO GREAT LENGTHS

The ring fit perfectly on Glinda's finger. Plated in summoning Magic, its shimmer was even brighter than it had been before.

"Well done, Zephyr," said the Priestess.

Glinda looked up from her ring. "Why do you call me Zephyr?"

"Because a zephyr is a draft, newly born," the Mystic said, perturbed at having to explain herself. "A breeze that has not yet become a gust. And there is something slightly windy about you. In your company I sense breezes, sometimes powerful blasts. As if you will one day enjoy some mystical communion with the Fairies of the air."

"You mean like Ria?"

"What do you know of Ria?"

"Only that she is hiding," said Glinda with a shrug. "But I picked up the emerald stone from the map before the game could show me where." Suddenly her eyes lit with realization; indeed, she could not believe she hadn't thought of asking sooner: "Grand-mamá . . . I mean . . . *Priestess* . . . you were King Oz's Mystic. *You* must know where Ria is!"

Mythra hesitated. "Yes," she replied softly. "Two bore witness. And I was one."

"I know you're sworn to secrecy and all," Glinda rambled on, as a thrill of hope shot through her. "But Miss Gage said the secret would only be kept until Oz was ready for its rightful ruler and the time to unleash the Fairies had come. Surely, with the Revolution underway, this is that time!"

"So it would seem," Mythra averred, then abruptly motioned to the last two items from the Paragon Chest. "Now, take up the rope."

"Wait . . . *What?*"

"You heard me! There's still work to be done here."

"But . . . you just agreed to tell me where to find the Air Fairy!"

"I agreed to no such thing," the Priestess snapped. "I merely said it seemed as if the time had come."

Frowning and frustrated, Glinda snatched up the tight

coil and saw that although the rope was thick and sturdy, it was not particularly long. If she were to hold one end at the tip of her nose, she suspected the other end would barely reach the floor.

"Can you think of a use for it?" Mythra inquired.

"Perhaps I could use it for skipping," said Glinda, with a sarcastic curl of her lip.

"Excellent idea," Mythra retorted, matching Glinda's tone, "because as we all know, Wicked Witches live in mortal fear of a Sorceress with a jump rope."

"I was joking," Glinda grumbled. "And besides, it's too short."

"Is it? Look again."

Glinda looked; the length of the rope was now twice her own height. "You didn't even need an incantation," she noted, reluctantly impressed.

"I've been at this awhile," was the Mystic's modest reply. Then she snapped her fingers, and the rope shrank back to the length it had been. "I would like you to use that rope to move all the rocks in this cave."

Glinda made a quick survey of the rocks in question and was glad that she had Magic at her disposal; many of the larger ones would be too heavy to lift otherwise.

"Move them where?" asked Glinda.

"Wherever you want. As long as you use the rope."

Use the rope? Glinda scowled. *Like a plow horse?* But she bent down over the rock closest to her, wrapped the rope around it, and tied a good strong knot. Then she looked up at the Mystic for approval.

The Mystic looked back with an unreadable expression.

Glinda sighed, turning her focus back to the rope. "*Move!*" she instructed.

The loose end of the rope squirmed obediently, but the rock stayed where it was.

Mythra let out a little snort.

"Well, it *did* move. I guess I just wasn't specific enough." Clearing her throat, Glinda tried again. "Move *the rock*."

The rope obeyed, moving the rock forward exactly one inch.

"Looks like we're going to be here awhile," Mythra muttered, settling into a chair.

Glinda glowered at the rope and ordered, "Move the rock *across the cave*!"

This time the rope leaped up, yanked the rock off the ground, and spun it in a wide circle, just as Trebly had done with her sling. Glinda ducked in time to avoid being clonked in the head as the rope released the stone, flinging it across the cave to crash against the wall like a cannonball, where it shattered into several small pieces that showered down all over Mythra's bed.

Mythra sighed.

"Can you at least tell me what I'm doing wrong?"

"It's not *what* you're *doing*. It's *how* you're *thinking*."

"I'm thinking like a Sorceress," Glinda countered. "I'm

using Magic to enchant the rope to do my bidding, just like you said."

"You're using *small* Magic," Mythra corrected, indicating the number of stones on the ground. "This is a big chore. You must always adapt the Magic to the size of the undertaking, and trust that it will be equal to the task. Sometimes a Sorceress must go to great lengths to accomplish her Magical objectives."

Great lengths, huh? I'll show you 'great lengths.' Glinda snapped her fingers at the rope, and it unwound itself from the stone to jump into her hand.

> *"To move these rocks from hither to yond*
> *This determined Sorceress will use all her*
>   *strengths*
> *These stones are to be relocated, above and beyond*
> *As I stretch my Magic to the greatest of lengths."*

Clutching the center of the rope with two fists, Glinda slowly pulled her hands outward until it had doubled in length. She repeated the process until the rope's span had tripled, then quadrupled. By her fifth pull, the rope seemed to understand what she wanted and accommodatingly began to grow on its own.

When she finally let go, the rope leaped into action; while one end went meandering across the cave floor, wrapping tightly around every stone it encountered, the other end climbed the air and squiggled to the high ceiling, where it secured itself around the sturdiest of the stalactites.

"Now hoist!"

The enchanted rope seemed happy to oblige, making a sort of primitive pulley system of itself, dispersing weight and energy to lift the stones upward to the full height of the cave. Stone after stone rose up, and whenever the rope paused to grow longer, the rocks hovered, suspended at different heights like fruit from a tree.

When at last the task was completed, an enormous rope web had been woven overhead, dotted with rocks of all shapes and sizes.

She turned a satisfied smile to her mentor. "Is this what you had in mind?"

"The better question," said Mythra knowingly, "is, is it what *you* had in mind? Look closely now. Do you recognize the arrangement of those stones?"

It took Glinda only a moment to make the connection. She bobbed her head excitedly, for she knew exactly what she was looking at! A particular portion of the diagram hovering from the cave's ceiling mirrored precisely the results of the pebble game that had informed her of the Entrusteds and their charges. A large rock at the midpoint clearly represented the embroidered compass rose stitched into the center of Tilda's map, while the placement of the four rocks hanging closest to it echoed the four landing places of the stones from the velvet pouch.

At first, anyway . . .

But the section of rope that had suspended its rock over what would have been the eastern quadrant of Tilda's map—Munchkin Country—was slowly beginning to swing the stone southward, toward Quadling.

Glinda opened her mouth to comment.

But what came out instead was a bone-chilling scream.

26

DOUBLE-EDGED SWORD

Where Thruff had been now stood a towering dragon-like creature, shining with purple scales, flapping two huge, powerful wings.

"What is *that*?" cried Locasta. "What did my brother just turn into?"

"It's a Rak!" said Shade. "I saw one once in the Oogaboo Valley of Winkie Country. It's believed they are exceedingly vicious."

"Gee . . . you *think*?" hollered Locasta, sidestepping a slap from Thruff's newly acquired claw foot. "Get behind me, Shade. Or better yet, get invisible."

Shade wavered, then disappeared as the Rak opened his

mouth and spit out a column of flame. Locasta jumped back just in time to avoid being seared. With a roar of fury, she reached for Illumina.

And realized with a jolt that someone else had reached for it too.

The scream was so brutal it had shattered the Magic of the ropes. Mythra threw herself between Glinda and the shower of stones as they slipped from their snares to crash around them.

But Glinda was barely aware of the falling rocks; she was too busy groping madly at her sash.

"What is it?" asked Mythra. "What's happening?"

"A battle," Glinda rasped. "No, more like a duel. Someone against someone—or some*thing*—very large. And very, very mean."

"You must engage."

"But how? My sword—"

"Draw it!"

"But it isn't here!"

"Because it's *there* . . . at the duel. Now draw it. Feel it in your hand, remember it."

Fingers trembling, Glinda let her grip close around the place where Illumina's handle should have been and gasped when she felt the cool firmness of the braided metal against her palm. With a yank, she removed what wasn't there from the sash that did not hold it, and brandished the memory of her sword against an opponent she could not see.

"What do you feel?" Mythra prodded.

"Heat. Fire, maybe. And a wind, as if from wings."

"Rak." Mythra's tone was grave. "Listen to me, child. Someone a great distance from here needs you desperately."

"Needs me to do *what*?"

"To guide this weapon! To join in this fight from afar."

"You want me to fight a beast I can't see?"

"Illumina can see it. Illumina is there. You must tell whoever is wielding your weapon exactly what to do by doing it yourself. This is Connection Magic at its most powerful!"

Glinda raised her sword arm and closed her eyes. She imagined Illumina glowing in her grasp, emitting the power of Truth Above All. In the next moment, she sensed the invisible mass of violence that was the Rak attacking with all its might. With a yelp, she thrust her unseen blade into the emptiness.

And above, a very amazed Locasta thrust Illumina at the beast.

The Rak that was Thruff yowled out in agony when the searing light of Illumina connected with the tip of its wing. Stamping closer, it swung its other enormous wing at Locasta.

In Mythra's cave, Glinda parried, swooping the sword downward to intercept the blow.

And with no conscious effort on her part, Locasta sent Illumina streaking into the path of the dragon's giant paw, blocking the assault and eliciting another growl of pain.

When Glinda two-handed her grip, Locasta did the same.

Together, they lifted the sword over their heads, just as Thruff's long, scaly tail reeled around to knock Locasta to the ground.

Glinda went down hard, landing on her hands and knees and losing her grip on the invisible sword. "I dropped it!" she cried, fumbling in vain for something that was not there.

Mythra's eyes searched frantically, helplessly.

Both Glinda and Locasta struggled to gain their feet, ducking the hot cloud of the Rak's salty, peppery breath.

Dazed, Locasta scanned the area for Illumina, panicking when she saw that it had skittered several feet out of reach. Suddenly it was being lifted from the ground by unseen hands.

"Shade!" Locasta reached out and the blade came arcing toward her through the air; she caught it by the braided handle.

In Mythra's cave, Glinda reached out, and though she could not see the sword, she caught it, clean. Leaping forward, she aimed Illumina at what she was almost certain was the Rak's broad chest.

At the same moment, Locasta felt the force of Glinda's swing in her own muscles and slammed the illuminated blade hard against the beast's scaly body.

Light exploded in a deafening *hiss*, and Thruff let out a keening wail as the brilliance of the sword seared his scales. The sound of his agony made Locasta's stomach lurch. She quickly withdrew the sword.

And Glinda did the same.

The beast threw his head back and howled, swaying above Locasta.

Glinda felt the massive force of the motion and retreated. Locasta stepped back and craned her neck.

Glinda craned *her* neck . . . and knew that the eyes she could not see belonged to Thruff.

The Rak snarled, then whimpered. And as the enormous dragon beast began to fall, both Glinda and Locasta whispered in a single, strangled voice, "*No* . . ."

But the beast dropped forward onto his belly, his wings outstretched behind him, shaking the ground beneath Locasta's feet, shaking the ceiling above Glinda's head.

The Rak was still.

Locasta's hand was empty.

And Glinda found herself blinking into the brilliant glow of Illumina, returned to the safety of her own two hands.

Staring at the fallen Rak, Locasta was vaguely aware of Shade emerging from the atmosphere. Her cloak was

fluttering even before it had fully materialized as she ran to crouch beside the Rak—beside Thruff. She stroked the Rak's horned head, which was bigger than she was. Pale sparks, not hot enough to burn, dripped from its pointed fangs, and its fluttering eyes were aimed at Locasta.

They were Thruff's eyes, exactly as they'd looked when she'd watched the soldier carry him off to the castle.

"I'm sorry," she whispered. "Thruff, I'm sorry."

As the words escaped her lips, the form of the dragon began to fade away until all that remained was the boy, sprawled on the ground.

When Shade helped him to his feet, Locasta saw that the front of his ragged shirt was scorched black; she could only imagine the severity of the burn underneath. She wished her father were there to help him, and at the same time she was glad that he wasn't. To see what she'd done to her brother—to see what her brother had *forced* her to do—would have surely turned Norr's heart to stone.

A slight buckling appeared in the ground—but to Locasta's surprise, the cobbles were not rising at her feet, or Shade's. The stones pressing up from under the ground were for Thruff. She was further confounded by the fact that there was not just one road of cobblestone, but two. One red, the other purple.

Thruff seemed startled to see the roads appear, and even more perplexed by the fact that when they had both fully surfaced, he was standing with one foot on each of them.

The small portion of the Road of Red Cobble that had availed itself to Thruff looked just as it always had—smooth and sure and safe. The purple path was much bumpier, paved with haphazard indigo, violet, and purple-toned stones, all slanted and uneven.

If he were truly dangerous, Locasta reasoned, *the red road would have repelled him.* "Renounce Marada!" she implored, her pulse racing with both terror and hope. "There's still hope for you, I know it!"

Only now did she notice that Thruff was gripping something in his curled fist. "What've you got there, brother?" Locasta asked, striding toward him. "Some charm from your Wicked new friend?"

Thruff glared at her, but said nothing.

Emboldened by his silence and the red bricks beneath his feet, Locasta took another step forward. "Whatever it is, don't do it. Thruff, please. Just this once . . . do what is *right*, not what is *easy*."

"I tried to do what was right once before!" Thruff spat, wincing at the sting in his chest. "And if you knew what I did, you'd hate me."

"I'd . . . *what*? No! Listen to me. It doesn't matter what you did. Because I'll soon have the means to vanquish the Witch of the North."

"Locasta," Shade warned in a voice like slivered ice, "tell him no more. He may use it against us."

Thruff's breath was coming short and shallow, and his

eyes were dull with the pain of his injury. "You think you're going to destroy Marada?" he sneered. "Then what? There are two more, and they are just as Wicked. Do you really think you can save Oz all by yourself?"

Locasta shook her head. "There are fairyfolk all over Oz who are prepared to join me. You saw it yourself, when you came flying in on that monkey! There are teachers, and apothecaries, and seamstresses and clumsy bears who will fight beside me; there are tree choppers and daughters of wagon-wheel salesmen, and silly girls with chronic cases of hiccups, who have already proven themselves brave enough to stand shoulder to shoulder with me in this fight. But I want my brother beside me too."

"You won't." Thruff's eyes flared, and he shot a glance at Shade. "You won't want me when she tells you what I've done." With that, he lifted the foot that rested upon the sturdy promise of the red cobbles and as they sank away, more purple ones pressed themselves up from the ground, lopsided and jagged. He leaped onto the path and took off, stumbling over the poorly laid stones.

"Don't you dare run away from me, you coward!" Locasta screamed, and made to give chase. But the purple path refused her passage and flung her backward, so that she went skidding on the seat of her overalls across the place where the red road had been.

Thruff looked back only once, just before his rocky trail curved out of sight in the distance. Then, like its red-cobbled cousin, the purple path retreated beneath the indigo grasses of Gillikin Country.

Locasta stared after him for a long moment, then spun to face Shade. "Be glad you're an only child!" she huffed. And stomped off toward the North.

27

THE MAGIC PEARL

Illumina was metal again when Mythra took it from Glinda's hand. Her fist closed as comfortably around the jeweled braid of the grip as if she had never let it go.

"Hello, old friend," she whispered, turning it this way and that, following the smooth motion of the blade with glistening eyes.

"I owe you a thank-you for that magnificent sword," Glinda realized. "I don't know what I would have done without it."

"I'm sure the brave someone who just used it against the Rak would share that sentiment," Mythra observed. "Have you any idea who it might have been, wielding our beloved Illumina up there?"

Glinda hadn't until just this moment, when Mythra said "brave." "Locasta!" she cried, her heart thudding with joy. "I'm certain of it, for I can't imagine Illumina allowing anyone else to take such a liberty. Which means she survived the monkey battle! With any luck, they all did!"

"I am happy to hear it," Mythra said, twisting her wrist to make Illumina dance in the candlelight. Then she spun it over her head and whirled into a lunge-and-thrust.

"You've missed it," Glinda observed. "Haven't you?"

Mythra expertly flipped the sword in the air, caught it by the handle, and offered it pommel-first to Glinda. "The creator cannot help but love the creation, whether it is a poem, or a world"—she smiled at Glinda with hazel eyes that spoke of Tilda—"or a child. This is how we extend ourselves from our past, through our present, and into our own future, whatever it may hold."

"Like you and my mother and me," said Glinda, accepting the sword and slipping it into her sash. "We've inherited much from your spirit, haven't we? After all, I am said to be your likeness. Was your hair coppery like mine, when you were a girl? And my mother has your eyes."

"Enough!" said Mythra sharply. "I did not intend for this to become an exercise in sentimentality. I was simply surprised to see my old weapon, that's all. There is no time for gushing. Not when we still have work to do."

Mythra snatched the pearl from where it lay on the

gossamer cloth, slapped it into Glinda's hand, and began to strut around the cave.

"You shall enchant it, like the rope."

"Enchant it to do what?"

"That is up to you. This pearl was a gift from the Sea Fairies and as such, it is irreplaceable. The Magic it will be capable of should reflect that. So ask yourself: Is there something this pearl can provide—*one* thing—that in this world and every other, is so precious as to have no substitute?"

Glinda considered the question and guessed, "Knowledge?"

"That's what Illumina is for."

"Friendship?"

Mythra waved this off with a dismissive flick of her hand. "You have friends. One of whom is trapped in a collide-o-scope as we speak, so let's hurry this up, shall we?"

Rolling the large pearl over in her hand, Glinda continued to think. "Great strength, perhaps?"

Mythra snorted and folded her arms. "You wish to be the strongest of all the fairyfolk in Oz, do you? So the next time you pluck a peachyplum from a branch, you will uproot the whole tree in the bargain?"

Glinda frowned.

"Think, Zephyr! What is the one thing, above all others, that a Sorceress needs in order to make good Magical choices, and proceed rightly with whatever she must do?"

Glinda thought. "The one thing, above all others . . . Oh! The truth! I will always need the truth . . . above all. Always!"

Mythra's eyes shone with approval. "Excellent. And how will you achieve this? What will you enchant this precious pearl to do?"

"Um . . . well . . . sometimes a lie can look very much like a truth, can't it? And despite her expansive knowledge, her great strength, and good friends to advise her, even an experienced Sorceress can be tricked by the Wickedness of a lie."

"I could not agree more," said Mythra, and there was a note of something dark—like guilt—in her words. "Now tell me, what charm will you give to this gem?"

"I will enchant it to glow with its own creamy brightness whenever I am in the presence of honesty." Glinda paused to reconsider. "But then, I would like to believe that most Ozians are good and honest, in which case the pearl would be glowing more often than not. So perhaps the opposite is wanted? Perhaps it would be better for the pearl to react to falsehoods, when someone or something is *un*truthful." She smiled. "Yes. I think that is the answer. In untruthful situations, the pearl will turn black. For a lie is a thing of darkness, and the pearl's Magic should reflect that a shadow is being cast over the light of truth."

Mythra looked away, as if the word "shadow" had struck a chord. When she again met Glinda's gaze, her face was unreadable. "As enchantments go, it's a sound one. Well-meaning and purposeful. And now, an incantation."

Glinda held the pearl in her palm and spoke these words:

When in the presence of this pearl
If ever a falsehood shall unfurl
The liar will be revealed to me
For black as shadow this pearl shall be."

The pearl shone brightly for a moment, as if welcoming the Magic into itself, then returned to its usual sheen.

"Did it take?" Glinda asked. "Will it work?"

"I suppose you will have to wait until someone tells you a lie," the Priestess reasoned with a shrug. "Now I think it's high time we get you back to where you came from. Frankly, I'm growing quite bored with your company and am eager to see you gone!"

In Glinda's hand, the pearl grew cold and black.

"Ah," said Mythra, grinning. "So it *does* work."

For the second time since her arrival, Glinda threw her arms around the Mystic. And this time, the Mystic did not pull away.

28

SO MOAT IT BE

Locasta was still shaken from battling Thruff the Rak.
It had been a trying journey from the Gillikin border
through the vast purple fields and over the rocky hills to
the heart of the country, where the Witch's castle stood.
She'd been forced to tie back her mane of purple curls and
tuck it into the collar of her old shirt. It itched terribly,
but she knew her hair was her most distinguishing feature, and if Marada's minions were on the lookout, those
ringlets would surely be the death of her. Fortunately, her
tattered mining clothes and rusted manacles were all she
needed to blend in with the other Gillikin citizens. And
nobody seemed to take any notice of Shade at all.

It was almost dark when they reached the valley that marked the edge of the Warrior's grounds. The castle loomed in the distance.

"Do you have a plan?" asked Shade.

"Of course I have a plan."

"What is it?"

"I'm going into the castle to retrieve the compass."

"That is an objective, not a plan."

"What's the difference?"

"An objective is a desired end result. A plan is a series of well-thought-out maneuvers that takes into account all the requirements and dangers associated with the task in order to achieve said result."

"Oh." Locasta shrugged. "Then, no, I don't have a plan. But my *objective* is still to get that compass and perhaps, if time permits, to free my mother and sisters from servitude."

When she took a step toward the castle, Shade caught her arm and pulled her back. "Locasta, there's something you should know."

"What?" Locasta urged. "Tell me! What do I need to know?"

Shade flicked her cape, as though debating what to say next. "The place is riddled with dark Magic and four-footed soldiers with tails and horns."

"I'm aware of that, Shade. Why are you being so peculiar?"

"You will not like what you see in there, Locasta. Trust me on this."

"I don't have to like it, I just have to find the compass, and my mother and sisters. Now are you going to help me or not?"

Shade turned away, her hair swinging like a dark curtain. When she turned back, she looked resigned. "To the moat," she whispered.

And as she did, the Road of Red Cobble buckled up from the ground at last, right at the tips of Locasta's old mining boots.

"It's about time," Locasta remarked. "I guess it's decided I'm worthy."

"Or stubborn," Shade mumbled. But she stepped onto the road behind Locasta, who was already humming, and followed her up the sloping sides of the valley toward the castle.

When they were close enough to see the castle clearly, Locasta stopped humming. The Witches, it seemed, had made good on their plans to increase their personal guard. Three Gillikin soldiers and their bulky yak and buffalope mounts were minding the stone bridge that crossed the moat. Behind them, the portcullis was securely in place, blocking the way into the zwinger, also known as the outer ward. Thanks to the Road of Red Cobble, the guards would be oblivious to their arrival. But Locasta knew the road would go no farther than the bridge, and getting past the spike-bottomed bars of the iron-plated gate was a challenge she had not anticipated.

The red cobbles brought them to the edge of the moat, where the water's glassy surface held a reflection of the half-moon in the sky. Shade swung her cape over it and it rippled. Then the moon was gone and another wavering image appeared.

Locasta gave a breathless little cry. "My father!"

"The moat and I share this memory," Shade explained. "It's the story of a boy who thought he could reason with evil."

She flicked her cape and again the water ruffled; this time it was an image of Thruff's face that rose up from the depths, to become part of a scene animated by the gentle motion of the water. And it was here that the moat began its tale:

WHAT THE MOAT SAW

There is a chill in the air and the ground crunches with frost. But this does not deter the barefoot boy. He slips by the Witch's guards and gains entrance to the broad gap between the inner and outer curtain walls, the area known as the zwinger. For Marada, this space is part gallery, and part prison.

His name is Thruff. He is young and angry—a dangerous combination, to be sure.

Behind him, his father, who is called Norr, creeps at a distance. He is a miner, and a soft-spoken rebel. He has followed his son from their shack in the village, hoping the lad was merely on his way to gamble at marbles or kiss a pretty girl.

But no, the boy has led Norr to the castle of the Witch.

Thruff is swift and stealthy and is over the bridge before his father can get close enough to grab him. Inside, Thruff shouts for the Witch, demanding an audience.

Deep in the guts of the castle, Marada, who dislikes being shouted for, leaps from her throne. Her heavy sandals tromp down the stairs of the keep and through the great hall; in no time she has marched through the inner courtyard and toward the outer ward.

"I heard the bellow of a peasant!" she snarls as she goes. "Show yourself, and prepare to perish!"

Thruff's father acts with the speed of devotion, pushing the boy behind a grouping of statues just as the Witch arrives. She might have spied the boy if not for the glare of the white winter sun shining off her gauntlets.

Instead she sees his father. "Is it you who hollers for me?" she asks through pointy teeth.

Norr thinks fast, explaining that he has come to

confess to the crime of vandalism. He does not let on that the true purpose of the messages he has scratched into the walls of her mines is to recruit rebels for a Foursworn Mingling.

Marada kicks him hard in his rib cage, and he falls to his knees in the grass of the bailey, clutching his shattered midsection and gasping for breath. Thruff, hunkered down behind the statues, stifles a shriek. He makes to run to his father's aid, but a covert look from the writhing Norr stops him.

"Keep hidden," Norr mouths to his boy.

His boy, for once, obeys.

"Bring me Norr's grubby girl litter," the Witch commands a guard.

The soldier stampedes into the castle and returns with the miner's wife and five older daughters. Thruff's mother and sisters. He has not seen them since his babyhood and yet he knows them. For they are humming.

Thruff cannot take his eyes off his mother; she is gaunt and weary-looking, and yet she is the most beautiful thing he has ever seen. He wants to run to her, but he knows that such an act would not end well. Her hair is like his sister Locasta's, a riot of violet ringlets; he imagines this is what freedom would look like if freedom could be seen. Her hands, though, are the opposite of freedom—scarred and wrinkled from the work the Witch has foisted on her.

And his sisters! Five of them! All taken away from him before he was old enough to learn their names. He is certain they would share Locasta's spunk if it had not been pounded from them at the hands of the Witch.

His sisters are still humming and weeping. Mother looks brave. Or at least resolute. Father is nearly unable to breathe. His ribs are ruined.

Marada growls and clouds gather overhead. She approaches Norr and presses the blunt-tipped finger of her gauntlet to his shoulder. He screams in pain. Thruff winces where he hides. He would like nothing more than to strip the Witch of these heinous gloves and melt them down with the heat of his fury to naught but a molten memory. What he cannot know is that those gloves were once as pure of purpose as the silver from which they were fashioned.

But that was when they were worn by a king.

Marada's touch shoots stillness into Norr, and her incantation peals through the bailey:

"Drain away motion, spill away breath
Petrifaction to stone is a fate worse than death
Sculpt away feeling, carve away life
Then to your daughters, then to your wife!

In between heartbeats, with a touch cold as stone,
Why? So you miners will LEAVE ME ALONE!"

As she chants the ugly rhyme, she touches each
of Thruff's sisters and his mother in turn, with the
same gleaming fingertip. Horrified, the boy watches
as their pale skin hardens over to rock; their faces go
stony and vacant.

Satisfied with her vicious artistry, Marada spits
on the gauntlet's fingertip as if just touching Thruff's
family has tarnished it. Then she stamps back to her
castle, her spurs leaving a trail of sparks in their wake.

The guards examine the statues with distress.
Seven more hunks of sculpture that they will be
required to polish. One less able-bodied miner to
labor in the bowels of Oz, and worst of all, six fewer
dainty maids to serve them guggleberry cider in the
dining hall.

It is a bad day in Gillikin, to be certain.

But then, it always is.

Thruff waits out the remainder of the afternoon,
squatting behind the statues that saved him. Through
the blur of his tears, he memorizes the stony faces of
his family angle by angle, curve by curve, and for one
fleeting moment, he dreams of telling Locasta how
sweet his sisters were, how brave their father was,
and how lovely their mother looked, even at the end.

But he knows he will not do that.

For to tell her this tale would be to admit that he is to blame for the loss of them. So he hides until moonrise, then scuttles out of the zwinger and runs home to the shack where his sister Locasta waits.

Newly made an orphan. Thanks to Thruff.

Locasta kept her eyes on the moat until the final image sank to the muddy bottom.

"He went to rescue them," Shade whispered.

Locasta nodded, listening to the ripple of the water and wondering how they were going to distract the guard, raise the portcullis, and get inside the castle to search for the compass. Saving her family, it seemed, was no longer an issue.

Then from the grassy rise came an unexpected sound. At first Locasta thought she was imagining it, but as the sound drew nearer, it became unmistakable.

Someone was humming.

29

TRUE OR FALSE?

"Is it really time for me to go?" asked Glinda.

"It is," said Mythra. "There is much for you to do in Oz."

Glinda stepped out of the hug and looked up into the Mystic's face. "Come with me! The Revolution will be much stronger with you there to lead it!"

"It is not my place to lead it," said Mythra, smoothing Glinda's newly trimmed bangs. "That responsibility belongs to you. Here is where I must remain."

"You never told me why you had to leave Oz in the first place," said Glinda, surprised that such a tremendous detail had gone unaddressed. "Are you being punished?"

"Not in the way you're implying. But now that I know what I've missed—not being there to see my darling Tilda marry her knight; never even dreaming that you, granddaughter, had come to exist—well, I can tell you that my exile has become a far worse punishment than I ever imagined. Now, gather up your things. It's time to say goodbye."

Glinda trudged to the table to collect the rope and the shield; she was already wearing the pink tourmaline ring. But the pearl—she just couldn't bring herself to deposit it into her pocket without enjoying one more look.

Placing it between her thumb and forefinger, she held it aloft to admire its luster against the gray backdrop of the cave ceiling. This created the illusion that she was balancing a full, white moon between her fingertips.

"You should be very proud of that little bauble," Mythra observed. "The enchantment you cast upon it shows that you possess the true wisdom of a Sorceress's vision."

In Glinda's mind the word "vision" brushed up against her thoughts of the moon, and suddenly the horrid image of the four Witches torturing Elucida came crashing back to her.

The moon vision.

At the same moment, Mythra's brows arced up. "Moon vision?"

Glinda quickly told Mythra about the dark phantasm that had set everything into motion—how the Wickeds had stepped out of the future and onto her back lawn. She described the compass formation, the Witches' cruelty, and how the poor Moon Fairy had seemed helpless against this confluence of evil.

She was just getting to the part in which the sinister fifth Witch had appeared and two of the three captives had been revealed when Mythra held up her hand.

"There is nothing to fear from that nightmare," she said calmly.

"Are you sure? Because my mother said it was from a time yet to come, and that it was possible—"

"Possible," Mythra repeated, "means a thing is as likely *not* to happen as it is *to* happen. In this case, the not happening is what applies."

"So you're familiar with this moon ceremony?"

"Quite." Mythra gave a little shudder. "It would have been called the Ritual of Endless Shadow if it had been allowed to take place. The fifth Witch hoped to release her master—a Shadow called Urla—from where I had imprisoned her, with Elucida's help, in the moon. I imagine you were just about to describe a pair of terrible red eyes?"

"Yes! The fifth Witch. You know about her?"

"It was she who, on the night of King Oz's demise, attacked Elucida. My extremely unwilling presence was the only thing that could have enabled her to succeed, and she very nearly did, by seizing the Magical strength of my past, present, and future and turning it against the moon."

As Mythra spoke, Glinda was racked with a feeling of being torn apart, split into three pieces—the sensation was not quite agonizing, but vastly unpleasant, and she understood that what she was experiencing was something Mythra had already endured.

Connection Magic.

Now Glinda felt herself flanked by two familiar forms: to her left was the glistening reflection of her past self. On her right stood the spirit of her own future.

"So I called upon the lingering power of Oz, the King Uniter," Mythra continued solemnly, "and with the help of four stolen pieces of silver, the last of his Magic helped me to escape the fifth Witch and foil the ritual. I was made whole again, made whole forever."

A violent force came pounding in on Glinda from both sides, and she felt herself slamming back into a single being. The action—Mythra's memory of it—was so jarring that Glinda's teeth rattled and her bones felt as if they might splinter.

"The fifth Witch knew that she could not rescue the Shadow without the full arc of my past, present, and future Magic, and since neither she nor anyone else could ever again divide what Oz's Magic had united, the Shadow was lost forever. This enraged her, and her rage, I am sorry to tell you, made her grow even stronger, right before my eyes. She turned herself to smoke and vowed that she would not rest until she had destroyed me and every last bit of Goodness in the Land of Oz." Here Mythra crooked a sardonic grin. "But mostly me."

"So that's why you pretended to be dead. To escape the fifth Witch."

To Glinda's surprise, the Mystic's cheeks flushed slightly. "I hope you do not think me a coward."

"No!" said Glinda with an emphatic shake of her head. "I recently did something similar, though instead of fleeing to the Underlands, I hid in a toolshed." She cocked her head, still trying to understand the complex tale. "But what do the Elemental Fairies have to do with this ritual? Madam Mentir said they were involved."

"Had the fifth Witch succeeded in freeing the Shadow, she planned to infuse her with one of Oz's Gifts. In the absence of the next Ozma, claiming even a single piece of the Oz spirit would have allowed the Shadow to take the throne of Oz."

"But doesn't Ozma need to accept all four Gifts of Oz to live on as the rightful ruler?" Glinda asked, remembering what Squillicoat had told her.

"Key word: 'rightful,'" said Mythra. "In that vocabulary class of yours, did you happen to learn the meaning of the word 'wholesome'?"

"It's another way of saying Good."

"Exactly. To be wholesome, our Oz ruler must be *whole*. Wicked, however, is not quite so concerned with balance. In fact, Wickedness thrives on being incomplete, off center, crooked. Fortunately, after Oz's death the fifth Witch had no Gifts at all."

"Because the Fairies hid them!" Glinda exclaimed. "But you knew where all four were hiding. So if she had rescued the Shadow, she would have forced you to tell her the whereabouts of Ember . . . or Terra, or Poole, or . . . *Ria*." Her eyes widened. "That reminds me! Where *is* Ria? She was the only one the map didn't point to, and the rope-and-rock diagram burst before I could decipher it."

"The Elemental Fairy of the Air," Mythra began, her voice filled with reverence, even as it trembled, "the lovely and powerful Ria, guardian of the Wind, was entrusted to Mistress Dottie Jane of Munchkin Country. Appropriately enough, Ria chose to conceal herself in what was Dottie Jane's signature accessory." Mythra grinned and fluttered her fingers as a hint.

"A fan!" said Glinda. "A pretty paper fan! Of course. I know just what it looks like, because I saw her holding it when the zoetrope revealed the unveiling party to us. What of Terra? Where did he choose to hide?"

"The Lurl Fairy is in the groundskeeper's compass," Mythra said, "and Poole—well, he took himself into Dallybrungston's fussy little pocket square!"

"The hankie!" Glinda laughed. "Yes, the map told us that."

"I have every faith you will be as successful with Ria, Poole, and Terra as you were with Ember," said Mythra.

"As do I," said Glinda confidently (but not *over*-

confidently). "With the help of Locasta, and Shade and Ursie and—*Ben!* Oh, I nearly forgot. To release Ben from the collide-o-scope, I had to promise the Nome King a trade." Her eyes went to the beautiful gem-studded belt at Mythra's waist. "I truly hate to ask, but—"

"Say no more." Mythra unclasped the belt and fastened it around Glinda's waist. Then she picked up the gossamer cloth from the table, whipped it sharply around her head, and let it waft down to her shoulders, where it once again became a tattered shawl of rough brown wool. "Be as brave as you are and as wise as you've been," she said, giving Glinda a gentle nudge toward the stairwell, which had silently reappeared.

"I will," said Glinda, swallowing her tears. "You're sure you can't come home to Oz? Ever?"

The Mystic's answer was to give no answer at all. Then, just as she had done when Glinda first arrived, she turned her back to her visitor and hobbled into the gloomy recesses of her cave.

"Thank you, Priestess," said Glinda. "Thank you in abundant amounts."

With a heavy heart, she made her way up the steps, toting her shield and rope. It wasn't until she'd reached the orange door to Roquat's palace that she heard the faint echo of the Mystic's voice from below:

"Truth Above All, my darling Zephyr," it said. "Your grand-mamá misses you already."

Glinda burst through the orange door, swung open the iron gate, and found the Nome King right where she had left him. Kaliko, who was busy polishing the gemstones that dotted the marble walls, barely spared her a glance.

"I have the belt," she said, dropping into a curtsy before the Nome King's throne, her eyes fixed on the collide-o-scope in his hand.

Roquat looked less than pleased by her success. "Well done, Glinda Gavaria," he said grudgingly. "That is indeed the very item I had in mind. Give it here."

Glinda rose and handed over the belt and watched Roquat fasten it around his broad midsection. He gave her a smug look that made the hair on the back of her neck prickle.

"You'll release Ben now," she said. "Won't you?"

"Hmmm." The monarch scratched his stone chin. "No. I don't think I will."

Glinda was aghast. "But that was our agreement. You said you would let him go if I brought you the belt. We had a deal."

Roquat spun the collide-o-scope between his fingers. "You make an excellent point, but I remain disinclined to release the earth child. He's making progress in there, you know. Learning to see through other prisms. So you may as well be on your way."

Leaving Ben behind, trapped in a spinning collide-o-scope, was simply not something Glinda was prepared to do. "How about," she said, mimicking the king's earlier offer, "I play you for him!"

"Wondiferous! If you win, the boy goes free. But what if I win?"

"Then, in addition to keeping Ben spinning in that contraption, you will also collect *this* valuable prize." Glinda handed him the enchanted pearl.

Kaliko, interested now, stopped polishing and raised his stony brows.

"What is the game?" asked Roquat, gazing at the pearl, his eyes shining with appreciation. "Multiple choice again?"

"True or False, if you don't mind."

"He doesn't," Kaliko blurted. "True or False it is! What are the rules?"

"Well, I assume there is some Magic involved in releasing my friend from that contraption."

"There is," Roquat confirmed.

"So you will describe a Magical act, or spell, or anything else that may or may not achieve the desired result, and I will tell you if what you've described is true or false."

Kaliko bounced exuberantly on the balls of his stone feet. "Delightful!"

"And no cheating," said Glinda.

"Fine, fine . . ." The king nodded his consent and handed the pearl back to Glinda.

"Begin," she said, curling her fist around it.

Roquat cleared his throat; it sounded like sand skittering over stone. "The way to release your friend is through a Witchly dance, which involves tapping the heels, wiggling the hips, and spinning on tiptoe."

Glinda opened her fingers ever so slightly to peek at the pearl. In response to Roquat's statement, the creamy hue had changed to the color of coal.

"Or"—Roquat crossed his arms over his chest—"removal from the interior of the collide-o-scope requires a potion containing one dram of the Water of Oblivion, four tail scales from Quox the Dragon, and five whiskers from the chin—no, no, I mean the mustache—of a shaggy man."

Again, Glinda's eyes went to the pearl, which this time had turned as black as onyx.

"Then again," the king continued, "it's entirely possible that the charm of the collide-o-scope can only be broken by the utterance of a Magical chant, which goes as follows: *Tumble, stumble, spin about; what went in must now come out.*'"

Glinda opened her hand; the pearl was once again a lustrous white.

"Well, what is your answer?" Kaliko prompted.

"It's quite obvious that the king's first statement was false," said Glinda with authority.

Roquat frowned. "That's right. How did you know?"

"Highness, you are made of solid rock, and quite a bit

of it at that. Did you honestly think I'd believe you could wiggle your hips and twirl on your tippy-toes?"

"She does make a very good point, sir," Kaliko allowed. "Graceful you're not."

The king pouted and slouched in his chair.

Now Glinda bit her lip, pretending to ponder the two remaining options. "The potion you described certainly *sounds* like it could be effective."

"Yes, yes, it does, doesn't it?" said Roquat eagerly. "Nothing like a bit of Quox to break a spell, I always say."

"But then again," Glinda hedged, tapping her chin, "that incantation you recited was quite lovely."

Roquat's face paled to the color of talc.

"Which is why my guess is that your second statement is false, and the third is true."

"She's right!" cried Kaliko, amazed. "On all three counts!"

But as Glinda reached for the collide-o-scope, the king jerked it away. "Double or nothing!" he croaked. "The boy *and* the belt, for the pearl."

Glinda shook her head.

"There must be something you'd be willing to wager!" The king's metamorphic fingers fumbled over the gleaming gems of his new belt until he'd plucked one from its setting. "What about this?" he asked, thrusting the stone into Glinda's hand. It was a particularly shiny one—the same glinting green as Glinda's eyes. "If you can name this stone, I'll let you keep the collide-o-scope!"

"I believe I've named enough stones already, thank you," said Glinda tersely.

"What if I throw in Kaliko?"

The steward gasped, looking utterly affronted. "Perhaps, my liege, it's time you considered giving up gambling."

"My 'sediments' exactly," Glinda said under her breath, and handed the green stone back to the king.

To her surprise, Roquat waved it away. "Consider it a parting gift," he mumbled. "It *is* the answer, after all."

"The answer to what?"

"To all the questions you have not asked yet," Roquat replied cagily.

Glinda eyed the twinkling gem, then cast a curious glance at Kaliko, who seemed to approve.

"Thank you," she said, slipping the stone into her pocket along with the pearl, then motioning to the collide-o-scope. "King Roquat, would you care to do the honors?"

"No," he huffed, slumping against the back of his gilt throne. "You go ahead."

Glinda spoke loudly, aiming her words at the collide-o-scope. *"Tumble, stumble, spin about; what went in must now come out."*

In the next instant, Ben was standing beside her. He looked mussed, and more than a bit dizzy, but on the whole, he seemed unharmed.

"Thank you again, Your Undergroundliness," said Glinda. "Now, if you could just tell me the way back to the upstairs land, I would very much appreciate it."

"You!" Roquat boomed, so loudly that the torches trembled in their brackets. "You are always asking for directions! I am quite tired of it. I thought the purpose of a quest was for the quester to find her own way!" From thin air the king pulled out a little pipe, which he lit by producing a red-hot coal from his pocket and tamping it into the bowl. Then he took a deep draw and blew out a long ribbon of white smoke. The smoke floated away from the throne to twist between Glinda and Ben.

Taking another pull from his pipe, he exhaled again, this time expelling a giant curlicue cloud of smoke that filled the cave. When it cleared, Glinda and Ben found themselves standing in the torch-lit cave with no one but the chief steward. The marble floors, the impressive throne, and the troublemaking king were gone.

"What a scalawag!" said Ben. "He's left us stranded."

"Not true," said Kaliko, still clutching his polishing cloth. His stony eyes looked sad. "My liege is complicated, to be sure, and I fear one day he will become truly troublesome. He bears watching by the forces of Goodness. But for now he is naught but a roguish trickster, and there is decency in him still."

"I don't see it," Ben muttered.

"Don't you?" Kaliko motioned to the long strand of smoke still hovering between Glinda and Ben. "He's left you a most excellent hint as to how to find your way home."

Only then did Glinda realize that the twisting ribbon of smoke from the king's pipe looked very much like a length of rope. She handed the formerly lead shield to Ben and slid the coiled rope from her shoulder. Then she aimed one end toward the ceiling of the cave and said, "*Climbable!*"

"Climbable?" Ben echoed. "That's the spell?"

"Do you want poetry, or do you want a way out of here?" Glinda replied with a grin, tossing the rope into the air.

Sure enough, it did not fall back to the ground; rather, it began to grow, wriggling upward just like the slender wisp of smoke, until the end of it vanished into the high shadows. She gave it a yank and was pleased to find it secure.

"Amazing," said Ben. "But do we have any way of knowing where it will take us?"

Glinda turned curious eyes to Kaliko.

"As I told you back at the lagoon, we are directly beneath the Witch of the North's castle."

"You mean to say," said Ben, "that we might just find ourselves crawling up through the floor of Marada's throne room?"

Kaliko shrugged. "Depending on your aim, and of course, the Magic, that is entirely possible."

"I doubt the rope would deposit us into danger," Glinda reasoned. "And besides, something tells me that when we break through into Gillikin, someone will be there to welcome us."

"And who will that be exactly?" asked Ben. "An army of yakityaks? The Warrior Witch herself?"

Glinda grinned. "Locasta!"

"But the battle at the academy . . . we don't even know if Locasta is—"

"She's fine," Glinda assured him. "I'm sure of it."

"And what makes you think she's found her way to Gillikin?"

"Because," said Glinda, "that's home."

"Home," said Ben with a wistful sigh. "There's no place like it, is there?"

"No, there isn't," Kaliko agreed cheerfully. "Good luck, up-stairs girl. I hope those chatty pebbles will soon bring us news of your success."

"I hope so too." And with that, Glinda began to climb the Magic Rope.

30

AS GOOD AS HEALED

As Locasta's brother approached, pieces of the purple road rose and retreated under his feet in a haphazard fashion. His humming, too, was unpredictable—high, then low, in and out of key. His eyes were anxious, snapping and sparkling as though he were trying to decide whether to be thrilled or terrified. But he sallied forth toward the three guards on the bridge.

Thruff of Gillikin, it seemed, was on a mission.

Locasta's first thought was to throw herself between her brother and those burly soldiers.

But Shade held her back.

When Thruff's bare feet hit the bridge, all three of the

soldiers drew their weapons. This was the boy who had embarrassed their comrade by stealing his dagger at the Levying; they were not inclined to trust him. But his voice was commanding, even as threads of pain caused by the burn on his chest ran through his words.

"I have seen the fugitive Locasta Norr!" he announced.

Locasta felt as if she'd been kicked as Thruff's eyes slid sidelong and she understood that he could see her on the Road of Red Cobble. He knew she was there, mere yards away from where he stood.

"Where is she?" the stockiest of the guards demanded.

"She was just now running along the shantytown lane," Thruff informed him. "And the enemy Sorceress Glinda was with her. The honor of capturing them can go to you, if you hurry."

Locasta grinned. "He's such a liar!" she whispered to Shade.

"I think you mean 'hero,'" Shade whispered back.

One of the guards leaped astride his buffalope, which reared up, snorting; its front hooves came down so close to Thruff's bare toes that Locasta cried out. The guards, of course, could not hear her.

"We shall storm the village," the soldier announced from the saddle. "Tear it to pieces until someone gives them up."

"No!" said Thruff quickly. "If you waste time pummeling miners, you will never catch her."

"He's protecting your neighbors," Shade noted with admiration.

Locasta nodded, then gasped when the stocky soldier pressed the tip of his dagger to Thruff's throat.

"You would tell us how to do our jobs?" he seethed. "We don't take orders from children."

"Suit yourself," Thruff replied sharply. "But my sister is nothing if not fast. Give chase now, or lose her forever."

"What about the Witch?" asked the third guard, looking over his shoulder through the portcullis gate as he mounted his yakity steed.

"I will go and find her in the castle and tell her you have gone to seize my sister and the redheaded menace." Thruff promised this with such sincerity that Locasta almost believed him.

"But you must go now," he went on. "They are probably halfway to the Forest of Gugu by now. Summon someone to open this gate for me and then be off. Marada will most certainly reward you for taking such swift action!"

"She will indeed," the stocky guard agreed, climbing into the saddle of his yak and sneering down at Thruff. "But we are not about to help you share in that glory."

"Filthy little scamp," the second soldier spat. "Find your own way in."

"H'yah!" growled the third rider, spurring his yak.

The three beasts galloped across the bridge. To avoid

being crushed, Thruff scurried out of their path and fell into the moat with a splash.

Locasta rolled her eyes, then followed the red road to where her brother was crawling out of the water and offered him her hand. Thruff reached up to accept it, and when his palm met hers, she felt him transfer something into it, a round metal object. Locasta's heart thudded, for she knew without looking exactly what it was: their father's compass.

With a firm tug she pulled her brother out of the drink, and as he stood there dripping, Locasta stared at the golden prize in her grasp, dented and scraped, but more precious than she could say. Not only because it contained the mighty Lurl Fairy, Terra; not only because it had belonged to her father. But because, despite his errant ways, her brother had taken the great risk of retrieving it.

The words of the verse inscribed on the parchment came back to her, and she recited them aloud: "*Errant* souls can soon return to those who yearn and there shall learn to welcome that which surpasses hurt . . . all wounds are as good as healed."

And as the words echoed into the night, Thruff's expression turned to one of disbelief. His hands went to his charred shirt as the scorch mark and the burn beneath it disappeared. His wound had healed.

"Healing Magic," whispered Shade.

"I've never been much for poetry," said Thruff. "What does that all mean?"

"You were an errant soul and I yearned for nothing more than to return you to the side of Truth," Locasta explained, smiling. "Now that I've forgiven you, your wound has healed. All we have to do is open the compass, release Terra, and send her storming into the keep to vanquish Marada."

Locasta held the compass steady. Her fingers went to the lid, and slowly, purposefully, she lifted the hinged cover.

"Nothing's happening," said Thruff.

"I can see that," Locasta snapped, giving the compass a good shake. When Terra still did not emerge, she turned it upside down and smacked the bottom with her palm.

"Locasta," said Shade, biting back a rare smile. "I don't think pounding is going to help. The Lurl Fairy isn't *stuck* in there, like the last drop of molasses in a jug."

"Well, if she's not stuck, what other explanation can there be? Terra should be as eager to come out as Ember was. The amethysts said, 'Terra, compass, as healed.' Well, I've healed Thruff's burn. What else could that mean?"

"Maybe you've misinterpreted something," said Shade. "In the first version of this poem, the word 'independent' was broken into three words, spelled differently to mean something else."

Locasta considered this. "As healed," she muttered. "As he led? Ashe aled?" Both options were nonsense. Frowning she tried again. "A . . . shealed?"

Thruff was suddenly wiggling his wet toes in the mud

of the moat bank. "Do you feel that?" he asked, panicked.

The ground beneath their feet was beginning to tremble; Locasta could feel it through the worn soles of her old mining boots.

"A lurlquake," Thruff rasped.

But even as he spoke the words, the trembling ceased and the ground parted gently to reveal the end of a rope rising up from it.

A rope to which clung their two missing friends.

And one of them was holding *a shield*.

In the moonlight that shone on the grounds of Marada's castle, four friends celebrated this most unexpected reunion.

"I feared the monkeys had won," Glinda gushed, squeezing Locasta so tightly that the purple-haired girl had trouble catching her breath.

"They *did* win," Locasta told her as she slid the compass safely into her pocket. "But that's a long story. And how about you? Did you find what you were looking for?"

"Much more," said Glinda as her wary gaze went to Thruff, then back to his sister.

"You can trust him," Locasta assured her. "He's with us now." In a flurry of explanation, she recounted what she had learned from the amethyst stones and the altered poem. Taking the shield from Ben, she quickly examined it, and smiled when she noticed the round indentation in the center. It was the perfect size to accommodate her father's compass, just as there had been a place for Tilda's red beryl stone in the handle of Glinda's sword. "To release the Elemental Fairy Terra, we must unite the compass and the shield. I'm sure of it."

"Astonishing," Ben remarked. "You'd think I'd be done with being astonished by now, but there it is."

"We have to get into the castle," said Thruff, eyeing the abandoned bridge and the heavy portcullis. "Before the next watch arrives and discovers their fellow guards have fled. They're bound to send up an alarm."

"How?" Shade flipped her cape in the direction of the portcullis and looked grim. "Even I would have difficulty sneaking in there."

But Glinda did not need to contemplate. "This is Locasta's quest," she said with complete conviction. "Her Witchcraft will open the gate."

So Locasta handed the shield to Glinda, positioned herself in the center of the stone bridge, and in the pale light of the moon, began to dance. Her feet moved like skipping stones flitting across a quiet lake; her arms swayed like branches in a breeze.

And slowly . . . slowly . . . the portcullis began to lift.

Glinda thought it looked as if the castle were a giant fanged creature opening its mouth to devour them. Fortunately, Marada kept her machinery well-oiled, and the creaking was minimal. When the pointed bottoms of the bars were high enough to duck under, Locasta ceased her dance and they all tumbled under it into the zwinger, where countless statues—formerly innocent Gillikins—loomed like stone ghosts. Many of them, who were miners by Marada's decree, had been cursed into stone while still toting the tools of their trade—pickaxes, sledgehammers, dolabras, oil lamps. . . .

"Where will we find the Witch?" asked Glinda, rolling to her feet on the wide grassy swath, facing the outer massive wall of the inner bailey.

Thruff pointed to the towering keep beyond the wall. A deep archway—unguarded—would bring them to the inner ward. But who knew what they would find on the other side? "Locasta, make sure you have the compass handy," Glinda advised. "And I will be ready with the shield."

But Locasta didn't seem to hear. She was heading in the opposite direction, making her way through the maze of statuary toward a grouping that had caught her eye. The others exchanged worried glances and hurried to catch up.

"Locasta," Glinda called, "what are you doing?"

"Isn't it obvious?" Locasta retorted, her words heavy with sarcasm. "I'm visiting my family." She had stopped at the figure of a man, frozen in stone on his knees. Above him, in a tight huddle, were the shapes of five girls of varying ages and a woman. Thruff sidled up slowly, looking sick and ashamed, but to his credit, he did not back away. And Locasta, to hers, did not utter a word of blame. Instead they stood together, side by side, staring at the seven faces, so very like their own.

"This is what Marada does to those who displease her," Locasta explained to Glinda and Ben. "I've heard that the Petrifaction is unspeakably painful, for the heart hardens first, and the eyes last—so the Witch's enemies can see themselves change over to stone. It is believed to be the most agonizing punishment in Gillikin." Here she flashed a wry smile. "Second only to actually *being* a Gillikin, that is."

"I can still remember the spell the Brash Warrior used," Thruff muttered. "'In between heartbeats, with a touch cold as stone . . .'"

"'Why? So you miners will leave me alone,'" Shade finished. "I'll never forget it either."

Something about the phrasing of the incantation struck a chord with Glinda, but before she could think further on it, she noticed that a strange look had come over Locasta's face.

She was reaching into her pocket, to pull out two purple stones.

31

TAKING SHAPE

The iron gate of the dungeon cell slammed open. Tilda looked up from where she was curled on the floor to see the Wicked Warrior's shape trudging convulsively toward her.

Marada's gauntleted fist shot out, aiming straight for Tilda's skull, but the Sorceress dodged it and the Warrior's silver-clad knuckles slammed into the wall just behind the prisoner's head.

Taking in the lifeless eyes and dirt tongue, Tilda knew she was once again speaking not to Marada but the fifth Witch. "Took the compass right out of the Warrior's hand, did he?" she taunted, grinning. "Honestly, for the liege of all Wickedness, you'd think you would have seen that coming."

Inside the body, the fifth Witch roiled with rage and Marada's jaw worked madly, trying to keep up with the fury of Mombi's words. With each utterance, a shower of dirt and pebbles spilled from the sides of her mouth; a verbal landslide.

"Is it what I believe it to be? Is that grubby little compass the hiding place of the Elemental Fairy and the Gift of the king?"

Tilda gave an insouciant shrug. "If it is, then that big, bulky host-body of yours had better be careful. Terra's prowess is not to be taken lightly."

"Where is the scamp?"

"I'm sure I don't know," Tilda replied calmly. "Is *his* Magic too raw for you to scry for as well?"

Mombi was now put in the somewhat awkward position of talking to the one whom she was talking *through*. *"Go, Warrior!"* she barked. *"Go and muster your cattle. March out upon Gillikin in search of the scamp, and employ a hawkish spy with news of the boy's defection."*

Marada's shoulders jerked upward and her hands flopped as though she were trying to remind Mombi that it might be difficult to find a bird willing to volunteer, since she'd *eaten* the most recent one. This only infuriated the fifth Witch more.

"Just get word to your sisters in the East and West," the

voice that was not Marada's screeched, "*however you can. Warn them to be on the watch for a purple-haired scoundrel in possession of a battered compass!*"

Marada's head gave a spasmodic shake, as though to once again fervently disavow any sisterly relationship to Daspina and the Munch.

"*I want that Fairy and the Gift he protects!*" Mombi's voice roared. "*Make haste, Warrior, or I shall destroy you myself!*"

Marada expelling the fiend that inhabited her was a sickening separation to behold. The Warrior's armor clanked and rattled as paroxysms overtook her; she flailed and shuddered until, with one mighty twitch, she ejected Mombi in a kind of full-body belch, spewing her out whole, her head ripping out from Marada's head, her torso disgorged from Marada's torso. It happened so quickly that the fifth Witch did not have time to turn herself to smoke, or fire, or lurlquake, or anything else.

And so she stood exposed in her true form before the great Sorceress of the Foursworn. It would not have been her choice, but there was nothing for it now. Besides, the expression of shock on the Grand Adept's face was almost worth it; this breach of anonymity wouldn't matter anyway, once the Gavarias had been sacrificed.

Tilda could not stop herself from staring. She had no idea what she'd been expecting the Krumbic one to look like, but she certainly had never imagined *this*.

Marada, now rid of the Wicked parasite, hunkered there, momentarily stunned. She blinked, spitting soil from her mouth.

"I want that compass," the fifth Witch directed softly. "Now go."

And Marada went, the pounding of her spurred sandals shaking the stone corridor, the rusted grating of her Warrior's voice calling her soldiers to arms.

Not until the clatter of Marada's exit had faded did the fifth Witch speak again. And she did so in a melodious tone that was chillingly civil.

"Well, Mistress Gavaria," she said, propelling herself eerily across the cell without the benefit of touching her feet to the floor. "Now that you know who I am, I suppose we should have a bit of a chat. One revered leader to another, as it were."

"Revered," Tilda echoed. "I believe you mean feared."

"It is all the same to me. As long as I am in charge. And before you attempt to inflict some bright-and-shiny Good Magic upon me, I must remind you that this cell is quite heavily enchanted by Wickedness. Nothing will come of your pretty Sorcery here."

"And yet, I still managed to get out of Aphidina's cocklebur dungeon, didn't I?"

"Which brings me to the topic of your little girl." The fifth Witch settled herself on the stone floor directly across from Tilda, so they were facing each other, looking for all the world as though they were two schoolgirls about to play a game of patty-cake.

Tilda recoiled, but the stone wall against her back prevented her from putting any real distance between them. And still, she could not stop staring.

Staring, in awe and confusion.

The Krumbic one seemed to understand—and relish—the fact that the Grand Adept needed to fully absorb the profoundly unexpected sight of her. "Let's talk for a bit," she suggested. "You can tell me all about Glinda and her plans to smite my loyal Wickeds, and I will tell you some surprising and interesting things about me—such as, for instance, the fact that I know your mother. And that I am very much looking forward to seeing her again."

Tilda felt a shiver of concern. Could the fifth Witch have discovered that Mythra was alive? Or was this just a wise but Wicked bluff?

"It's been so long since we've seen each other," the Witch went on. "I was hoping you might tell me where to find her."

"Never," Tilda said through her teeth. "Even if I knew where she was, I would die before I'd share that secret with you."

The Witch gave a silky laugh. "Well, you're going to die anyway, Sorceress. So I really don't see what difference it makes."

Tilda kept her eyes firmly on the Witch's, which were flashing with dark mirth.

"But let's not let the fact that you are doomed prevent us from getting acquainted," Mombi drawled. "After all, I am a Krumbic shadow of a Shadow, and you are the most powerful and benevolent Magician in all of Oz. I'm sure there is plenty we can discuss. And from that, who knows what might . . . *take shape*?"

32

THE GROUNDSKEEPER

hat're those?" asked Ben, peering at the stones in Locasta's hand.

"Amethysts," she said. "They were my father's. I never put it together before, but I realize now that whenever he told me anything Magical, he would be holding them in his hands. They were how I learned about the compass and the shield. When I read the poem in the library, they sort of jiggled."

"Are they jiggling now?" asked Shade.

Locasta nodded, squinting at the stones. "I didn't realize before how similar they are to my father's eyes. Same color, same shape." Steeling herself, Locasta stepped closer to the statue of her father and leaned down to gently fit the oval gems into the place where his eyes had been. The addition of the stones made the statue eerily lifelike.

They all held their breath, watching as the amethysts began to twinkle. The next thing they knew, a scene had sprung up around them like a dream come to life.

"What's happening?" asked Thruff.

"I believe we're seeing something your father saw," said Glinda. "Something he once witnessed, that he wants us to see now."

"The setting looks familiar," said Ben.

"It's the Reliquary," said Locasta. "On the night of King Oz's defeat."

"How can you possibly know that?" asked Glinda, though it was clear that Locasta was right.

"I know it sounds impossible . . . but I think perhaps I was there."

"We're seeing the past through the eyes of a statue," Ben pointed out. "Once again, I submit that 'impossible' is a relative term."

"There's the groundskeeper from the teakettle's story," said Shade, pointing into the flickering scene. "I recognize his purple cap."

"And that's Mythra!" cried Glinda. Her grandmother looked terribly shaken, frightened even, and Glinda knew why: she had, just moments before *this* moment, been Magically rent into three pieces and nearly sacrificed in a ritual that, if not for her own quick thinking and Oz's Magic, would have retrieved a Wicked Shadow from the moon. Even in terror and disarray she looked majestic in her white dress and gem-studded belt; its stones—especially the green one that was now nestled in Glinda's pocket—glistened, despite the dark presence of the smoke.

It was everywhere, heavy with malice, swirling and sweeping over the Reliquary terrace in a thick, black whorl. Deep within it flared the red eyes of the fifth Witch, the strength of her Wicked Magic increased by her rage. A rage that was directed at Mythra, who stood tall in the face of it, her back to the emerald statue of King Oz as if she would protect him from this enemy cloud.

They all fell silent, watching as the desperate young groundskeeper struggled to lift a rectangle of lead from the ground.

"Is that—?" asked Ben.

"Yes, I think it is!" said Glinda, gaping at the beginnings of her shield.

The groundskeeper spoke: "Magic, please . . . let this not be more than I can *handle*!" As he said the words, a handle appeared on the lead slab. He lifted it easily and dashed across the terrace just as a bolt of black fire shot out from the heart of the smoke. Deflecting it with the corner of his makeshift shield, he stayed his course, running so fast that the cap flew off his head, revealing his face at last.

Shade gasped. Ben's mouth dropped open. Thruff blinked in amazement.

And Locasta cried out, "Papa!"

"So *Norr* was the groundskeeper at the unveiling party!" Glinda breathed.

"*That's* how he came to be entrusted with Terra," said Locasta.

They watched as Norr ran to place himself between Mythra and the smoke, just as she had placed herself between it and the statue.

"Step aside, lad," Mythra ordered.

Young Norr shook his head.

"The smoke grows more lethal with every passing second! Now, go!"

Another rope of dark energy exploded out of the cloud.

Norr flung himself at Mythra and pulled her to the ground. "It's you she wants!" he shouted in her ear. "You're the one who has to leave."

"I will not abandon this battle just to save myself!" Mythra rasped.

"*You* need to stay alive," Norr urged, "for whatever comes next!"

For one tense moment, they stared at each other, and then Mythra gave Norr a curt nod and, if Glinda was not mistaken . . . a *wink*!

It was all the encouragement Norr required. Moving behind the statue of the fallen king, he pressed his shoulder to it. "I do this with a heavy heart," he said softly, "it's not an end, it's just the start." Then with a roar, he hurled himself against the heavy statue . . . once, twice, and finally, using all his strength, a third time . . . to send it toppling forward, pinning Mythra to the slate tiles of the terrace.

Enraged, the smoke spun forth like a black cyclone, enshrouding Mythra where she lay lifeless beneath the rock. The red eyes burned with fury as the fifth Witch conjured a second bolt of dark fire to launch at Norr.

With his last bit of strength, he held up the shield; the Magic hit dead center, carving a small indentation into the lead.

The smoke raged again, spinning in on itself so ferociously that the glowing eyes became two sightless blurs against the darkness. It was the opening Norr needed. Clutching the shield, he ran into the vastness of the ruins and disappeared.

As the dreamlike images faded to a white haze, Glinda and the others caught their breath. But Norr's amethyst eyes continued to shine, throwing forth another scene.

This time he was showing them the parlor of a cozy little house in Quadling.

It was Glinda's house—ages upon ages before she would ever call it home, but it was as familiar to her here as it had been on the morning of her Declaration Day.

Tilda was seated by the fireplace, her face tight with worry. The light of the fire made the red pendant around her neck glow, casting red sparks on the scrap of linen in her lap. A woman in a scarlet gown sat in the rocking chair beside her, observing her work.

"I know you're nervous, dear, but you will need to make those stitches tighter if you want the Magic to take hold. Particularly there, around the edge of the compass rose."

Glinda's heart nearly cracked at the sound of that sweet voice.

"Maud!" whispered Shade. "I recognize her from the trapestry."

An elegant woman dressed in blue stood behind the rocking chair; she had one hand resting on Maud's shoulder. In the other she held a blue paper fan.

"That must be Dottie Jane," Glinda said. "And look . . ." She pointed to the Winkie gentleman seated across from Tilda, his fingers anxiously smoothing the neatly folded edge of his pocket square. "It's Dallybrungston!"

"The Entrusteds," said Ben.

"Three out of four, anyway," Locasta noted.

There was a tall man pacing the floor, and Glinda gasped when she saw that it was her father. She could not find the words to describe how it felt to see him in the house where she had grown up, or to know that she would only ever see him there through someone else's eyes.

When a faint knock came at the door, Tilda yelped and Stanton rushed to open it. He ushered a hunched figure in a woolen hood into the parlor.

"That's Mythra," said Glinda.

Stepping through the front door behind Mythra, carrying his shield, was Norr.

"Mother!" cried Tilda, throwing her arms around the Mystic while the knight hurried to draw the curtains.

Locasta, Ben, and Shade all turned to Glinda at once. *"Mother?"*

Glinda shrugged.

"You were attacked!" said Tilda, noting the cuts and bruises.

"By whom?" Stanton demanded. "Tell me the name and I shall slay the villain myself. Was it a Witch? A Wizard? A dark Sorceress, perhaps?"

Mythra said nothing. Stanton whirled to glare at Norr. "Did you see who it was?"

When Norr kept silent, Stanton drew his sword so quickly that even the five observers in Marada's zwinger jumped. He held the blade to the groundskeeper's throat.

"Now I see where you get it from," Locasta quipped.

"Shhhhh," said Ben. "This is getting good."

"Tell me what you know," said Stanton through gritted teeth. But Norr looked him in the eye and spoke not a word.

"Stanton," sighed Mythra. "That is quite enough of that."

Looking immediately contrite, the knight lowered his sword. "My sincerest apologies," he said, offering his hand to Norr.

"I accept your apology, friend," Norr replied with a grin like Locasta's. "These are trying times, and spirits are bound to run high."

"Trying times indeed," said Mythra. "And I fear there are more ahead. The evil we just witnessed is unprecedented in the Land of Oz . . . perhaps anywhere. And the longer it is allowed to fester, the more powerful it will become."

Dottie Jane sighed, and Dally nodded gravely.

"Suddenly we find ourselves with secrets," Mythra went on, her gaze going to each Entrusted, her voice filled with regret. "It is difficult to say yet which ones should be shared. I will leave that up to the four of you to decide . . . after I have gone."

Tilda frowned. "Gone?"

"This enemy is Wicked, but she is also wise. Right now, thanks to Norr, she believes that I am dead."

"*Dead?*" Tilda gasped the word out as if she were choking on it.

"Yes. And from now on, you must behave as though I am. Spread the word of my demise to any who will listen."

"But why?" asked Dottie Jane.

Mythra shook her head. "That is all I will say for now. My hope is that my exile will be brief; that the good fairyfolk of Oz will rise up quickly, before this Wickedness has a chance to take root." She reached out to stroke Tilda's russet hair. "But the longer I remain, the more danger you are in. The last thing I want is for this enemy to know that we share a connection."

"Connection! Mother, we can still use our Connection Magic, can't we?"

"I must forbid it. Even if we are lucky enough to feel it, we must ignore it. Discourage it, in fact."

"Where will you go?"

"It is better you do not know." Mythra's tone did not allow for argument. "You should not be worried about protecting me. You all have more precious charges now."

At this, Tilda's fingers went to the red beryl. Norr's hand slid into his vest pocket to wrap around something inside. Dally adjusted his hankie, and Dottie Jane fluttered her paper fan.

None but Mythra took note of these gestures.

Taking her daughter's hands in hers, she said, "I know you had dreamed of being Ozma's Cherished Chamberlain, but for now, caution and secrecy must take the place of dreams. I am sorry. Now, the Paragon Chest, please."

Tilda hurried into the bedroom and returned a moment later with the chest; Glinda recognized it as the same one that had provided her with the rope, the ring, the pearl, and the shield. Mythra took it, then leaned close to her daughter and said, "Be as brave as you've been and as wise as you are. And when the time is right to act, you will know it. In the meantime—"

She was cut off by a horrible noise from outside. Norr and Stanton ran to the window and saw a tall Witch in a silk headdress gliding down the peaceful street.

"Aphidina," said Glinda, the name bitter on her tongue.

"It seems Wickedness is quicker than I imagined," Mythra remarked, sounding fearful for the first time since the scene seen through the amethysts had begun.

As the Haunting Harvester strode past the quiet houses of Glinda's street, she flicked her long fingers at their front doors, or thatched roofs, or garden shrubs, and as she did, they each burst into flames.

"I am your new queen," she proclaimed. "The Witch of the South. Whosoever harbors the king's Mystic shall be punished. Turn her over to me, and all that you wish for will be yours. For this is Quadling and all is well."

"You must go!" said Stanton, placing his strong hands on Mythra's shoulders and guiding her toward the kitchen door. "Run! Please. And don't look back."

"Run!" said Tilda, then covered her mouth with her hand and wept.

Outside, the Witch was nearing the front walk of Glinda's house.

"I shall go out the front door and run off in the opposite direction," said Norr, handing the shield to Mythra. "It will give you time to go . . . wherever it is you're going." He gave Tilda a reassuring look. "I will come back as soon as I can," he promised.

With that, he opened the door and stepped out into the lane.

Into the path of the Witch of the South.

And as he did, the amethyst eyes of the statue went dark; whatever Norr had seen and done next faded into the moonlight.

In Marada's zwinger, no one moved or spoke or even trembled for several moments.

"But he never did go back," Locasta said at last. "He couldn't. The Witches wasted no time in forbidding their subjects to travel from country to country."

Suddenly a terrible thumping shook the ground beneath them.

They all turned to the archway, through which was thundering an army of draft animals ridden by Gillikin soldiers. And the Wicked Warrior Witch herself was leading the charge.

33

No Stone Unturned

The Witch looked surprised to find her quarry already in the outer ward of her castle. "How fortuitous," she shouted savagely, "the enemy has brought themselves to me!"

Glinda swept Illumina from her sash and held it high so that the glow of the sword mingled with the light of the moon, giving them all a clear view of the army rampaging toward them.

The Warrior's soldiers were numerous and mighty. Their heavy armor and metallic weapons shone and glinted as they galloped on their war-yaks and buffalopes toward the five intruders.

Reaching out with one gauntleted hand, Marada grabbed a fistful of darkness, a piece of the night itself, which she rounded into a sphere and bowled across the purple grass toward Thruff, but he was spry and jumped over it.

Without so much as slowing her march, the Witch lifted one hideous sandaled foot, snapped the razor-edged spur from the heel, and with a searing sidearm toss sent it slicing through space toward Shade. Shade leaned out of the circle's path just in time to prevent the loss of her right ear, but the lethal little disc tore through the hood of her cape and sheared off a lock of her sleek black hair.

With the hand that wasn't holding the shield, Glinda gathered up the rope. "Find, bind, leave no soldier behind!" she instructed, and the rope went whirling through the air, growing longer and longer in flight. When it was directly above the stampeding Gillikin regiment, it dropped around them, pulling itself tight. The animals lowed and shrieked, digging their hooves into the grass. As the soldiers slid from their saddles or were bucked off their beasts, the sound of armor clashing against armor seemed to shatter the night.

"Knot!" Glinda cried, then thought better of it and shouted, "Double knot!"

The rope dove and pulled, winding itself into a secure binding, trapping the platoon; they struggled against Glinda's Magic to no avail.

Locasta was scrambling toward Glinda and the shield,

clutching the compass. But Marada dropped to one knee and slammed her fist on the ground in Locasta's direction; the world reared up, throwing them all high into the air. But Locasta got the brunt of it, landing like a cannonball.

Glinda came down on the purple grass in a crouching position behind the shield. Ben landed sprawled beside her, and Shade crashed down on top of him. As Ben and Shade frantically attempted to disentangle themselves, more soldiers swarmed from the inner bailey on foot.

Locasta still had not moved.

As Marada continued her advance, she began to beat her fists against the breastplate of her armor. The pounding of silver against metal produced a violent explosion of purple sparks, which coalesced into a single bolt of Wicked Magic, shooting like purple lightning in Locasta's direction.

"Noooo!" Glinda's voice was part plea, part war cry as she grabbed the shield and ran to protect her friend from the Witch's brutal Magic.

The shield caught the purple bolt, deflecting it back on Marada, where it slammed into her midsection and sent her flying backward, crashing into another trio of soldiers who'd just appeared through the arch. She fell on one of them, the weight of her armor and her own muscular bulk crushing him instantly. The power of the purple bolt bounced off her breastplate, dissolving the other two in a burst of darkness. But the impact of her own Magic had left the Warrior severely stunned.

As Glinda continued her sprint toward the fallen Locasta, the shield began to grow heavier in her grasp. Struggling to keep her hold on it, she recalled Mythra's words: *Give your fears to the shield . . . give voice to that which threatens to hold you down. . . .*

"I'm afraid for my friend," she whispered to the shield, "I'm afraid for my friend. . . ."

And just as it had in the Mystic's cave, the shield threw off its own heft and took on Glinda's burden instead. With the shield nearly weightless, she made it to where Locasta still lay motionless, and quickly dragged her behind a grouping of six burly miner statues, each holding a pickax or hammer. Thruff arrived a moment later, and Shade and Ben were not far behind.

"Ben," said Glinda, motioning to the next wave of guards pouring through the gate, "can you take care of them?"

"I think so. As long as I have the right weapon."

She drew Illumina, held it close to her lips, and whispered to the sword, "Fight, my friend; fight as though both Mythra and I are guiding you!" Then she handed it to Ben. "Illumina will know what to do," she promised. "Just listen to the light!"

Despite the odds, Ben did not hesitate. He ran toward the heavily armed soldiers, leaving Glinda and the others unarmed, with only the minimal protection provided by the half-dozen statues behind which they crouched.

"If only they could help us, " Glinda murmured, her gaze taking in the stony forms of countless Gillikin miners and their families who had been Petrified at Marada's hands—all enemies of the Witch, and therefore allies of Glinda.

As she studied their sculpted faces, thoughts began to race in her mind:

Why can't these statues just awaken?

If only I knew *how* to reverse Marada's Magic.

What words did Shade and Thruff speak *when* they quoted the Wicked spell?

And with a jolt she realized why Marada's curse had struck a chord. *There is always a how, a why, and a when.*

"Shade!" cried Glinda. "Thruff! I need you to repeat Marada's curse for me, right now. I need to hear the words again—not all of them, just the active phrases, but please, make sure to say it with nothing but Good intention in your hearts." She lowered one eyebrow at Thruff. "Especially you."

Shade and Thruff exchanged curious glances but did as they were told, speaking the Witch's ugly lines in a kind of wary harmony:

> *"Drain away motion, spill away breath*
> *Sculpt away feeling, carve away life*
> *In between heartbeats, with a touch cold as*
> *stone . . ."*

"Excellent. Now I need you to say them again, only *backward* this time."

Thruff looked confused. "But it won't mean anything."

"No, it won't," Glinda agreed. "But it will be the opposite of Wicked. Now, please . . . just keep saying it."

Thruff might have challenged her command a second time, but Shade, with her cloak whipping around her, was already shouting in a voice louder than Glinda had ever heard from her before. "Breath away spill, motion away drain."

Thruff chanted with equal zeal, "Life away carve, feeling away sculpt."

Glinda was not naive enough to imagine that simply saying a spell backward could reverse it, but this particular curse had included a very particular how, when, and why. Her hope was that if she could reverse these points as well, the combination might be powerful enough to negate the spell.

As Shade's and Thruff's voices continued to ring out, Glinda positioned herself in front of the stoutest of the six stone-ified miners. "*When?*" she asked herself. And because the answer was the oddly poetic "in between heartbeats," she forced herself to focus on the frenzied pounding of her own heart, clocking not the "in-betweens" but the beats themselves.

"*How?*" she said. "With a cold touch." Well, that certainly wouldn't be a problem, since her whole body felt overheated, thanks to her exertions with the heavy shield.

Lastly she asked, "*Why?*" And the answer to this was

the precise opposite of the answer the Warrior had given in the curse. Because the last thing Glinda wanted was for these cursed victims to leave Marada alone!

She reached out and placed her warm palm on the statue's arm in perfect time with the next thud of her heart.

"Away drain . . ."

"Away sculpt . . ."

"Away spill . . ."

"Away carve . . ."

The Magic began, just as a woozy Locasta opened her eyes. The hard stone of the statues was slowly crumbling in a series of small cracks, echoing from every corner of the zwinger.

"Motion . . .

. . . feeling . . .

. . . breath . . .

. . . life."

When the words registered in Locasta's dazed mind, she jumped to her feet. "That's Marada's curse. They'll turn us all to statues!"

"No, they won't. They aren't Wicked, and besides, they're reverse-incanting it."

Locasta frowned. "You made that up."

"Well, yes, I suppose I did. But it's working! Look!"

Sure enough, the outer surface of the statues was falling away to reveal the faces of the startled Gillikins beneath.

"They're alive?" Locasta gasped.

"It seems so," said Glinda.

Ben came speeding back from his battle, beaming with triumph, and handed Illumina to Glinda. "Truly, if the colonial militia had swords like this, we'd have no trouble defeating England!"

"Who's *England*?" Locasta asked.

But a growl from across the ward had them all swinging their heads around. Marada was hoisting herself up from the ground. They could only just make out her burly form through the thickening cloud of stone dust created by so many crumbling statues.

"Show yourselves, brats!" she roared, peering through the dust cloud.

"We have to free the Fairy!" said Glinda. "Now! While Marada can't see us!"

"Hurry," said Ben as Marada's footsteps stamped toward them.

"Hold the shield steady," said Locasta, and Glinda obeyed. As Locasta fit the compass case into the small indentation in the center of the shield, her words boomed into the dusty haze. "I call upon the Elemental Fairy of Lurl! For Oz! Forever! Truth Above All!"

The golden lid of the compass flipped open and from it rose what Glinda could only describe as a living mountain. Terra! Enormous, imposing, and rock-solid, climbing up from the compass, the force of her arrival sweeping away the cloud of stone dust.

Terra's girth was not without grace; her boldness not without beauty. Her legs shimmered with flecks of quartz, and her arms were smooth and shining like marble; indeed, she contained bits of every handsome stone represented in the Arc of Heroes—emerald, alabaster, obsidian—but most exquisite were her wings: delicate sheets of gleaming mica, which gave off a silver-white frosted sheen in the moonlight.

The Gillikins who had been statues just moments before gaped first at the Fairy, then at their loathed leader, the Wicked Witch of the North, who had stumbled to a halt at the sight of her nemesis.

Raising her arms above her head, Marada slammed the wrists of her gauntlets together to form an X, and the sharp noise of their contact solidified into a weapon. She was now holding a vicious-looking spiked ball—a bludgeon—attached to a long handle by a short chain.

"It's a flail!" Thruff rasped. "And I'm sure she's cast a Wicked enchantment, making it strong enough to fight this Fairy."

Terra's mica wings had already carried her across the zwinger to meet Marada where she stood. The Witch was expertly rotating the weapon's haft, causing the bludgeon to circle wildly on its chain.

Terra lifted one gigantic stone foot, but the Warrior and her weapon were swift. The swinging spiked ball slammed into the Fairy's ankle. As chips of stone showered down on

Marada, pinging off her armor, the Fairy let out an agonized wail; it was the sound of an avalanche.

Marada dropped the flail and clapped her gloved hands together, and this time a crossbow appeared in her grasp. When she released the arrow, it sailed arcing up into the night, as high as the Fairy's towering shoulders—and as it flew it divided itself into a whole shower of arrows, all of which lodged into the Fairy's chest.

Another scream of pain, this one as loud as a lurlquake.

Laughing maniacally, Marada tossed away the bow and was about to clap her hands again when a pickax came spinning through the atmosphere, catching the spaulder on her left shoulder. She stumbled backward, howling.

Next a dolabra with a lethal blade followed, its blunt end pounding her in the knee.

"It's the miners!" cried Ben. "They're using their tools to hold her off."

Glinda looked around and saw that Ben was right. From every part of the outer ward, the freed-from-stone Gillikin miners were advancing on the Witch, hurling their tools at her, preventing her from using her Magic to conjure more weapons to use against the Lurl Fairy.

Just as Glinda had hoped they would.

And in the midst of it, she spied a familiar face. A former groundskeeper to the king.

And beside him marched his fiery-eyed, curly-haired wife and their five daughters. They had each picked up a chunk of rock from the ground—perhaps pieces of their own prisons—and were hurling them at the Witch who had cursed them.

High above, Terra was jerking the arrows out of her stone flesh. The brave intervention of the Gillikins was all she needed to regain her control of the battle. As Marada ducked from the rocks and hammers that flew at her, Terra made her way forward, motioning for the miners to stand down.

This left only the flustered Witch and the Elemental Fairy to glower at each other.

Marada did not shriek or beg as Aphidina had; instead she sent up a ferocious war cry that rocked the night. But the sound was swallowed up by the force of the Fairy's foot stomping down upon her, grinding her into the very ground that long ago, Terra herself had had the great privilege of creating. The soldiers bound in the Magic Rope sank where they stood, disappearing into the rocky soil of Gillikin as if they had never even existed. Only Glinda's Magic Rope remained to mark the spot where they had met their fate.

Glinda, Ben, Shade, and Thruff ran forward just as Terra was lifting her foot.

Amazingly, the purple-tinted grass looked utterly undisturbed; there was no hint of the Witch to be seen, except for the Silver Gauntlets—which had not suffered so much as a dent.

Thruff scooped them up and turned hopeful eyes to Glinda. "May I have these?"

"Absolutely," she said, grinning. "As long as you promise you won't use them to pummel your sister. Right, Locasta?" She turned to where she expected Locasta to be, and was surprised to see that she wasn't there.

Her heart flipped over, fearing her friend might have accidentally stepped into the path of a flying pickax or sledgehammer. But Shade's voice came to her, soft as a summer rain:

"Don't worry. She's safe."

"Where is she?" Glinda pressed, still frantic. "Where did she go?"

Smiling, Shade flicked back her cape and pointed across the ward. "Isn't it obvious? She's visiting her family."

Glinda smiled when she saw that Shade was right—Locasta, surrounded by her parents and her five sisters, looked very, very safe indeed.

34

FOOTSTEPS OF THE FAIRY KING

The Road of Red Cobble had no trouble surfacing through the rocky rubble left by the crumbled statues. Once again, it delivered Miss Gage to them, and this time, as a pleasant surprise, Ursie Blauf had come along too.

"Ursie, could you—" Glinda motioned to the Magic Rope, which still lay knotted in the purplish grass.

"Certainly!" cried Ursie, skipping off to do what she'd been asked.

"She has a way with knots," Locasta explained to her sisters, who had all gathered along the edge of the road so that their father could introduce them to his Foursworn friend, Miss Gage.

"Allow me to introduce my family," Norr said proudly to the teacher-Sorceress. "This is my wife, Norlasta. My boy Thruff, and these darling fairygirls are my older daughters, Calamita and Margolotte, and the triplets, Edith, Schuyler, and Suzanne."

Plump, sweet-faced Margolotte curtsied while the other four smiled and nodded.

"Another Fairy safe, another Gift freed!" said Miss Gage. "But where are the footsteps of the king?"

"Perhaps we should ask *her*," said Ben, his voice filled with admiration as he pointed to the towering form of Terra hovering in the air behind Locasta.

"Good Fairy of Lurl," said Miss Gage. "Can you show us the Gift of the king's final footsteps?"

Terra ceased the flutter of her tremendous mica wings and slowly descended. The moment the Fairy's stone feet touched the dust-coated Lurlian ground, Glinda felt the soles of her boots begin to pulse.

"Hey!" cried Ben, looking down at the ground. Although he was standing still, a trail of green footsteps was suddenly stretching out before him.

The same was true for Glinda, Locasta, Shade, and everyone else. The ground, which felt firmer and sturdier now that Terra was free, was covered with hundreds upon hundreds of emerald-green footprints in the precise size and shape of King Oz's silver boots, creating trails all over Marada's outer ward, heading out through the main archway and crossing over the stone moat bridge.

For one fleeting moment, these thousands of footprints glowed green in the moonlight, then faded softly away. And when they were gone, so was Terra.

"Dazzling," said Ben.

"But what does it mean?" asked Thruff.

"It means," said Glinda, "that King Oz's footsteps will forever be found upon the Lurlian landscape." On a hunch, she took a step forward; a green shimmer appeared where her foot touched the ground . . . but this time it was not the outline of King Oz's footprint, it was in the shape of Glinda's own. "And so will ours. Because the path we forge will be a continuation of the trail he blazed, but we must walk it with our own intentions, at our own speed, toward our own goals. The past gives us direction—we learn from it—but how and when and why we travel must always be of our own design."

Locasta looked at her with wide eyes, thoroughly impressed.

Norr and Miss Gage nodded, and Ursie beamed. As though to prove Glinda's theory, Ben took a step in the Makewright's ancient boots, and they all gasped when the green shimmer beneath his foot rose up from the ground and into the sky, exploding with a soft *pop*.

"What do you suppose that means?" he asked, laughing.

Glinda shrugged, but she suspected it meant that Benjamin Clay of the New York colony was destined to leave *his* footsteps—newly informed by his time in

Roquat's collide-o-scope—on another land, a great distance from Oz. It was a thought that made her feel both hopeful and sad at the same time.

Mistress Norr, the five girls, and Thruff (who for some odd reason insisted on calling each of them "swister") said their farewells and left the castle, eager to be home again. Norr would stay behind to walk back to the mining village with Locasta.

Locasta . . . who was suddenly looking at Glinda with a very grim expression.

"What is it?" Glinda asked, her stomach winding into knots that even Ursie wouldn't be able to untie. "What's the matter?"

"There's something you need to know," Locasta began gravely. "Something Shade discovered on the road of yellow brick."

"Your mother was taken by the smoke," Shade whispered, her eyes sad behind the sweep of her dark hair.

"Taken?" Glinda echoed. "Where is she?"

"I'm sorry," said Shade, shrugging inside her cape. "I don't know."

"I do," said Thruff. Grinning, he nodded toward the arch that led to the inner bailey.

They all turned in the direction Thruff had indicated, and Glinda let out a cry of sheer delight.

Because walking through the archway, utterly unharmed, was her mother.

35

A PEARL OF WISDOM

Tilda approached them with a serene expression, as though there was nothing at all out of the ordinary about stepping over chunks of broken statue parts outside the Wicked Warrior's castle.

"Mother! Thank Goodness you're safe!"

"I'm perfectly fine," Tilda assured her. "And I'm so glad to find you well as well." She cast her warm hazel gaze around at the gathering as she drew nearer. "All of you! You all look so very, well . . . *well.*"

With a broad smile, Norr stepped forward to greet Tilda, for, as Glinda now knew, they were very old friends who'd been present at the birth of this cause. But Tilda

spared him only the scantest of nods, as if she didn't recognize the groundskeeper-turned-Foursworn at all. With
her eyes locked firmly on Glinda, she walked right past
Locasta's father, and did not pause until she was standing
toe to toe with her daughter. "My darling, Glinda," she
said.

"Hello, Mistress Gavaria!" said Ursie.

"Hello there"—Tilda gave Ursie a polite smile—"little
girl."

Ursie's cheeks turned pink with embarrassment. "It's me,
ma'am. Remember? Glinda and I used to walk to school
together every day. For six years."

"Oh, yes, of course!" said Tilda. " I'm so sorry. I suppose I'm just a bit frazzled from being in that dungeon all
this time."

"Mother, I have so much to tell you," Glinda exclaimed,
throwing her arms around Tilda. "There was an attack on
the academy! You'd never believe it, but it turns out that
Trebly Nox is quite the expert with a sling. And Ursie can
untie anything."

"Ursie?" said Tilda, as if she'd never heard the name
before.

"Me," said Ursie again. "Ursie Blauf? My father sells
wagon wheels?"

Tilda gave her a loving smile. "Yes. Of course."

"And then I was part of a battle between the Sea
Fairies and the Sea Devils," Glinda went on. "I saved the

Sea Fairies, so they gave me a gift." She reached into her pocket, feeling around for the pearl.

"Sea Fairies?" Tilda repeated with interest. "How fascinating. Tell me, how exactly did you happen to come across those elusive creatures? Where were you?" She reached out to stroke Glinda's copper-colored hair. "Where *exactly* were you?"

"Something's wrong," Gage whispered to Norr, at precisely the same moment that Norr said, "Glinda, come over here. Quickly."

Glinda gave Locasta's father a bewildered look. "Why must I come there?" she asked, still searching her pocket for the enchanted pearl. "I'm just standing here talking to my—oh! Here it is!" Her fist closed around the pearl.

"Please, Glinda," said Miss Gage with an anxious wave of her hand. "Please come join us . . . over *here* . . . now."

Glinda frowned, withdrawing the pearl from her pocket. "I don't understand why you're acting so strangely, Miss Gage. I'm just talking to my mother. Isn't that right, Mother?"

"Yes," said Tilda. "That's right. You're just talking to your mother."

It was at that moment that Glinda opened her hand to reveal the pearl.

Which was cold.

And completely black.

CLOSING LETTER

GABRIEL GALE

To Whom It May Confuse:

Perhaps you are wondering about . . . well, a lot of things. That's what readers do, after all, isn't it? They *wonder.* They puzzle over literary hints, and make educated guesses about plot, and generally try to imagine with some degree of accuracy what could possibly happen next, even though they fully want and expect to be surprised by it.

In particular, I hope you are wondering (at least a little bit) about how it came to pass that my name appears in this book as the author of *The Compendium of Archaic Ozian Legendencia.*

Legendencia, by the way is not a word . . . anymore. But it was then, when the *Compendium* was penned, a very, very long time ago. When I was younger than I am now, when you were older than you might be later today.

(And now you are wondering about *that,* aren't you? If you are, then Lisa Fiedler and I have done our jobs.)

There is more to tell.

And more to wonder.

Not just for you, Reader, but for all of us. Here at home, and there, in Oz. Because the story isn't over yet. And that of course, is the best part of stories. They keep going.

Even after they have happened.

Even while they are happening.

And sometimes even before they happen.

There are still two Wicked Witches. And there is Magic just waiting to occur. There is Glinda, of course, and there will be . . . oh, what is her name again? The little girl in the blue gingham dress?

Ah, yes . . . Dorothy. Dorothy *Gale*.

And if you think that's a hint, then you are undeniably correct!

I remain, as ever, a most faithful Royal Historian of Oz and your eager guide on this Ozian adventure,

Gabriel Gale

ACKNOWLEDGMENTS

I'm lucky to have gained so many new friends from across the country since the first Ages of Oz book was published! My greatest joy has been to meet—either electronically or in person—all the readers and their families, teachers, faculty, librarians, and local bookstore owners that have chosen to join me on this journey through Oz's past, present, and future. Together over the past year we've unleashed so many mythical hybrid beasts that the Wards of Lurl will need to work overtime to clean up after us!

In addition to all those I mentioned in the first book who continue to join me side-by-side on this adventure, namely the incomparable Lisa Fiedler; Ruta Rimas and the team at McElderry; Sue Cohen and the team at Writer's House; Sebastian Giacobino; Craig Howell; Maria and Nick Makrinos; and Ralph, Joanna, and Karina Succar, I would like to mention here the wonderful people who have been particularly supportive during the time between the first and second Ages of Oz books.

To Marc Baum and his family, and everyone else at Oz-Stravaganza and the All Things Oz Museum in Chittenango, New York, I want to thank you for being the first group to bring Ages of Oz aboard your annual plans. To Clint Steuve and everyone at The Columbian Theater, thank you for bringing me to Wamego, Kansas to enjoy my first OZtoberFest. To Laura Schaefer, we know your Chappaqua book bunnies can speak just like Billina the Hen, so remind them to stop being so scattered and tell us how they prefer their carrots cooked. And to Sally Roesch Wagner, your indomitable spirit and channeling of Matilda Joslyn Gage is a source of continued inspiration through my travels.

To Christine Freglette, your energy is unfathomable. To John Alexander, your magic with words is swift and mighty. To Peter Glassman, the champion of all books of wonder, thank you for your love of Oz. To Victoria and Joseph Cardinale, Wendy Davis-Lupo, and Maryanne Visconti, thank you for introducing this adventurer to new dimensions. To Barbara Vellucci, Irene Hanvey, and Stella Panagakos, you are true loyalists. To Paulette Poulos of the Leadership 100, thank you for your counsel. And to Christina Tettonis of the Hellenic Classical Charter School and Lexy Mayer and Paquita Campoverde of the Brooklyn Public Library, thank you for being the support I can always return to in my hometown.

To Cassie Carlina, who was born from the ethereal magic of her parents Katie and Tom, may that magic guide and support you in all your endeavors as you and your parents have supported me in mine. To Steve Mancuso, Tommy DiLillo, and their families—Bossie and Genevieve Mancuso, and Roseanna, Troy, and Jagger DiLillo—I know we'll always find the fun in any situation on Earth or in Oz. And to Noelle Luccioni, Maria Georgiadis, Cassandra Meyer, and Stephanie Cicatiello, I will continue to seek your insight and advice.

The Royal Historian and Headmaster of Fireside Institute, John Bush, who has been my chief comrade in the full chronicling of Ages of Oz, would like to thank his lovely wife, Johanna Bush, for her earnest and continual support, Catherine Bush for her lifelong encouragement, Alyssa Delaney and Eugenia Long for their faith and humor, and Dan Delaney and Ryan Long for their dedication. John wishes to specifically acknowledge the contributions of Emerald City Scholars Maahi and Pranav (Moji) Patel, Royal Scout Marcus Pintilie, and Fairy Envoy Autumn Greco.

And finally, to John Fricke, who is always there to keep this adventurer on the Ozzy path. I'll keep it fun John, not too dark, I promise! Mark my words, we'll have a hug with the Scarecrow before we reach the end of this road.